Mind *of* Her Own

DIANA LESIRE
BRANDMEYER

MIND *of* HER OWN

Tyndale House Publishers, Inc.
Carol Stream, Illinois

Visit Tyndale online at www.tyndale.com.

Visit Diana Lesire Brandmeyer's website at www.dianabrandmeyer.com.

TYNDALE and Tyndale's quill logo are registered trademarks of Tyndale House Publishers, Inc.

Mind of Her Own

Cover and title page designed by Jacqueline L. Nuñez

Published in association with the literary agency of The Steve Laube Agency.

Mind of Her Own is a work of fiction. Where real people, events, establishments, organizations, or locales appear, they are used fictitiously. All other elements of the novel are drawn from the author's imagination.

Library of Congress Cataloging-in-Publication Data

Brandmeyer, Diana Lesire.
   Mind of her own / Diana Lesire Brandmeyer.
      pages cm
      ISBN 978-1-4964-0128-1 (sc) — ISBN 978-1-4143-8102-2 (ePub) —
      ISBN 978-1-4143-8101-5 (Kindle) — ISBN 978-1-4143-8103-9 (Apple)
      I. Title.
      PS3602.R3585M56 2015
      813'.6—dc23   2015008437

Printed in the United States of America

21	20	19	18	17	16	15
7	6	5	4	3	2	1

Nancy Brown Whitley, thank you for your

excitement about Jazz's story.

ACKNOWLEDGMENTS

Rhonda Langefeld, for being there from the beginning.

Jennifer Tiszai, Jenny Carry, Julie Lessman, Liz Tolsma, Robin Bayne, and Laura V. Hilton, for all your critiques.

Marty C. Lintvedt, thank you for your help on researching retrograde amnesia.

Danika King, thank you for your amazing editor skills and kindness.

CHAPTER ONE

RAIN PELTED THE ceiling-to-floor windows of the family room. The grayness of the evening invaded Louisa Copeland's mind and home. The oversize chair she snuggled in helped hide her surroundings. The thick romance in her hand further darkened her mood as she read how the hero whisked away the heroine for a surprise dinner on some pier. Were there relationships like that? She didn't know of any.

"Give it to him!" Joey, her five-year-old son, joined the fray as Madison, her twelve-year-old daughter, dangled a plastic horse over the head of Tim, her youngest son, just out of his reach.

Jolted from the fantasy world into the real one, where

rainy days turned children into caged animals, Louisa gripped the book tight and took five deep breaths. "Madison, if you don't give it back to Tim now, I will take your phone away for the rest of the day."

Madison's eyes narrowed. "Daddy won't let you."

"He isn't here at the moment. He is working but will be home for dinner, and you can discuss it with him then. But for now give it to Tim."

"Baby." Madison sneered at Tim. "Take your stupid horse."

Problem solved, Louisa retreated into the book to finish the chapter. Done, she sighed and laid the book faceup on the side table next to her reading chair. The love-struck characters standing in front of a houseboat mocked her from the cover and filled her with jealousy. She longed to be the woman between those pages. She closed her eyes, pursed her lips against her hand, and tried to imagine the feel of Collin's lips on hers.

She couldn't. Her hand didn't smell woodsy like Collin. Why would it? They hadn't slept together in over a week. Not since that hurtful night when he'd accused her of not loving him enough. And until he apologized, he wouldn't be back in her bed. She wasn't going to give in this time, even if she did toss and turn all night in that enormous bed because she missed him. But letting him back in her bed without a true "I'm sorry" would mean he'd won, and she couldn't accept that. He would have to come to her first, and sending her those two dozen roses didn't count either. She knew he had his secretary call the florist, and Louisa didn't want a quick-fix apology. No, she wanted a heartfelt, grand gesture of some kind. She hadn't quite figured out what it would take for Collin to make the sting of his words dissolve, but she knew it would have to come from him, not his office staff.

"Mom? Are you kissing your hand?"

Startled by her son, Louisa felt her face flush. Her thoughts twirled around themselves as she tried to come up with a reason for her action. "I was pretending to be a jellyfish. See?" She put the back of her hand against her lips and wiggled her fingers like tentacles.

"Why?" His serious face moved closer to hers to inspect the gesture.

"Because I was reading a book that has the ocean and jellyfish in it." She could tell Tim believed her the minute his hand went to his own face. He walked away with his own pretend jellyfish flailing its tentacles.

She considered the morality of lying to her child but dismissed it. Her children didn't need to know she couldn't remember how their father's kisses felt. She and Collin had lost the spark, the excitement and joy. Even their communication had dwindled to no more than a few small phrases—"Where's the paper?" and "Have you seen my phone?" Did his commitment to her exist any longer? Had he found someone else?

Her head started to pound again from a migraine that had first made its appearance when a save-the-date for her family reunion had arrived in the morning mail. She still couldn't believe it. *A save-the-date? When did my family get so fancy?* A phone call from her mother had followed minutes later. She demanded that Louisa tell her whether or not she and Collin would be there. An argument had started about Louisa being a snob and not wanting to know her own family, not wanting to spend time with her mother, which then led into why Louisa and Collin weren't taking the children to church. The call ended with the usual rebuttal of "We will when we find a church we like."

Her mother always brought out Louisa's obstinate side. Louisa knew she had that effect on her own daughter, but she wasn't sure how to fix either problem. She rubbed a thumb knuckle into the center of her forehead the way the neurologist had shown her to ease the pain. She wouldn't be scratching "clean the van" off her list today. Bending over made the pounding worse.

This morning, Collin promised he would be home for dinner—for the first time since he'd announced he wanted to make partner this year at his firm. He'd informed her that he would be working extra hours and expected her to take care of the family. So she did her part and his. Then, less than a month later, he'd accused her of loving the children more than she loved him. How could he make that judgment since he was never home? The roses his secretary sent the next day didn't even make it to a vase. She'd trotted out to the curb and stuffed them in the trash, where he'd see them when he came home that night. Since then, the two of them had lived like oil and vinegar unshaken in a jar.

Thunder rolled and lightning sparked in the distance.

Maybe Collin wanted to make amends tonight, and that was why he was making an effort to be home early. Or maybe he wanted to tell her something else, something she might not want to hear. Would she listen? What if he wanted to tell her she wasn't the kind of wife a partner at his firm would need? She did complain about having to attend office functions. They made her feel small—just a stay-at-home mom. She couldn't compete with the woman lawyers, especially Emmie, the tall, stick-thin beauty who had an office next to Collin. Louisa could share a recipe or where the best dog park was located, but nothing brilliant or witty crossed her lips anymore. She rose from her chair and walked to the glass door. The waves on the lake had increased in height. Cleo, their dog, was out there somewhere.

Did Collin love someone else? Like a virus, the image of Emmie with her cute clothes and bright smile at the Fourth of July party threaded from Louisa's mind and invaded her spirit. She swallowed back the fear that rose from her heart and lodged in her throat. That just couldn't happen. Collin was hers and only hers. He didn't belong to the firm or anyone else. She had to find a way to make him understand that she did love him, that he came first in her life. She wished she could open up and tell him everything. Maybe then he would . . . No, he would never love her if he knew her secret. No, that story could never be told. She would have to find another way.

The first thing she'd do was prepare a meal so delicious he wouldn't want to miss another one. She knew it was foolish to put such expectations on her cooking but held out that there might be a fraction of hope, a glimmer of a possibility.

Behind her, Madison shrieked at her brother, lurching Louisa back to her own reality show. "Give me back the remote!"

"It's my turn!" Joey tried to outshout his sister.

"Yeah, it's our turn!" four-year-old Tim echoed.

The noise brought fresh, sharp spears of pain to Louisa's head. With a sigh, she ignored the opportunity to jump into the fray and yell herself. In her stocking feet she crossed the great expanse of the golden oak floor to the kitchen, which was located to the side of the family room. When they first moved in, it had seemed like a great floor plan, all open, but now she regretted having chosen it. It made her always available to the children, and if one room wasn't picked up, the whole house looked like a mess.

The clock in the entryway chimed five times. The hour had come! If only she could cook like Emeril, she might have a chance to win back her husband's love—or at least his presence at the table. Then again, Collin might break his promise to her and the kids again and not even come home for dinner.

She flipped through the cookbook that rested on top of a cobalt-blue stand, where it usually sat for looks.

"Mom?" Tim ran circles around the kitchen island. "Joey and me want a snack."

"Not now." The page in front of her held a beautiful prospect for a meal, just not one made by her. *Who cooks dinner like this?* She flipped the page. Why had she bought this book? Surely she didn't think she would ever have time to prepare a dish from it or be able to get her children to eat it. . . . She read the ingredient list. *What is jicama?*

"Mom, can we have Crunch Squares for dinner?" Tim interrupted her thoughts, tugging on the bottom of her shirt.

Louisa turned her attention from the cookbook pages. She placed her hands on her hips in her don't-mess-with-me stance and stared down at two small, pleading faces. Her sons craved anything coated or sprinkled with sugar. "Sorry, boys, you cannot have cereal for dinner. You need protein and vegetables so you grow big and strong like your daddy." She pried Joey's fingers from the bright orange-and-red cardboard box.

"The commercial says it has all the vitamins and nutrients we need." Madison bellowed her opinion from the family room.

"Don't believe everything you see on TV, Madison." Making dinner night after night for three kids and Collin had never entered her mind when she said "I do" at the church thirteen years ago. She closed the book, weary of its glossy pictures. She couldn't pull off a gourmet meal tonight, not with this roaring headache. She'd be better prepared this weekend. Possibly Collin would eat with them Sunday night if she gave him enough notice.

"We're having grilled chicken." She looked down at the two waifs standing in front of her. Joey and Tim both frowned in unison. She blinked at their action and shrugged it off. Some days she thought those two had to be twins, even though that was physically impossible since she had given birth to them twelve months apart. "You two, pick up the fort you've assembled in the other room. I don't want to see or step on even one plastic block tonight."

"It's not a fort. It's a space station." Tim scrunched his face in disgust. "I told you a hundred times, Mom."

"It's a grand space station, but you still need to put it away." She watched them leave the room, thinking a sloth could move faster than those two when it came to cleaning up.

Chicken—that's what she was doing, wasn't it? What else should she put on the table? Maybe a salad and mac and cheese, she thought. Yes, that would be best. It would cause less tension around the table if they all had something they liked.

Cleo whimpered at the back door. Her nails scratching against the glass felt like tiny needles pushing into Louisa's optic nerves. It ratcheted her headache higher on the pain-management scale. She had never wanted a big dog, but Collin wouldn't settle for anything small. Not even medium size. It had to be a brindled Great Dane, the gentle beast, to make him happy. It didn't matter to him that *she* would be the one hauling the dog to the vet and puppy day care for socialization and training classes. She tried to ignore the pathetic whining coming through the door. Maybe the kids would let the dog inside.

Peering through the open archway, Louisa checked to see if anyone was moving. She could hear a satisfying plunk of plastic hitting plastic—the boys were picking up like she'd asked. Slow, but at least the rug had begun to appear. She had been cleaning for most of the day and wanted to enjoy an orderly space after dinner. Madison lay on the couch with her head hanging over the end. Her blonde hair almost touched the floor as it moved in time to a music video.

"Madison, let Cleo in before she chews through the door."

"But, Mom, this is my favorite song," Madison whined from the couch. "Can't Joey let her in?"

"No. I told you to do it." Louisa squatted down in front of the cabinet and grabbed a pot for the macaroni. As it filled with water, she rubbed her temples with her fingers. Cleo scratched against the door again.

Louisa felt herself stiffen as she prepared to go into battle with Madison. She turned to see what her daughter was doing. Madison had stood but had not moved in the direction of the door. Instead she watched the television screen and swayed to the beat of the music.

"Madison, step away from the TV."

"I'm going. You don't have to tell me everything twice. I'm not stupid." She glared at her mother.

This is what the counselor they were seeing called a standoff. She and Collin were supposed to be stern in their commands and follow through with them. Well, she didn't have any problem with following through, but Collin did. All Madison had to do was turn her lower lip down into a pout and Collin backed off, afraid to upset his little girl. *There was a time when Collin would do anything for me too,* she thought. Those days disappeared the minute Madison said "Daddy."

Louisa removed her glasses and rubbed her eyes. The intensity of the headache rose. "Thank you, Madison, for promptly doing what I asked."

Madison clenched her lips tight, straightened her back, and stomped over to the door and yanked it open. Cleo came bounding through, her nails clicking over the wooden floor like fingers on a keyboard. Madison turned, whipping her long hair around like a weapon, and stared at Louisa as if to say, *"I did it. Don't ask me to do anything else ever again."*

"Thank you." Louisa slid her glasses back on and smoothed her hair behind her ears. She checked to make sure the boys were still doing as she'd asked. They were making progress.

The clock in the entryway weakly imitated England's Big Ben at the half-hour mark. It wouldn't be long before Collin came home. Maybe he would relieve her tonight. A hot bath—no, a long, hot bath, she corrected herself—sounded wonderful if not dreamlike. *Please, God, let him be in a good mood and willing to play with the kids tonight,* she offered in silent prayer. She loved these kids; she really did. It was just that today, with all their requests, they had drained her of the will to live. School had begun less than a month ago. Why the school board felt the teachers needed to take off already for a two-day conference escaped her tonight.

Back in the kitchen, Louisa picked up a glass from the counter, a dribble of milk left in the bottom. A quick rinse under the faucet, and then she placed it in the dishwasher. All the small chores were done. The counter no longer held books, toys, or dirty dishes. Louisa opened the pantry door and caught a cereal box as it fell. She shook it. Almost empty. Someone had been snacking in secret, probably Madison. She reached for the indoor grill on the top shelf. The cord dripped over the edge and dangled in her way. She wrapped it around her hand to keep it out of her face. Standing on tiptoes, she used her fingertips to work the grill out.

Barking, Cleo burst through the kitchen, chased by Joey.

"Stop running in the house!" They wouldn't; she knew from past experience. Once Cleo began a game, she wouldn't quit until she wanted to. Louisa almost had the grill in her hands. If she were just a little taller . . . There! She balanced it on her fingers.

"Look out!" Joey screamed.

Louisa jerked her head around and saw the tiger-striped 120-pound dog skidding across the floor, straight for her. The "gentle giant" rammed into her leg. She felt her sock-clad feet give way and slide out from under her. The grill slipped from her grasp as she fell to the floor. Her last thought was that dinner would be late.

Salt water burned her lips as she floated onto a white, sandy beach. Piccolo notes from seagulls called to her as they landed in an uneven line onshore. They hunted for forgotten corn curls and abandoned sandwich crusts, their tiny claws etching the sand behind them. A flash of white danced into her view. She glanced at the gauzy skirt grazing her ankles and wondered when she'd changed clothes. Then she noticed her hand held a bundle of calla lilies tied with a dark-green satin ribbon that trailed to her knees.

Next to her, the ocean increased its crescendo. Froth swirled around her bare feet, and the small white bubbles tickled her toes. Like a child, she wove up and down the shore, playing a game of tag with the swash marks on the sandy shoreline. She slowed her steps as a man ahead of her grew larger and larger until she finally stood next to him. He didn't have a name, but she knew she would marry him this day. Her lips began to form the words "I do" when a voice crashed her wedding.

"Come on, baby, wake up." Warm fingers brushed across her cheek. Startled, she tried to open her eyelids, but they felt weighted as if someone had stacked pennies on them. Peeking through her lashes, she discovered a pair of chocolate-brown eyes gazing into hers. And not the milk-chocolate kind but the dark, eat-me-now-and-I'll-solve-your-problems kind. She tried to sit, but the onslaught of pain in her head stilled her like Atlanta traffic in a snow shower. Bright light lit the room around her, but it wasn't a room she knew.

"Louisa, baby. You gave me quite a scare. How do you feel?" His hand trembled as it gently swept across her forehead.

"I'm Jazz." Her words oozed like cold honey past her thickened tongue. She was desperate for information and a cool drink of water. "Wrong woman. Where am I?"

His hand dropped to his side, and he stepped back from her. "Dr. Harrison?" His weight shifted from one foot to the other.

The man she assumed to be the doctor maneuvered past

Mystery Man. From his pocket, he pulled out a penlight and shone it into her eyes.

"Evil man. That's a bit torturous to my brain." She swatted at his hand but pulled back before making contact, realizing his purpose was to help, not hurt her.

"You're in the ER. You suffered a nasty bump on the head, Louisa. You have a concussion, which is making your head hurt." He clicked off the light and placed it back into the pocket of his lab coat. "Your scan came back clean. There is no bleeding in your brain. I'll have the nurse come in and unhook the heart monitor in a minute. You can go home with your husband in a little while."

"Husband?" The monitor showed a jump in her heart rate. "Please, I'm not who you think I am." She wished for them both to dissolve from her sight and for someone, anyone, even a disgruntled fan, to appear in their place. Something like wind seemed to roar in her ears, and she struggled to catch her breath.

"Just calm down. Take a few breaths." Dr. Harrison patted her hand.

The old, reliable remedy—take in oxygen and the world's problems will be solved. Somehow that made her feel normal. She could go home soon, or at least Louisa could. She closed her eyes, willing the two of them to go away.

"Open your eyes, Louisa," the doctor ordered.

Still not willing to play their game, she compromised and opened one. "Light hurts. I'm not Louisa."

"You're just a bit confused right now. Your name is Louisa, Louisa Copeland. The bang on your head gave you quite a headache, didn't it?" The doctor patted her arm as if doing that would change her identity. "This is all to be expected, just a bit of disorientation. Don't worry. Once the swelling goes down, you should remember everything."

Respect for his position kept her from saying that maybe he needed to switch places with her. After all, she knew she was Jazz Sweet.

The doctor turned his back to her. "Collin, I think you need to take her home. Once she's home in familiar sur- roundings, I believe her memory will return."

Collin. She considered the name. *Irish,* she thought. *A romance hero's name.* Maybe she would use it in her next book. He certainly looked the part—strong chin and thick brown hair that begged for a path to be wound through it with willing fingers.

"What if she doesn't?" Collin asked.

"Take her to your family doctor for a follow-up tomor- row. Wake her a couple times tonight and ask her questions. Make her answer with words; full sentences would be even better." She heard the familiar rough scratch of pen on paper. "Give her acetaminophen or ibuprofen tonight." He tore the paper from his pad and slapped it into Collin's hand. "Fill this for pain if she needs it."

Home? Whose home? Jazz dropped the characterization of her newest hero. *Home with Collin?* She focused on those three words. That couldn't be right—she loved adventure, but going home with a man she didn't know went beyond what she would do for book material. She didn't go anywhere without a folder full of notes, and she hadn't spent any time researching living with this man. Panic ran like ice water down her neck.

She struggled to prop herself up on an elbow and demand an explanation. The end of the bed wavered like a desert mirage, causing her to wonder if the head injury had affected her sight. She squinted, trying to sharpen her vision, but it didn't help much.

She needed to tell the doctor—maybe then he wouldn't send her with this man. Jazz started to call out, but the white of the doctor's coat blurred out of her sight before she could recall his name.

Collin bent over her. She noticed that for a man who'd probably been working all day, he still smelled nice. "Well, honey, you heard him. Let's get you back home."

"Water. Please." She pointed to a sweating water bottle that beckoned just out of her reach. Collin put it in her hand but held on to it. For a moment she thought he planned to help her bring it to her lips like an invalid. Good thing he didn't or he'd be wearing it, she wanted to say, but thirst won over talking.

The liquid slid down her parched throat. Feeling better, she returned the bottle to him and then hit him with the big question. "Tell me who Louisa is and why you think I'm her!"

Collin sank down in the chair next to Louisa's bed. She looked paler than his daughter's collectible porcelain dolls. "You don't remember us?"

"Remember you? No. I've never met you. Wait, you

weren't at Jen's party, were you?" Hope touched the edge of her voice.

"Who's Jen?" He rubbed his earlobe while he went through a quick list of Louisa's friends.

"My agent. Jen is my agent."

"Agent? For what?" He knew they hadn't been communicating well, but when did she decide to sell their house? No, she'd said *her* agent, not *ours*.

"I write inspirational romance novels." She crumpled the edge of the bedsheet between her fingers.

"Romance?" Collin felt like he had fallen into another dimension. Louisa had never written a word, much less a book or books. She had said *novels*, as in more than one. Hadn't she? He assessed the situation. It had to be a grasp for attention. He had been working hard, and yes, he probably deserved this. He'd play along for a little bit. "Who do you think you are?"

"Jazz Sweet. I live at . . . on an island or the coast. Florida, I think." She rubbed her forehead with the tips of her fingers.

"Louisa, you win, okay? I'm sorry—I really am—about what I said." He squeezed his hand into a fist and then released it, a futile attempt at ridding himself of the tension in his body. "Let's not play games here. It's late, and it would be nice to go home, wouldn't it?"

"Games? What games are we playing?" She cocked her head at him, her eyebrow raised in question.

The look she gave him wasn't one he recognized. She truly looked lost and confused. His gut clenched. She really didn't know who she was. "Never mind, it's not important. Once you get home, I'm sure you'll be back to normal."

"Go find your wife. Maybe she's in the next room." She waved her hand at him as if to dismiss him. The diamonds on her finger caught the overhead light and winked at him.

Collin grasped her hand out of the air. He felt a tug at his heart as she struggled to pull away from him. "Wait. Look at your hand. See, you have a wedding ring; it belonged to my great-grandmother." He traced it with his finger. "Honey, you're not a writer. And you live with us in Hazel, Illinois."

She brought her hand close to her face and inspected the ring as if she had never seen it before. She jerked her face toward his, and comprehension of the plural word rode across her face. "Us? How many people make an *us*?"

"You, me, and . . ."

She tapped her lower lip with two fingers as she concentrated on the information he was giving her.

". . . the kids." He leaned back in the chair, confident she would remember the children.

Louisa splayed her hand against her chest. "Kids? What kids?" she squealed as if he'd said she lived with a rowdy bunch of sailors. "I think I had better call Kristen now."

Collin grew even more confused, starting to doubt that he was looking at his own wife. Louisa loved those kids. How could she not remember them?

"Who's Kristen?" he managed to ask while massaging the back of his neck with his hand.

"She is my assistant. She's organized and knows all my

plans. I can't keep any deadline without her." She peered around him. "Is there a phone in here?"

Collin looked at the ceiling and counted the white tiles over the bed. He took a deep breath, then let it out. "I'll call Kristen if you give me her number."

"I–I don't know it," Louisa stuttered. Her blue eyes filled with tears, and she whipped her face away from him. The tension in his shoulders eased. This was a behavior he recognized. Louisa never let him see her cry.

"Then for now, why don't you come home with me?" He used the persuasive voice he typically saved for jurors.

"But . . ."

He placed his fingers on her lips to silence her. "I know you're my wife, even if you can't remember. So I'm thinking, why not come home with me and see if your memory returns?"

"You really think I'm your wife?" She glanced at the door expectantly as if waiting for someone to come and tell him differently.

"I know it. And I can prove it when we get home. I'll show you our wedding pictures." Louisa had organized their photos in matching albums. It wouldn't take any effort to find the right year.

"Did we get married on the beach?" Uncertainty shone on her face, but her voice held confidence that he would say yes.

Collin took another punch to his gut. She didn't remember the expensive wedding—her very own fairy-tale day, she'd called it. He shook his head. "No, Louisa. We were married in your parents' church."

"Again, not me." Louisa swung her legs over the edge of the bed. She grabbed her head with both hands. "Ouch. What happened to me, anyway?"

"The indoor grill fell on your head."

She snorted. "Right, like I own one of those."

"You do. While you were getting it off the shelf, Cleo knocked you down."

"Is Cleo your daughter?"

Collin rubbed his chin with his hand and held back a groan of frustration. "Cleo is our dog, a Great Dane, our gentle beast."

"Collin?" Her voice softened, and he leaned in closer to hear. "How many kids are there?"

"Just the three," he said.

"Three? *Just* three? Do you—we—have a nanny?" She rubbed the side of her face with the palm of her hand.

Collin laughed at the absurdity of the question, then sobered, realizing she didn't know the answer to her own question. This could not be good. He summoned his patience before speaking. "Louisa, you didn't want a nanny for them, remember?"

"No. I don't remember. I'm Jazz—have you forgotten? And I've decided. I will not be going anywhere with you. Who knows? You might be a serial killer or a stalker." She crossed her arms and held them against her chest.

"I'm not either of those things. Look, honey, I'm tired. I've worked over twenty-five hours this week and it's only Tuesday. I shouldn't even have come home when I did, but I promised you that I would make it for dinner."

"Please don't call me 'honey,' 'cutie,' or any of those couple names. We're not a couple, and besides, they sound silly."

He didn't know what to say. Louisa liked his terms of endearment. Didn't she? The differences between the wife he had left at home this morning and this seemingly new one dumbfounded him.

"Why did you get married and have a family if you weren't going to participate? What kind of important career do you have? Do you save people's lives? Are you a surgeon?" She glared at him, waiting for an answer.

Her rapid-fire questioning made him feel like he was standing on the courthouse steps facing a battalion of reporters. It didn't matter that the question was one he'd been asking himself lately—right now, being home wasn't feasible. Not with several trial cases and the promise of a partnership dangling in front of him. He didn't have time for anything. If Louisa wanted to be Jazz, he didn't care as long as she kept their family life intact. "I'm a lawyer. That means I have a lot to do tonight. So get dressed and we'll go home. I'm sure you'll remember everything when we get there."

"I'm not going with you." Louisa slid her legs back onto the bed and pulled the sheet up under her chin like a child refusing to go to school. "I'll get dressed as soon as you leave, and then I'm going to—to—"

"To what? Where are you going to go?" He waited to hear her plan, watching her eyebrows bob up and down while she thought. "Well?"

"I'll go to a hotel. So there, problem solved. You don't

have to worry about me anymore. You're free to go." Again, she waved her hand toward the door, dismissing him as she lay back against the pillow. "If you don't mind, would you hand me my purse before you leave?"

"It's at home." He looked down at her. Her blonde hair feathered across the pillow and caught the light from overhead, softening the silky strands. He reached out to touch it, as he often did, but her icy look kept him at a distance. "That's what you want? To be here alone in a hospital, in this town, and not knowing anyone?"

She nodded and pointed to the door.

"Then I'll go." Collin paused at the doorway and turned to give her a chance to change her mind. She didn't say anything, just lay there looking like a lost child, eyes wide and fighting tears. "Nice meeting you, Jazz Sweet." He knew he needed to convince her to come home with him. He couldn't leave her here until her memory returned. There had to be a way, but for now, he'd let her think she'd won this battle. He left the room and didn't look back.

CHAPTER TWO

JAZZ WILLED THE SHARP SPEARS of light to stop stabbing at her closed eyelids. She curled into a ball on the coarse sheet. The thin pillow encased in plastic and covered with cloth crackled under her head. Shivering under the rough blanket, she tried to plan.

She needed answers to basic questions, like where to sleep tonight. Was there a hotel close by? Did she have money or a credit card? Then she remembered—unlike a fashion doll, she didn't come with accessories. No purse. Did she have shoes? She continued to stress over her lack of information. Her easy option had walked out the door the minute she sent him. Now was not the time to celebrate finding a man who would do what she told him. She'd have to do this alone. *Not alone. God is with me, all the time.* At least her faith remained.

She needed to be strong and courageous. She didn't know about her own strength, but she knew she could rely on Christ to get her through anything, even this. They'd been through tougher times together. Hadn't they?

Removing the covers, she sat and slid her feet onto the floor. For the first time, she realized she had on socks. Odd socks. They were white cotton with tiny red hearts across the toe line where they would be hidden by any kind of shoe. Kind of like wearing lacy underwear under plain clothes to keep the real person a secret. A chill went through her. What kind of bra did she have on? Fearful she might find a sheer, black, racy number, she dipped her head and with one finger slowly raised the neckline of the hospital gown away from her chest. *Sports bra in white, nothing to fear.*

The cold from the tile soaked into her toes. Did they keep the room cold in case someone died? *Too morbid, Sweet. Think of something else—like if you don't have shoes and cash, what taxi is going to take you anywhere? A taxi to nowhere.* Forget that, what hotel would let her stay without paying for the room?

It didn't matter. She was determined to find a way once she passed through the exit of the hospital. But first she had to locate the clothes she'd been wearing. Trotting through the exit door clad in a hospital gown wouldn't work. She stood. Unprepared for the sudden slice of pain that ripped through her head, she yelped like a puppy. In defeat, she sank back onto the bed.

The door opened, banging against the wall. *Collin.* She tried to still the odd feeling of happiness that leaped in her heart at the sight of him. "Did someone call a code?"

"You yelled. I came." He loomed over her like a large ape. All he needed to do was beat his chest to complete the image of a male on the loose.

"How very manly of you." She wouldn't admit it to him or even to her best friend, but having him rush in to save her plumped her self-esteem to another level. Maybe he wouldn't be so bad to have around.

Collin scowled at her. She'd made him angry, or at least she thought she had. Maybe she'd embarrassed him. Her mother always said she'd never win a man with her quick tongue or her cooking. So far her mother had been right.

"I can't leave. It's my duty to take care of you because you're my wife. I can't leave you here."

Duty? That was a loaded word, and she had a feeling he'd like to leave her here. "Your duty? You're not a policeman, too, are you?"

"That might have been a wrong choice in words. I meant I'm not leaving even if you don't know who I am. Like the vows say, in sickness or in health. This qualifies."

"Still not going with you, sick or healthy—which I am, by the way. There's nothing wrong with me except you." That stung, and she knew it the minute the words charged from her lips like a dog after a squirrel. She realized she should be a little nicer. After all, he had been sweet ever since she woke up in this place.

"I have proof." He reached into his back pocket and pulled out his wallet. "Look." He flipped it open to a picture. "That's you and me in front of our home." He turned the plastic page. "Here's a school picture of our daughter. Now do you believe me?"

Jazz took the wallet from him and turned back to the picture of him and his wife. "You think I look like her? I don't."

"There's a mirror over there." Collin grabbed her wrist and started to pull her from the bed.

She resisted. "Stop it. I'm not getting out of this bed with you sitting there."

"Why not? It's just a mirror."

Her face flushed. "Because there isn't a back to this lovely gown, and I'm not married to you. You aren't allowed to see my backside."

His lips twisted into a grin. "I've seen it before, but I get it. You don't remember." He slid his arms out of his suit coat and placed it over her shoulders. "Slip this on; it will cover enough to protect your virtue."

The jacket was warm from Collin's body, and the heat relaxed Jazz in a way that made her feel safe. The exotic smell of spice and cedar surrounded her as she clutched the front together. "Thank you."

Collin held out his arm for her to grasp. He led her to the tiny mirror over the sink. Jazz found herself looking not at her familiar reflection, but at the woman from the picture. "My hair is shorter. And it's not red." She reached up to touch the foreign blonde locks.

"It's never been red, but you threaten to dye it at least once a month. And you cut it a few weeks ago; that's why it's shorter." He reached for her hand to bring the photo next to her face, its image reflected beside hers in the mirror. He pointed to it. "Look at the grin and then compare it to yours. It's you. You are Louisa."

She stared at the familiar face standing against the back-drop of an unfamiliar world. She felt the corners of her lips reach for the ceiling in an attempt to replicate the smile. *Could I be her?* The wallet felt heavy in her hand, and a few bills peeked over the edge, tempting her to find a way to take them. If he were so concerned about her, he could pay for a hotel room, at least for the night. But he didn't offer and she didn't ask. She gave him back his wallet, wishing for more options.

She wouldn't be in this mess if she had her BlackBerry with its vast lists of e-mail addresses and cell phone num-bers of friends, but she didn't. She considered going back to his house. At least she would have a place to stay tonight, and maybe in a few hours she would remember where she really lived.

Still, he could be crazy. Convincing, but crazy. *But where did he get the picture?* The arguments for not going home with a stranger bombarded her already-overloaded brain. She decided only one thing could ease her mind. "Are you a Christian?"

"What?" His eyes blinked fast as if processing each word letter by letter. The astonishment on his face didn't offer her comfort. "I don't think anyone has ever asked me that before." He gazed past her head as if he would find the answer inserted between the upside-down *E*s on the eye chart behind her. "Yes. I am."

Not exactly the quick response she'd hoped for. But maybe she could trust the answer since he did take time to think about it. "I'll go home with you for a while—until morning, anyway. If I decide to stay, you have to call me Jazz and hire a nanny. I don't know anything about children."

"Great. Your stuff—"

She glared at him.

"Sorry, *Louisa's* stuff is in here." He retrieved a bag with the name Copeland emblazoned on the side with a thick black marker. He reached in and pulled out a pair of black-frame glasses. "Maybe you'll recognize me if you put these on."

"Glasses? Am I losing my sight?" She held her hands in front of her face. She could see them fine, ten manicured fingers. With *pale-pink* nail polish? When did she stop biting her nails? And light pink? That had to come off.

"You've worn glasses since the sixth grade." He held them out to her. "You need them for distance."

She pushed them away from her. "No thanks. I don't require them."

"Sure. This is one you'll find out on your own soon enough." He tossed them back into the bag. He pulled out a white cashmere sweater and some jeans and set them on the bed. "Why don't you get dressed?"

"But . . ."

"I'll wait outside. Don't worry." He left, closing the door behind him.

She wondered if he was standing guard so no one would enter, or had he walked down the hall? It didn't matter. Here was an answer to one of her problems. Clothes—not what she would choose, but they seemed to be her size. Tossing Collin's jacket on the bed, she picked up the soft sweater and slid it over her head, then climbed into the jeans. She tried to wrap her mind around the fact that they fit. Fit well, even.

Jazz called out to Collin that it was safe to enter. She watched his expression to see if there was any reaction to her appearance. Did she look like his wife to him? He went straight for the bag on the floor.

Picking it up, he reached in and withdrew a pair of navy Crocs and handed them to her. "I brought these from home. Slide them on and we'll get out of here."

She shuddered. "I don't wear Crocs." Kristen would know something was terribly wrong if she saw Jazz in a pair of Crocs, and navy ones at that. "I suppose Louisa wears these too?"

He nodded. "Since these are the only shoes we have right now, I'd suggest you put them on your feet."

She took the offending shoes from him. The rubber felt clammy in her hand. There were scuff marks stretched across the toe. Nothing like the expensive leather she usually wore. Would they fit or feel strange on her feet? She'd worn her cousin Amy's old shoes when she was younger, and she had vowed never again to wear another person's shoes. Yet here she was, sliding a cold navy Croc on her foot. "It fits."

"Yes, Cinderella, it does." He plopped on the bed next to her and watched as she slid on the other one. She slipped a quick glance at him, startled to find him staring at her. He smiled. She didn't.

"You have a sense of humor—funny. One more thing, Collin."

"What?" He put his hand in his pocket and jingled his keys.

"I'm not sleeping in the same room with you."

She watched as his lips moved, but he didn't say anything. She wondered what he held back. "Collin?"

"I'll sleep on the couch. Anything else, *Jazz*?"

"That's it—except I'm hungry. What did the cook make for dinner?"

CHAPTER THREE

AFTER GOING OVER all the things Jazz couldn't do or shouldn't swallow in the next eight hours, Emily the nurse thrust her official clipboard into Jazz's hand. "Sign here, by this *X* and this one." Both were circled in red ink on the canary-yellow paper. For emphasis she tapped one *X* with her index finger, where purple polish lingered in the edge of her cuticle. *Are nurses told to remove all the color from their nails before coming to work? Does Emily paint her nails, then take it off before her shift every day? If she didn't, would her supervisor stick a note in her permanent file?* Rules and how they got broken fascinated her. She started to ask but then remembered she had bigger problems. How to sign her name stood first in line.

Louisa? Louisa what? She couldn't remember. With a flour-ish, she wrote *Jazz Sweet*, scribbling across the two required lines and thinking if they didn't like it, they could keep her here. Finished, she handed Emily the clipboard and waited for her reaction.

"You can go home now," Emily said without looking at the signature. She ripped off the sheet of instructions and handed a flamingo-pink copy to Jazz. "Make sure you follow all of these tonight. And you—" Emily turned to Collin on her way out of the room—"don't forget to wake her every two hours."

"Sure, no problem." Collin straightened his back and moved away from the wall. He retrieved the plastic bag from the chair where he'd dropped it. "Do you want to keep this bag? It has your name on it."

"No." Did he expect her to take *that* with her? She would stuff things in her pockets and increase the size of her hips before she carried a cornflower-blue bag with plastic handles anywhere. Besides, *her* name wasn't on the thing. "You take it. There's nothing I can use in there—no phone, no purse, no cash."

Collin reached inside the bag. "You need your glasses." He tried to hand them to her. She slapped his hand away.

"I don't need those. I told you before; I don't wear them." He shrugged his shoulders and muttered something as he tossed them back into the bag. The only word she could make out was "stubborn."

"Let's go, then." He scrunched the neck of the bag in his large hand. She doubted it would fit through the handles.

He offered his elbow for her to grasp, but she ignored it. She still didn't feel comfortable leaving with him and didn't want to touch him or give him any sign of encouragement at all.

"Are you coming?"

"Yes." She grumbled inside about committing to going with him, knowing she wouldn't go back on her word. It was a matter of principle. She remembered a lesson from sixth-grade Sunday school class about "letting your yes be yes and your no be no." Or something like that. Often she reminded herself of the promise she'd made to do that. Right now it seemed like a foolish vow. He still held his arm out for her. Despite her misgivings she grabbed on, and granite connected with her hand. Under that suit coat lurked a muscular man.

After a few strides, her confidence grew and she let go. She could walk on her own. Determined to prove it to him, she rushed ahead. Except everything seemed out of focus, like Vaseline had been smeared across the lenses of her eyes. She banged into someone on a gurney, sending it squeaking a few feet down the hall. "I'm sorry." She tried to retrieve it, but instead of metal, she grasped air. She waited for him to laugh.

"There's no one there. Now will you try the glasses?"

With exasperation instead of humor, she didn't turn to face him. She wouldn't give him the satisfaction of seeing the frustration she felt. "Fine, but they won't work. It's just this head injury." Behind her, she heard the crinkle of the bag. Rubbing her eyes failed to remove the offending film. Giving up, she held out her hand.

He slapped them into her open palm without a word. She winced as she slid the cool plastic frames over her ears. The hallway in front of her sharpened into view. She gasped. "I can see!"

Collin remained silent.

"You were right about the glasses. And the shoes." She hated to admit that to him but was still thankful he didn't use the opportunity to gloat. One more piece of the puzzle to cram into place. Her gut twisted at the unknowns waiting for her at Collin's home.

They walked to the parking garage like bordering states with a river between them. The lights on the ceiling cast a yellow pall over the concrete floor, and the oil stains resembled dried blood. Car exhaust hovered low, making it difficult to find a breath of fresh air. Her stomach threatened to uproar if she didn't leave the premises immediately.

Collin stepped out in front of her, turning her with his body and herding her like a lost sheep. "That's ours."

A minivan. A red one. *Could it get any worse?* Collin held the door open for her. "Do you do this for your wife?"

"Always."

The way he looked to the side when he answered made her think he might be stretching the truth. But he did it right, waiting until her entire body was safely inside, unlike her experiences with other novice gallant males.

Settling in the seat, something crunched underneath her foot—a fast food bag, trash. She wrinkled her nose as her stomach almost bolted. The smell made her think about investing in one of those multicolored, polished-page cook-books. Almost.

A glance into the back proved Collin told the truth about having kids. Soccer balls, greasy fingerprints on the window, and a French fry poking out between the seats proved it. A chilly wave of reality broke over her head. She struggled to breathe.

He touched her arm. "Hey, something wrong?"

"No." Her eyes linked with his. The intense ache of long-ing shocked her. *Who is this man? Could he be my husband?*

Collin looked away first. "Buckle up."

Her heartbeat slowed at his suggestion. Did he think her a child? "I intended to."

"Sorry, it's a habit. You—Louisa—always get distracted with the kids and forget to buckle yourself." He reached across the console and brushed away her hand when the clip refused to connect.

The belt clicked and he retreated. Jazz tried to ignore the warmth his hand left on hers. "She must be a good mother if she cares more about her kids than herself."

"The kids always come first in Louisa's life."

"Where do you fit in?" Using her foot, Jazz pushed the trash on the floorboard into a neat pile in the corner.

Collin gave her an odd look she couldn't decipher. He flipped the blinker with his hand and pulled onto the street. "I don't want to talk about my life with Louisa. Not until you remember who you are."

"I thought I could gather insight into marriage. Research I can use, since I've never had the experience of being married."

He didn't reply but stared ahead as if she didn't exist. And she didn't, at least not the way he wanted. Something deep inside suggested to her that this wouldn't be just a gleaning of insight into marriage—more like stumbling into the mother lode of knowledge.

Collin wrestled with his feelings about bringing Louisa home with him. The doctor had assured him there wasn't anything more they could do for her. Still, it felt unethical to be shuffling her to a place she didn't want to go. But what else could he do? He was married to her, and he couldn't leave her at the hospital. Maybe he should offer her a hotel room for the rest of the night. *It's still not too late to do that,* he argued with himself as he weighed the pros and cons like any good lawyer. His problem? He didn't have a judge and jury to make the decision for him.

To drown out his thoughts, he pushed the knob to turn on the stereo. A CD Louisa had in for the kids began to peal. He didn't want to listen to high-pitched children's voices singing about swallowing flies right now. He switched to the radio and began a scan. Sound bites crowded the airwaves. He let it run through its cycle until it circled back to the university station and soothing, soft jazz notes fragmented the quiet of the van. Increasing the volume, he sneaked a peek at his wife to see if it bothered her. Her eyes remained closed, so he settled back against his seat.

His thoughts went to the work stowed in his briefcase. The case would be going to trial in a few weeks. That would bring more trouble into his life. Louisa hated how much time trials took from their family. And he knew she was right, but he loved the thrill of the fight and the excitement of the victory.

A small moan came from the other side of the van. He glanced over at Louisa. Streetlights silhouetted her head, angled back against the headrest. Blonde bangs partially covered her face. *Beautiful.* He watched the gentle rise and fall of her chest as another soft moan escaped her lips. Dreaming? About what? Even without the turn of events, he was clueless about his wife and her dreams these days.

When had the two of them drifted so far apart? He missed sleeping next to her, listening to her soft breathing, the scent of jasmine in her hair from her favorite shampoo. He missed the way she would snuggle next to him while she slept.

He sorely regretted the argument that had sent him to the couch to sleep. In his defense, he'd been tired when he yelled, saying she cared only about being a mother, not about being his wife. The crestfallen look on her face as she ran into their room, sailing a pillow and blanket into the hall before slamming the door and locking it, haunted him tonight. He had knocked and pleaded at the door, trying to apologize and only walking away when he heard the bathwater running. The next day, the flowers he sent didn't melt the ice from her gaze. *Roses.* Lots of them, something like two dozen, with a sappy *I'm sorry* card. When he came home, they were stuffed in the trash can at the curb.

Get over it, Collin. She doesn't even know she's your wife anymore. He suddenly sucked in a sharp breath as another thought followed, generating a ray of hope he hadn't known he craved. Maybe it was a second chance, a gift from God to make his marriage work. If ever there was a time, this would certainly be it. And he knew he could do it . . . that is, *if* he wanted to.

Jazz peeked at the strange man through her eyelashes. He appeared motionless, his neck frozen stiff, his head facing straight. His face glowed from the dash lights as he stared at the road ahead. She turned away and looked out the window. She didn't speak, instead choosing the comfort of silence against the backdrop of John Coltrane. The quiet suited her hurting head. And if she talked, she might find answers to questions forming in her mind, answers she didn't really want to know.

Cole, Camden, Clare . . . What was this man's name again? The road signs glimmered in the streetlights outside her window, and none of them were familiar. *Just an adventure,* she tried to reassure herself. *Think of it as material for a future book.* Yeah, right. She didn't write science fiction. But then again, according to tall, dark, and good-looking sitting next to her, she didn't write romance, either. What a mess she had awakened to. Did this man—*Collin,* she reminded herself. *His name is Collin, and he thinks you're his wife and probably expects you to sort socks and fold his underwear into perfect squares.* She snorted a laugh.

"What's so funny?" Collin asked, casting a glance her way. "Did you remember something?"

"No. It's the situation. I don't understand why you would take a stranger home with you." She tugged on the lap belt, which clung tighter than the new designer jeans she'd found on sale last week.

"You're not a stranger, but I will admit you're acting strange." With his brow furrowed, Collin paused as if in deep thought. "Louisa, do . . ."

"Jazz. Please call me by my name—not hers." She released the seat belt. It sprang back and hit the door with a clunk.

"Put your seat belt on. It's late, and I don't need to be pulled over for a ticket tonight."

"It's too tight. I'm trying to fix it." She pulled the belt hard and away from her, then reconnected it.

"Jazz, we—I have children, and they aren't going to understand why you don't know who they are." His hand clenched the steering wheel, and she imagined if there were enough light, his knuckles would appear white.

"This is not my problem, Collin. I didn't ask to go home with you. In fact, I demanded to be sent to my own house." She squirmed in her seat. The belt inched tighter, squishing her lungs.

"You can't even give me an address, Lou—Jazz." Collin

corrected himself at the last second. "How can I put you on a plane with a ticket for Someplace, Florida? Even if you weren't my wife, I wouldn't do it."

Jazz stuck out her tongue at him and showered him with a raspberry.

"Well that's a grown-up response," Collin said. "Louisa would never do something so juvenile."

"Guess that proves it. I'm not your wife." She crossed her ankles and then uncrossed them, fighting the feeling of being trapped.

"Sorry. You're married to me, unless Louisa has a twin sister I don't know about." An odd look passed over Collin's face, leaving her with an uncomfortable feeling. It bothered her that she didn't know how to interpret his facial clues.

"Do you think she does? Have a twin? It could happen." And what a story that would be to write! If she had her notebook, she could jot it down. She didn't see a piece of paper anywhere, not even a pen stuck in the sun visor.

"I'm sure she doesn't. Besides, if she did, what are the odds she would be knocked out and you would be put in her hospital bed with the same kind of head injury? On the same day?"

"You're a very logical person, aren't you?" *And I bet you aren't much fun at parties either,* she added for her own benefit.

"It helps in my career—allows me to connect the dots and find the best way to represent a client in his best interest."

"Is it hard to keep track of so many details in a case?" Drat, she wished she had something to write on. She had a

real-life lawyer just a few feet away and could ask him anything, but the way her head hurt, she knew she wouldn't be
able to recall his answers without notes.

"I have to be organized and make sure I've done all the
research."

"So that's why you don't come home until late?" In the
brightness of the streetlights she saw his lips tighten. "Bad
subject?"

"You know it is." He turned the volume up on the radio.

Feeling fatigued, she didn't argue with him. She twisted
the ring on her finger, and the motion felt oddly familiar. But
it couldn't mean anything. She must have worn a ring before
and naturally twisted it like any woman might do.

The diamonds caught the beam from an oncoming car
and flashed brilliant red. She shivered as a feeling of familiar-
ity floated through her mind. Déjà vu? No, not possible. *It is
pretty.* Maybe she'd written about a similar ring? She wouldn't
mind owning a diamond. She vowed to enjoy it until Louisa
returned. Then maybe she'd buy one for herself with her next
advance.

"So what are you going to tell your kids?" She posed
her diamond-clad hand against the window, where the ring
reflected the streetlights as they passed, occasionally sending
out prisms of color.

"I don't know. I'm still thinking about it." Collin slowed
the car and turned into a fast food place. He maneuvered the
van between two others. "Want to go in or eat in the car?"

The restaurant lights were bright enough for her to count

the buttons on a customer's shirt. "The lights might hurt my eyes."

"In the car, then. What would you like?" He waited for her order, his fingers tapping on the door handle.

"Fries and a soda."

"No chicken sandwich? I thought you were hungry."

He had to be kidding. Animal parts? He still thought she was Louisa. "I don't eat meat."

Collin turned the key and silenced the engine. He sat for a moment and pressed his palm against his forehead. "You don't eat meat?"

"Not since I was twelve and found out where hamburger comes from." She didn't care what Louisa ate or that she was wearing her clothes and going home with that woman's husband. Jazz knew she didn't eat meat and wasn't about to start.

He lowered his hands. "What other surprises do you have for me?"

"I don't know. I guess we'll find out. That is, if I'm your wife."

"You're my wife. You're just different."

Jazz hesitated, afraid of the answer. "Bad different?"

"Too soon to tell."

She slumped into the seat. How did she respond to that? Why did she care? "Please don't get me anything. I'm not hungry after all."

Collin started the car. "Me neither. I thought maybe the kids would be in bed if we waited a bit before going home."

"How old are they? The kids?" Jazz sensed this question

would bother Collin even more, but if she was going to help him, she needed more information.

Help him? She hadn't even met the kids, and she was thinking about helping him? *Just for the night,* she reassured herself. *Tomorrow, all of this will be over. By then I'll remember where I live and what Kristen's number is.*

"Tim is four, Joey five, and Madison twelve."

"Nice names. A little middle-class boring."

"And that is why you have a total of two close friends. Not many can stand your thoughtless blurting," her mother's voice burned in her ears.

"You named them," he shot back.

"Surely not. I would have named my children something more exciting." Indignant, she stiffened her shoulders and arched her back in her I-am-a-famous-author pose. "Like Chantel in *Prairie at Dawn,*" she went on when Collin looked at her oddly. "A book that I wrote. Chantel moved west as a mail-order bride. Her new husband had three children. They didn't like Chantel because she wasn't their mother. Those kids were mean to her, and they played all kinds of tricks to make her look bad to Ben. In the end it all works out, though. Chantel—"

"What does this have to do with you not remembering you have kids and a husband?" Collin demanded.

"Just that this whole misunderstanding will work out. Your kids will adjust until you find your wife." Jazz knew her voice sounded calm, but inside she wanted to scream. All she wanted to do was click her heels and go home—to her home, her life, not Louisa's and not his. "Let's just go and see what happens. I do have a bump on my head, so tell them I can't remember anything right now. I'm told kids bounce back from change quite well."

"Maybe in your world of romance, but not in mine," Collin grumbled. He slapped on the blinker and made a sharp turn, and the abrupt motion shoved her against the door. "Sorry," he said with a pinched grimace. "But it's been my experience that when kids bounce, somebody always gets slammed on their way back down."

CHAPTER FOUR

IT SEEMED LOUISA HAD fallen asleep or chosen to ignore him after his last statement. He couldn't blame her; it was harsh. Collin considered how the kids would react to her strange behavior. Madison would no doubt try to use it to her advantage by breaking rules any way she could. Tim and Joey—now those two would either embrace this new person or be afraid. He feared it would be the latter, especially in Tim's case.

Collin slowed the car to the pace of a lost man looking for a landmark. He would have laughed at the comparison if it hadn't rung true. He couldn't be more lost right now.

"We're almost home," he whispered, not wanting to wake her just yet if she was asleep.

No answer came from her side of the van, and he didn't attempt any more conversation.

He turned onto their street, past the Waites' house, then the Kerns', where he could see the television flickering through the window. Did they know how lucky they were to have a normal life?

He entered his driveway. The second-story windows were dark, and he sighed in relief. At least the boys were asleep. A quick glance at the illuminated time on the dash told him even Madison should be. Reaching above his head, he pushed a button to trigger the garage-door opener. The van lights reflected on the metal door as it slid up its tracks. The overhead fluorescent light blinked on and flooded the garage with its garish glare. He inched the van inside, careful not to snag the handle of a pink bicycle, before turning off the engine. Gently nudging Louisa's shoulder, he woke her. She jumped, startled at his touch.

She sat with perfect posture as she glanced at her surroundings.

"Does any of this look familiar?" Collin pointed out the windshield.

Louisa shook her head. "No," she said, her answer almost inaudible.

"Maybe the crime scene inside will jar your memory." Collin grinned.

Her face went even whiter, and she seemed to shrink in size. "Crime scene? I thought you said I fell or something?"

"It was a joke. Are you ready to go inside?" *Nice one,*

Collin. She almost didn't come home with you to begin with, and now you scare her with your sick humor.

"Not yet. Who's watching your children?" Louisa sat statue-still with the seat belt tight against her.

"Your best friend, Laurie." He reached across the middle console and gently rested his hand on her shoulder. "I didn't tell her you lost your memory."

Louisa jerked away from him. "Why not? Won't it be a bit awkward when I don't even recognize my best friend?"

"I find it a bit *awkward* that you don't recognize *me.*" He folded his arms. Collin knew he sounded like a pouting husband, but he'd been exhausted before he found Louisa spilled on the floor unconscious, with Cleo licking her face and the kids trying to save her. Tim was crying and Madison trying to do CPR from directions in a book Joey held.

"I'm sorry, Collin. I know this is upsetting to you," Louisa said. "It's a nightmare for me too. Can you even imagine waking in a strange place and being told you're someone you're not?"

"Not really. But I do feel like I've fallen into another world right along with you. If you don't figure out who you are by morning, I'll tell her. Trust me on this: Laurie will not notice tonight. Does that make you feel better?"

"It might be easier like that if I were Louisa, but I'm not. My headache is beating me down, and I'd rather not argue right now, so let's do it your way." She continued to sit motionless in the passenger seat. She made no effort to open her door.

She's scared. The sudden thought surprised him. Earlier she seemed full of bravado, but he realized it must have been an act. "Are you ready now?" He hoped his voice contained patience.

"I guess."

He watched her take a deep breath, slide her hand to the handle, and pull. The door gave its creaky groan as it opened. He hustled out of the van and maneuvered around the lawn mower. He waited for her, noticing her face still held a grayish cast that caused her ocean-blue eyes to seem twice their size. "This door goes to the laundry room. It's just off the kitchen."

Collin wondered if she realized she had grasped his hand. He missed holding her hand and feeling like her protector. How odd that this quirk of life had Louisa reaching out through someone else inside her mind. Louisa wouldn't have held his hand. She acted as if she didn't need him. He could hand over his paycheck on Friday and disappear for all she seemed to care.

Did he dare hope things might be different now?

Jazz's steps faltered at the kitchen threshold. She gazed in amazement at the expanse of white glass-fronted cabinets. Small lights beamed from underneath them, casting warm ambient light through the room. For a moment she thought she saw a swash of sparkles, the kind that follow clean sponges in commercials. She took a cautious step into the foreign territory.

Everything appeared to be in meticulous order, nothing like her home. Above the counter, white plates played bookends against yellow and blue saucers in a plate rack hanging on the wall. The surface of the kitchen island held only a bowl of glossy red apples. Had she stepped into a kitchen makeover show?

She ran her hand over the cool, gray soapstone counter as she continued the inspection. No mail resided there, no empty glasses next to the sink, nothing to show real people lived here. The door of the stainless-steel refrigerator sparkled. Not even a child's fingerprint graced it. Footsteps on wood followed by a clicking noise caused her to glance up to see a huge dog and a woman hurtling toward her.

"You're home! Oh, you poor thing. I always thought making dinner should be classified as hazardous."

A mass of curls flowed around the shoulders of a woman she didn't know. The woman enveloped Jazz into her arms for a quick hug. Jazz felt herself stiffen. She wasn't free with hugs, at least not with people she'd never met.

"Don't worry about a thing, dear. The kids are sleeping, even Madison. Tom said he would take the big kids to school tomorrow. Collin, you bring them to my house before you leave, and let Louisa sleep in. I'll keep Tim until around noon. Then, Louisa, I thought we could take Cody and Tim to lunch at McDonald's. They can play on the indoor playground while we figure out what to do next Friday night. Well, I'd better scoot home. I'm sure you're tired." She took a step toward the door and turned back.

"Oh, I put the chicken in the fridge. I didn't know if I should put it in the freezer, but then I thought maybe you had already taken it out of the freezer, so it wouldn't be a good idea to put it back in."

Laurie peered at her reflection in the stainless-steel refrigerator door and patted her wayward curls. "I must look a fright. I came right over as soon as Collin called. I'll probably scare Tom. Be good for him; maybe he'll notice me." She laughed and headed for the door. "I'm out of here," she said as she closed the door behind her.

"Thanks for coming," Collin said as the last of her curls bounded away.

"Who was that tornado?" Jazz said.

"Laurie, your best friend."

"Are you sure?" Jazz tried to process a friend that talkative. Her friends were introverted, always thinking about their characters or words to use that had angry alliteration.

"Positive."

"Is she always so . . ."

"Energetic? Yes."

She didn't care for the way he answered her question before she finished asking it. Too much like a married couple, which they weren't. "What's next Friday night?"

"They're having some kind of girls' night out. You and a few other friends are having a sleepover at Laurie's house."

Jazz leaned against the counter, exhaustion overriding her concerns about the strange way her life seemed to be going. "Seriously?"

"Yep. They've been talking about it for weeks. Come on, stay home with me instead." Collin grinned at her.

"I think not." Though Collin was charming, Jazz didn't care for the grin on his face. Didn't he want his wife to have fun with her friends? If she was still here that night, she planned on going to Laurie's girl party. No way would she miss this night out. Girlfriends—good ones, anyway—knew a lot about each other's marriages. She wanted to know about the one she might be participating in. Right now Collin could tell her anything, and she would have no choice but to believe him.

"I think I'll go. Might be fun." She ran her hand along Cleo's back as the dog passed by her.

"They'll be surprised if you do."

"Why? They asked me to come."

"They always ask you to come, but you never do." Collin opened one of the cabinets and retrieved a box of dog bones. He pulled one out. "Sit, Cleo." He waited for her to obey his command and then tossed the treat to her. The dog caught it in her mouth and trotted off.

"I wonder why? Maybe your wife is too busy to go? Or you aren't home to take care of the kids?" She yawned. Collin didn't answer her questions. That seemed odd, but right now all she wanted was to crawl into a bed and sleep for days. She'd figure it all out tomorrow. "Where am I sleeping?"

"Our room, upstairs, first door on the left. Come on, I'll show you." He held his hand out to her.

Now that she stood in his house, she again wondered at

the wisdom of her choice to come here with this man. She kept her hand by her side, refusing to reach out to him.

"Look, I can take you to a hotel for the night if you want." Collin scratched his chin as if that would help his confusion.

He stood close enough for her to hear the roughness of his beard under his thumb. She took a few steps back even though he was giving her a reason to think he wouldn't harm her.

He arched his eyebrow but didn't mention the space she'd put between them. "The problem is, I can't leave you there alone. I'll have to stay with you so I can wake you every two hours."

"Doctor's orders—I remember." She gave the kitchen another quick look, hoping to discover something familiar. Nothing there assured her of being in the right place.

"Maybe Laurie would stay with you? Or you can stay in their guest room? I can call her." Collin reached for the phone on the wall.

Jazz shuddered. She'd be the first to admit she was shallow enough to jeopardize her reputation for a peaceful night. She had a feeling a night with Laurie wouldn't include any sleep. "It's late. I don't think we should ask her."

He nodded in agreement. "And you seem tired, so why not stay at least the rest of the night?"

Tired of arguing with him and with herself, she gave in, deciding to trust God to look after her. "Upstairs on the left, right?"

"Let me walk you upstairs. I want to make sure you don't

pass out or take a tumble down the stairs. You don't need a broken arm or leg too." Again he held his hand out to her.

This time she grasped his outstretched fingers and wound hers through his. It felt right, familiar. "You can show me the bedroom and pick up your pillow to bring back down to the couch."

Collin let go of her hand. "My pillow is already down here, remember?"

At the release of his hand, she felt a shock of abandonment. "No. I don't remember. I have no idea why your pillow would be downstairs, but it doesn't have anything to do with me. So leave me out of it. Don't bother showing me upstairs. I think I know my left from my right hand, and I'll hang on to the banister." She didn't want him to know how much the removal of his hand bothered her. She took a few steps forward, stopped, and straightened. She wouldn't ask. The last few hours weighed on her. She squeezed her eyes tight against the sting of fresh tears.

"Keep walking, past the couch, and look to your right. You'll see the stairs. They're hidden behind this wall." Collin tapped it with his fingers.

"Thank you—" she trailed her hand along the top of a wooden counter stool, refusing to look at him—"for not making me ask." She crossed the wood floor, barely taking in the surroundings other than to notice the lack of clutter.

"Try to get some sleep. I'll be up to wake you and make sure you're doing all right a few times tonight, like the doctor said. I'll knock, so you'll know I'm at the door."

"I don't know if you should do that." She squinted her eyes against the sudden pain that sparked in her head. Right now she couldn't handle the thought of a strange man waking her in the middle of the night. It didn't feel right; it felt . . . what? She poked around her gut. What did she feel? Her stomach churned. She couldn't answer her own question.

"I won't come in the room unless you don't respond when I call your name. It's my responsibility to make sure you're okay. How would it look if you slipped into a coma or something? I may have to go to jail for life, and then who would take care of the kids?" The tilt of his head, with his wide brown eyes and puppy-dog look, caught her heart and gave it a gentle squeeze.

"You're a lawyer; surely you'd find a way to get a reduced sentence." She smiled to soften her words so he wouldn't think she was anti-lawyer. She slid her hand up the white railing and climbed a few steps.

"Jazz?"

She stopped but didn't turn to face him. "Yes?"

"Good night." His voice was as soft as a summer breeze on her cheek.

"Night." Unexpected happiness rose within her chest, and she smiled. She didn't want to admit it, but it felt good to hear someone say that, someone male.

In the upstairs hallway, a pool of light ebbed from the first room she came to. She peeked in. A night-light in the shape of a train bathed the room in warm peach. Books were lined by size on shelves, a basketball hoop had been painted on the wood floor, and a small table decorated with a wooden train sat at the end of the bed. She shuddered at the magazine layout. Yet it was a real child's room. The evidence lay in the bed tangled in sheets, brown hair in soft spikes across the pillow. A miniature hand dangled over the side. With great stealth she walked past, afraid to waken the boy within.

She found the master bedroom. The lack of personal belongings made her feel as if she'd stepped into a hotel room. No opened books were sprawled on the bedside table, no stray socks were on the floor, and the carpet still showed signs from a recent vacuum-cleaner attack.

The bed loomed large in front of her. The comforter faded from pale beige to tan in an indistinct pattern. She ran her fingers over the fabric. Cotton, no texture, but there did seem to be a fern motif. Hooray—some form of expression! Collin's wife—Louisa, Jazz reminded herself—seemed to be lacking a personality, more of a clean-slate brain. Maybe that's why Jazz couldn't remember being this woman. If she was her. No, that wasn't right; she wasn't the woman who lived in this house. She wasn't someone without a personality. Why, her name alone shouted that she had pizzazz!

The crystal clock on the nightstand echoed the time in her body—late. She longed to land facedown on the bed among the cream satin pillows stacked against the head-board. She pushed the door closed and turned. Then she saw it. A dresser stood to the right of the door, and over it hung a giant wall portrait. Of her. In a wedding dress, holding a bouquet of calla lilies tied with a forest-green satin ribbon.

Soft beige carpet muffled her landing as she sank to her knees. *Dear God, who am I?*

Collin watched the familiar stiffness of Louisa's back as she climbed the stairs. He had noticed her walking away from him all too often this past month. Even if she thought she was someone else, Collin had no doubts she was his wife, and his heart ached at the chasm between them.

He searched for some excuse to follow her, then remembered the ibuprofen. She would need that. Rushing back into the kitchen, he found a bottle of extra-strength hiding in the cabinet behind the cartoon-character vitamins Louisa doled out every morning to the kids.

Collin doubled-timed up the staircase to their room, stopping abruptly in his tracks at the closed door. He gave the door a quick tap with his hand, almost hoping she wouldn't answer so he'd have a reason to rush in, be her hero, and save her.

The door opened, but no more than the width of a cell phone. His wife peeked around the edge. "What?"

"Here." He thrust the bottle at her. "You might need these. Now you won't have to navigate the house in the dark to find them."

"Thanks. I didn't think about needing to take them later." Her hand stretched beyond the cracked opening, grasped the bottle, then closed the door.

Resigned, he went back downstairs to what had become

his bedroom—the family room. He yanked open the armoire doors and pulled out the pillow and blanket, tossing them onto the girly couch. Toile was what Louisa called the fabric. "Very chic," she'd said. He had wanted brown leather, not this cream and brown stuff.

He scratched the back of his head and stretched. He knew he should review the stack of papers in his briefcase, but instead he scooped up the remote from the top of the glass coffee table. He used his thumb the way it was meant to be used, turning on the TV and cruising through the stations to search for something interesting. The channels flew by. He didn't stop until a Japanese Western dubbed in English caught his attention. Realizing it was nothing but mindless entertainment, he relished the relaxation it would bring him.

Stripping off his shirt and suit pants, he draped them across a chair. In his boxers, he stretched out on the sofa, and his feet bumped the arm. Groaning in frustration, he twisted until his knees bent, hanging slightly over the edge. He prepared for another long night of trying to get comfortable. He dozed off and on, changing the channel as the night went by but never finding anything to watch except infomercials that attempted to sell him something he didn't need.

"Collin. Collin." A small hand clenched his shoulder, shaking him.

He sat up and rubbed his face with both hands. The television shot varied colors through the darkened room, creating a sci-fi vision behind his wife. "What, Louisa?" He blinked his eyes, trying to shake the sleep from them. He jolted, realizing he should have checked on her before now.

"My head hurts and so does my wrist, the one I need to open this." She held the offending bottle out to him. "Can you get the lid off this?"

Collin swept the blanket out of his way and reached for the bottle. "Childproof cap," he grumbled. "More like adultproof."

"Um, Collin. You don't have any pajamas on."

He glanced up in time to see her backing away, her gaze fixed on the ceiling. "Sorry." He retrieved the blanket and covered his legs before remembering it was his wife who stood before him. "I never wear pajamas. I guess you still think you're Jazz?"

"Who else would I be?" She rubbed her forehead with her hand. "Don't answer."

Collin lined up the arrows on the cap and squeezed. The lid popped off in his hand. He shook out two caplets and handed them to her.

She tossed them into her mouth and swallowed, without water.

He could feel the edges in his own throat. "Don't you want something to drink with those?"

"No, I never do. I learned how to take pills without liquid in Mexico. Good water is precious there."

"Mexico?" He felt like he'd been surprised by the prosecution. "When did you go there?"

"Long time ago, before my parents died."

"Your mom is still alive—or, rather, Louisa's mom is."

"No. I'm sure my mother is dead."

He had to admit this new Louisa fascinated him with her imagination. He patted the cushion next to him. "Want to sit and tell me about Mexico while you wait for the pills to kick in?"

Hesitation flashed across her face. Shades of Louisa not wanting to be near him? Then she surprised him by plopping down next to him.

"My parents were missionaries." She yawned and leaned against the back of the sofa. "I was about twelve when we went there."

He couldn't picture Louisa's mother as a missionary. She seemed cold to him, almost uncaring—even when it came to her daughter. "Can you speak Spanish?"

"*Sí.*" She tilted her head and rested against his shoulder.

Collin blinked in surprise. The only Spanish Louisa knew came from *Sesame Street*. Of course, she hadn't really spoken the language. One word everyone knew hardly counted as conversational. She relaxed against him. It felt nice to have her there again, her Eve to his Adam.

"I saw the wedding photo in the bedroom. It's my face, but I don't remember any of this," she said. "Were we happy together?"

He realized she couldn't know the depth of pain her question caused. He didn't know how to answer it. If he said yes, what if her memory returned in the morning? But if he said no, she might demand to leave him right now. He couldn't take that chance. Even if she never remembered being Louisa, he didn't want to lose her.

He glanced over, and her eyes were closed. Her smooth, even breathing eased his anxiety. Saved by the sandman! He wouldn't have to answer her question. Not yet, anyway.

CHAPTER FIVE

SOUNDS OF SCURRYING SQUIRRELS outside the door woke Jazz from an excellent dream she thought would make a great novel. Keeping her eyes closed to contain the idea, she reached for the pad of paper and pen she kept on her night-stand. Her hand slid across the smooth surface—nothing. It wasn't where she'd left it yesterday.

"Stop it. It's mine!"

A high-pitched voice shattered her idea, and the fabulous plot flew out of her mind. That wasn't a squirrel. As much as she wanted to keep them closed, she wrenched open her eyes. Bright sunshine caught the edge of a crystal frame throwing colorful rainbows across the duvet cover. It held a photo of three smiling children and a dog—a big dog. She slammed her eyelids closed again and clicked her heels together under the covers like Dorothy in *The Wizard of Oz*. She wanted to go home!

She peeked through her lashes. The room remained the same. Maybe it only worked with ruby slippers. Or maybe she was still dreaming? She plucked a hair from her arm and winced at the pain. "Nope, not residing in Neverland." She picked up the frame and tilted it to study their small faces. What did that man say his kids' names were? Something boring, she remembered, along with the argument that followed. And what was his name? Caleb? Collin. The name shot into her brain. That's good. Keep going. . . . Who are the others? She tapped her lip with her index finger and tried to recall. Mel, Misty—Madison! That was the daughter's name, Madison. The other two names escaped her. And the dog? She had no idea, and right now she didn't care. She slammed her head back into the pillow. Why was she here?

Jazz decided to maintain silence, hide out in the bedroom until the house was quiet, and then research the subject. There had to be something around this house with the names of the kids on it. Didn't moms write names on coats? If she were a kitten, she would have purred with satisfaction at her brilliance. This would be easy. Match the name, the size of the coat, and the kid—that's all she'd have to do. She lay back on the bed and prayed that no one would discover she was awake. As soon as they were gone, she planned to take a bath in that wonderful Jacuzzi tub she saw in the bathroom last night.

There were whispers at the door.

"It won't hurt to peek."

She sank her head back into the fluffy pillow, a pillow worthy of the most expensive hotel she'd stayed at one summer. Why had she been there? She pondered that question while she closed her eyes and feigned a deep sleep. Soon the soft sound of bare feet on the carpet alerted her of an invasion. She didn't move. Maybe the intruders would go away if they thought she was sleeping. She tried to slow her breathing and willed her eyelids not to twitch. Although in a dream state they are supposed to twitch, aren't they? She considered that thought for a moment, then let her eyes move a tiny bit. She was so involved in her acting skills she hadn't realized one of them had come closer. She almost jumped when a soft, cool finger poked her cheek.

"It's not Mom," a very small voice said, close enough that she felt the breath of the breather.

"Is too. She looks like Mom."

"If she's Mom, why is she still sleeping instead of making us breakfast?"

Jazz forced her body to continue to lie as still as possible. No way would she climb out of this nice, soft bed and make oatmeal or whatever kids ate for breakfast these days. Maybe if she stayed motionless they would go away and their father would get their breakfast for them. Besides, didn't he say last night he would take care of his kids this morning?

"Why doesn't she move?"

Jazz fought the urge to open her eyes to see who was leaning over her.

"Maybe she's dead," said another.

"No, she's not," wailed a small voice. "She's not dead! She's Mom."

Always a sucker for someone or something in pain, she couldn't handle the hurt in that small voice. She opened her eyes.

A small boy scooted away from the bed and screamed. "She's awake!"

The sound of Collin's voice came from the hall. "Kids, are you in there with your mother?"

"Shh, maybe he won't find us in here," someone whispered.

Collin entered the room. "I told you kids to stay out of here. She's not feeling good."

His aftershave wafted through the room, reminding her of the deep woods in the fall. She couldn't figure out where that memory came from since she didn't remember ever being in the woods during the fall season. Maybe she traveled from Florida to Tennessee and hiked the Appalachian Trail? Didn't matter; her nose liked the scent.

"Madison said she wasn't our mom and we wanted to see. She is our mom, isn't she, Dad?"

Collin cleared his throat. "Your mom hit her head last night, and she's having memory problems."

Jazz sat up in bed, wincing at the pain in her head. "I'm not dead, and I'm not your mom. You can call me Jazz."

"Dad, Mom's name is Louisa." Joey looked at her like she was insane, then back at his dad for reassurance. "Right?"

"Yes, Joey, it is, but after the grill fell on her head, she woke up thinking she is someone else. Someone named Jazz."

"That's a funny name." Joey scrunched his face as if he were thinking hard. "Is it like Jasmine in Madison's movie?"

"I don't have that movie anymore. It's a baby movie." Madison elbowed him. "Brat."

"This is not the time, Madison. Joey is just trying to help." Collin stood against the doorway. Jazz couldn't see his expression, but she had a feeling he wanted to know the answer as well.

"I have a headache and I don't remember right now, but I don't think it's a princess name. Ask me again later and maybe I'll know."

"If Mom is crazy, who's going to take care of me?" Tim asked. "Are you going to stay home with me today, Daddy?"

"I'm taking you to Miss Laurie's house for a little while. Then you'll come back this afternoon, and your mother, Jazz, will watch you until I get home."

"Is that smart, Dad?" Madison put her hand on her hip and squared off to face him. "How do you know she won't do something like . . . like lock him in the bathroom or let him eat candy all afternoon?"

"Miss Laurie is next door, and . . ."

"I'm right here. Why don't you ask me what I'll do to him?" Jazz brushed an annoying strand of hair from her eye. "I may not remember being your mother, but I think I can watch someone so small without hurting him." *Can you?* a nagging voice echoed inside her head. *How do you know? What does a boy child do or eat?*

"I'm sure you'll be fine with him." Collin turned to Tim. "You can watch your videos this afternoon and let your mother—Jazz—rest on the couch, okay?"

"Will she make me a snack?" Tim and Joey looked at her with huge brown eyes, like basset puppies begging for a piece of chicken from the table.

"I think I can manage a snack. Snacking is one of my favorite things to do, Tim."

"Okay, then. I guess it will be fun," Tim said and slid his hand into hers. "I like her."

Collin clapped his hands together. "Everyone, out. Breakfast is on the table, and I'm late for work."

He ushered the children from the room. With the edge of the door in his hand, he turned. "I'll leave my work phone number on the fridge. If you need to, call. And try to rest today, okay?"

"What time do you get home from work, Collin? Please say before school's out."

"Usually around seven, or sometimes eight."

"In the evening?" She moaned and fell back on the bed. "What about dinner? And what am I supposed to do with the kids?"

Collin rested his forehead against the doorway. "I'll leave early and bring home takeout, but please call me if you remember who you are, so I can stay at work."

"Sure." But no way would she call. The doctor said to rest, and that's what she planned to do—no matter who she was.

✑

A door slamming downstairs startled her. Silence crept through the house, no high-pitched voices or feet thumping on the stairs. The only sound came from the electronic hum of the bedroom clock. Had they all left for the day? She crept from the warm bed to the bedroom door, opened it slowly, and peeked around the corner. Nothing to see but beige walls and beige carpet stretching like a runway down the hall.

"Hello? Anyone still here?"

A clock chimed from somewhere in the house as her only answer.

Sighing with relief that there wouldn't be any questions for a while, she strode across the thick-carpeted bedroom to the bathroom. The whirlpool tub beckoned with its high-gloss ceramic tiles. With a quick twist of the brushed-nickel knobs, she started the flow of hot water for a well-deserved bath.

After her indulgent soak, Jazz realized she would have to wear yesterday's clothes or wear something else of Louisa's. Neither seemed appealing, but since clothing was not optional, she had to put something on. She dried off with a thick towel. Maybe Louisa had clothes worth investigating, if her linens were any indication. She decided to check it out.

As she opened the closet door, a light came alive overhead. Stunned, it took a moment for her to take in the size—the room had to be as big as her guest room! The cedar walls were lined with cabinets, shoe trays, and multi-level bars dressed with clothes. An essence of jasmine floated in the air, making her nose twitch. Suits in every shade of gray hung on Collin's bar. Louisa seemed to prefer navy and khaki.

Jazz ran a hand over the clothes and looked for a pair of jeans. Nothing. Doesn't the woman own any? She rapidly slid the wooden hangers aside. Their golden hooks scratched against the metal bar. Everything seemed to boast a designer label, and nothing had color—no reds, no pinks, and no bright blues; not even a plaid peeked from the mass.

And no denim.

A thrill of excitement ran through her. She wasn't crazy; she knew who she was! She'd worn jeans home last night that would prove to Collin that she couldn't be Louisa. He must have been so upset he hadn't noticed what she wore. It was evident to her the woman didn't even own a casual pair of pants. Collin would know that.

Dressed in Louisa's clothes, Jazz felt rather washed out from the vanilla sweater and khaki pants. Her own personality desired attention. Back in the closet, she twisted one of Collin's red ties off its hanger, wound it through the belt loops on her pants, and tied it at the waist. Feeling much better about her appearance, she trotted down the stairs. Collin had said he would leave a number to call him at work. She found it written on a yellow sticky note stuck to the front of the fridge. She punched in the number.

"Good morning. This is Mr. Copeland's office. May I help you?" a well-dictioned woman asked.

"I need to speak with Collin immediately."

"I'm sorry; Mr. Copeland is unavailable at the moment. May I take a message?"

"Yes. Tell him his wife is still missing."

"Missing? Louisa is missing? Has she been abducted? Have you called the police?"

"No, I haven't called them. It's like she's missing, but she's not. Collin knows what is going on; it's complicated. Just have him call home." She wondered how long it would take for him to return her call.

"Let me put you on hold. I believe he can take your call now."

The phone line swelled with soft classical music. Then, "Louisa?"

"Jazz."

"Jazz, what do you mean you're missing or Louisa is missing? Didn't we determine last night that you are Louisa?"

"But that was before I had proof that I'm not her."

"Proof? What proof could you possibly have?" Collin asked, disbelief dripping from his tone.

"Denim. Louisa doesn't have anything denim in her closet, or anything colorful. I only wear denim, and I had jeans on last night." Satisfied with her case, she waited for his rebuttal.

"Did you look in the dresser in the bedroom?"

"No." She rubbed her forehead as she considered the obvious conclusion—she was wrong. Louisa wore denim.

"Then you don't have the proof you need. That's where she—you keep the jeans."

"So she's not missing, or at least you're feeling confident that I'm Louisa?" She could hear him clicking a pen. Was it a nervous habit or was he frustrated with her? She didn't know, and that bothered her. "Quit with the pen; it's annoying."

The pen quieted, but he didn't answer her question about who he thought she was.

"Do you still have the pounding headache?"

The concern in his voice comforted her. "It's still with me and getting worse."

"I'm calling the doctor, then, and getting you an appointment this afternoon. I'll call Laurie and ask her to keep Tim. You lie down and rest. I'll be home soon."

She disconnected and realized that she no longer liked the adventure she had been thrust into, book material or not. This was not fun.

Collin sat in front of the doctor's desk and waited for him to come in after examining Louisa. The desk held a few family pictures but nothing else on its expansive oak top. *Unlike mine.* At this moment his desk overflowed with manila folders and stacks of papers, work he should have completed by now and would have if Louisa hadn't turned into Jazz. He should be at the office and would be if his wife hadn't called him insisting he needed to report her as a missing person. And all because of a pair of jeans. He had immediately called their family doctor for an appointment. On his way out of the office, he'd paused only long enough to tell his secretary he wouldn't be back for the rest of the day.

The door swished behind him. Collin rose from the chair and offered an outstretched hand to the doctor.

Shaking Collin's hand, Dr. Allen said, "Sit down and let's talk about your wife." Dr. Allen plopped a folder on his desk and flipped it open before he sat.

Collin perched on the edge of his seat. He pinched his pants and slid his finger and thumb down the crease on his thigh.

"Before she comes in, I'd like to make a suggestion to you," Dr. Allen said as he carefully turned a few pages over in the folder.

"Anything." Collin felt a moment of hope.

"Her memory isn't coming back, and I believe she has retrograde amnesia." He leaned his elbows on the desktop and made a triangle with his hands, tapping his nose. "Has she experienced an unusual trauma in her life?"

"Like what? We have three kids—sometimes that can be dramatic."

Dr. Allen shook his head. "Nice evasion, Counselor, but I said *trauma*, not *drama*. Retrograde amnesia can be triggered by a bump on the head or a seizure. We've determined that Louisa didn't have a seizure. The grill is heavy and could be the reason for the amnesia. Retrograde amnesia can cause a loss of memory from the time of a specific event. Is it possible your wife had something happen to her as a child that she hasn't told you about?"

"No, no. I don't recall anything that she'd want to forget."

"There is more you need to be aware of: it is likely she'll have problems remembering things from now on as well, although that shouldn't last long. We have seen in some cases like this that patients don't remember their past, so they fill in the details of what they think happened in their past, believing those details to be correct. They aren't trying to lie, understand, but they may offer an exaggerated version of some truth." He paused for a breath, steepling his hands again and resting them on the desk. "She'll likely have frequent headaches that will get worse as she gets closer to remembering."

Collin leaned back into the chair. "Does she know all of this?"

"I've explained it to her, but I'm not sure she'll remember it." Dr. Allen closed the folder.

"Is there anything good about this? Is there something I can do to move the process along?"

"Time will tell. You could try nudging her memory—sometimes a place or a smell will bring back the memory. It is usually a smell associated with the previous trauma that the patient doesn't want to recall."

"How am I going to accomplish that?" Collin would do anything to get his life back on track. He straightened his tie as if that would reinforce the need for normalcy.

"Talk to her mom and see if she remembers anything that might have happened to Louisa as a child—but to forewarn you, many parents are clueless about traumatic episodes, or they refuse to acknowledge them." Dr. Allen leaned back in his chair. "Perhaps you could start by re-creating how you first met, your first date, that sort of thing? I hope your memory is better than mine. My wife tells me she is the only one who recalls everything about our dating years."

"I'm not sure I can remember everything." Collin reached for the BlackBerry in his coat pocket. He typed in *Repeat dates*. What had they done together? They went for ice cream and to the movies, but he wasn't sure which ones. "How detailed do you think I need to be?"

"As close as you can get." Dr. Allen offered a consolation-prize smile. "Give her things to smell, pleasant and unpleasant as well."

"And that will work?" He keyed in *Smells, good and bad.* "Are you thinking like oranges and chocolate?"

"I don't know what might trigger a memory, but don't leave out negative smells like diesel fuel or cleaning supplies."

"Can't she do this herself?" He mentally started lining up those tiny candles with strong scents on the kitchen counter for Louisa to smell.

"There hasn't been a lot of success with that because the patient is able to prepare and push the memory back. If they come across the smell unexpectedly, it seems to have a more powerful effect."

Collin's finger tapped in *Use surprise attack.* "Got it. I can't plop her in front of a banquet of smells and think she'll snap out of this."

Louisa brushed through the doorway. "You aren't talking about me, are you?"

Collin stood. "No. Not really." He scooted over one chair, leaving her the one nearest the door.

"So what's the verdict? Am I ever going to remember my address or phone number in Florida?" Louisa said as she sat down.

The doctor nodded at her. "In time you'll remember things. For now, though, I think it best you continue as you are."

"As Collin's wife?"

"You are Collin's wife. Like I told you in the exam room, I delivered Tim, and Collin was there."

"So I'm to live as a fata morgana?" She sank back into the chair with a sigh.

"A what?" Collin asked. He tapped his foot, afraid of what her explanation would be.

"Fata morgana. It means 'mirage.' I'll be living as your wife, but it won't be real to me until I regain my memory of being Louisa." The words seemed to float with ease from her lips.

"Exactly. Not the words I would have chosen, but it works nonetheless," said Dr. Allen as he pushed his chair back from the desk. "Do you have any questions?"

"Are you sure there isn't a magic drug I can take or some kind of exercise, like standing on my head, to make my memory come alive?" Louisa asked. "It's just so hard to understand that I'm someone else when I feel like I am who I'm supposed to be, yet you keep insisting I'm Louisa." She clasped her hands around her head. "And I have children."

Collin reached over and took her hand. "Louisa, look at me."

She turned to him. Her eyes begged for some kind of reassurance.

"You'll remember and I'll help you."

"How can you? You don't know anything about me."

CHAPTER SIX

COLLIN PRESSED THE toaster button down. He shoved up the cuff of his white shirt and checked the time on his watch. He would be late, no doubt about it. He couldn't afford to come in past eight again tomorrow. Today Cranston would give him the famous stern stare; he just knew it. Maybe an e-mail would even be waiting in his in-box from the big guy himself, expressing concern—not for Collin and his family, of course, but for the firm. Everyone who received a "boss-gram" knew they were being watched and graded on their performance. Coming to the office early was something you knew you had to do in this law office. If you wanted to make partner, being late wasn't acceptable.

Not even when you had a sick wife at home. That was just it, though; he wasn't sure he had a wife. She looked like his wife, but she sure didn't act like it. He toyed with the thought that she might be pretending to not remember. He didn't think Louisa would jeopardize his career like that, but then again, she was angry with him for spending too much time at work. She had hinted more than once that he could afford to send her to the Chase Park Plaza with her friends for a girls' slumber party. He had checked the cost, but two hundred dollars a person was more than he wanted to spend. She would want to take along three of her friends. He made good money, but not that good.

"Daddy?" Tim pulled on his pants leg. "Can I have cookies for breakfast today?"

"No."

"Mom lets me."

"She does not. I'm not here for breakfast, but I know she doesn't let you have cookies." He was tired of these kids lying to him. Yesterday Joey had trotted into the room wearing his soccer uniform. He informed Collin that Louisa always let him wear it to school. And Madison had come to breakfast sporting metallic purple eyelids. He shuddered. His little girl was growing up, and he wasn't ready for that. He wondered where she had found the grape-colored sparkle stuff anyway. She had protested all the way upstairs to the bathroom, yelling that all the girls wore it and it wasn't fair that she had to remove it.

"Yeah, stop trying to fool Dad, Tim," Joey said. "Mom makes us pancakes or French toast in the morning."

"We only get cereal once a week," Madison chimed in.

He turned and stared at the three of them, unsure of who was telling him the truth now. He knew Louisa prided herself on taking care of the kids, but a real breakfast four mornings a week? Louisa had better find herself fast because he couldn't do this every day.

"Consider this your lucky week because you're going to get cereal more than once. That's all I can do in the time I have." The toast popped up. Collin pinched it between his fingers and dropped it on the plate, where it sent blackened crumbs into the air before settling in place.

"Eww. I'm not eating that." Madison plopped into her chair at the table and reached for the box of cereal Collin had placed there earlier. "We need the sugar bowl, Dad."

"You don't need any. There's tons of sugar in that stuff."

"But it doesn't taste good without it," Madison whined and then batted her eyes at her dad. "Please?"

Collin reached into the cabinet and pulled out the sugar bowl because arguing was what he did for a living, not as a hobby. He put the bowl and a spoon on the table. "Only a little." He watched in horror as Joey grabbed the spoon and put three scoops on top of the sugared flakes. "Hey!"

"Sorry, Dad, it's the best way to eat it."

Collin grabbed the cereal bowl from his older son and dumped the contents into the garbage disposal. "Change in the agenda. Now who wants scrambled eggs?"

"I want waffles." Tim bounded from his chair and opened the bottom cabinet where the pans were kept.

"I'm fixing eggs and that's it. If you don't want to eat them, you can eat the cereal without the extra sugar. Now I need a show of hands—who wants the eggs?"

Joey raised his hand. "I want two."

Madison scowled at him. "I'd rather eat cereal."

Tears streamed down Tim's face. "I want Mommy to make my breakfast." He slammed the cabinet door and scurried to the couch. He buried himself under the blanket Collin had left there.

Collin cracked the eggs and managed to keep the shells on the outside of the bowl. He grabbed the milk and poured. Lumps plopped into the bowl on top of the yolks.

Louisa walked into the kitchen and gasped at the chaos. "Is it like this every morning?"

Collin whipped a carton of milk from the counter. "Smell this." He held it under her nose, hoping the odor would change her back into his wife.

"That's disgusting!" She backed away from the sour smell in the plastic bottle.

"Doesn't pour very well when it's lumpy either. So yes, Louisa, breakfast is chaotic this morning."

"Not her, still not her, and if that's how you greet her in the morning, no wonder she checked out." She opened a box of marshmallow cereal and began eating from the carton. The occupants of the kitchen stilled. "What? I'm not allowed to eat breakfast?"

"Not from the box, not ever," Madison informed her. "It

isn't healthy. What if you had just petted Cleo and then stuck your hand full of germs into the box we all eat from?"

"But I didn't just pet the beast. So everything is germ-free, okay?" Louisa reached for one of the bowls stacked on the counter. "If it will make everyone more comfortable, I will conform to your standards of food preparation." She drained the rest of the box into the bowl. "Can I still use my fingers since there isn't any milk, or must I use a spoon?"

Collin turned off the burner. "It doesn't matter to me what you use. I'm just glad you're here and ready to take over breakfast duty. Madison and Joey, we're leaving for school in ten minutes, so eat fast."

Joey and Madison scooted from the table and ran for their rooms.

"Breakfast . . ." Louisa tried to speak.

"That's what I said. I have to be at work on time, and while you're here, this is your new job. Cleo needs to go to the vet this week, and I talked to Laurie; she's bringing the two older kids home from school this week. Next week you have to take over getting them there and back."

"But, Collin, I don't know how to do this."

"It's not hard; any woman could do this job. If you need help, call Laurie. She said she'd help you figure things out this week." He reached for the coat he'd placed on the back of a chair. Slipping his arms in the sleeves, he yelled for Madison and Joey. "Car is leaving in three minutes. Grab those book bags and an apple—at least they aren't spoiled."

Slinging his laptop messenger bag over his shoulder, Collin swiped an apple for himself. "Have a great day." And then he left for the garage.

⁓

Jazz stood in the kitchen, feeling dazed. Tim sat at the counter, marshmallow cereal heaped in small mountains around the outside of his bowl. Drawers and cabinets were open everywhere. She walked across to the fridge and pushed the door shut.

"It was quite chaotic this morning, wasn't it, Tim?"

"Huh?" Tim looked at her with wide eyes. He picked up a green tree and popped it into his mouth.

"Either you don't know what *chaotic* means or nothing seems out of the ordinary for you." Jazz grimaced at the mess before her. "What does Mommy do after Joey and Madison leave for school, Tim?"

"Cleans up stuff."

That much was apparent to her. Collin should really get a nanny. How was one mom supposed to take care of all of this every weekday? At least the weekend would be here soon, and Collin could take over. "After everything is put back, then what does she do?"

"Plays with me. We watch *Charlie Town*."

"Is that your friend from next door, Laurie's son?" Jazz felt a headache starting. She didn't think she could watch another kid today. What she wanted to do was find a pad of paper to write on. She had a great idea for a new story.

"No! *Charlie Town* is a cartoon. It comes on TV after exercise time."

Swift relief swept through her. Tim could be parked in front of the huge screen, and she could write all morning. "Wait, exercise? Do I take you on walks or something?"

Tim snorted, sending half-chewed cereal across the counter. "You exercise to the lady on TV. You know, she tells you to point, point, flex. I have to stay in my room or play on the couch. That's the rule."

"Do we do this every day?"

"Except when I'm at Discovery Preschool." His foot bounced with a steady rhythm against the base of the cabinet.

"Do I exercise every day, or do I take a day off when you're at school?" Jazz collected the empty bowls from the table and plunked them into the dishwasher.

"Every day because you don't want a fat fanny."

Jazz processed the thought of a routine where she lay on the floor, flexing her toes. She self-consciously felt her behind. "Maybe that's a good idea."

"How come you don't remember anything?"

"Because I hit my head on something." And I don't even remember doing that.

"Are you ever going to remember?"

"I hope so, but until then you can help me when I forget, okay?"

"Okay." Tim went back to eating his cereal.

Jazz closed three open cereal boxes and stuck them back in the pantry. She poured the chunky milk into the sink and ran the garbage disposal, trying not to heave at the sour smell. Then she closed the drawers and cabinets. By then Tim had finished his breakfast.

"Put your bowl in the dishwasher, and the spoon too."

"Mom does that."

"Not anymore. You're big enough to do it yourself." Jazz shook her head. How did Louisa have time to do anything if she picked up after everyone else all day?

"Tomorrow is pancake day," he said before sliding off the kitchen stool. "Do you remember how to make them?"

"Not a problem." Jazz made a mental note to check the freezer. She knew how to open a package and toss food into the microwave as well as any mom. Or maybe she'd sleep in one more morning and let Collin handle the early shift.

Tim, taking his new job seriously, tugged on Jazz's hand. "It's time to pick out my clothes for today."

Together they climbed the stairs. Tim informed Jazz of all the chores she had to do that day. Today was Thursday, and Louisa did laundry and went to the grocery store. Could they have lasagna for dinner? Tim wondered. The now-familiar rush of panic began to rise in her chest. Laundry for five, dinner for five, groceries for five. She couldn't possibly do this alone. She sank to the steps. "Tim, where's the phone book? I'm going to get us some help."

Flipping through the yellow pages, she found what she needed. Emergency House-Cleaning Service, available 24-7.

Collin watched to make sure Joey made it into school before pulling out of the car lane. He hoped Madison got through the door too. The second the car stopped, she had dissolved into a group of girls who looked just like her. He glanced at the clock on the dashboard. Even with this morning's fiasco at breakfast, he wouldn't be noticeably late.

In the rearview mirror, he caught his own gaze. "How do single parents do this?" He shook his head. Now he could add talking to himself to the strange things in his life. But who else could he talk to since his wife had disappeared? A bus passed by with an advertisement for health care written in Spanish. "Mexico," he muttered. That was one story he could check out.

Using the speakerphone, he dialed his mother-in-law and filled her in on Louisa's state of mind, or rather, lack thereof.

"She doesn't remember being married to you or having the children?" Beth Harris asked, her voice rising with shock.

"That's about right. She thinks she is a writer and lives in Florida."

"How odd! What does the doctor say?"

"He thinks her memory will return in time. He did ask if there was a trauma of any kind when she was a child. Was there?" He kept the car at the twenty-miles-an-hour school-zone limit, anxious to pass the sign that allowed him to move along faster.

"No, nothing out of the ordinary. Her grandparents

died and we lost a few pets. Her father has only been gone two years."

"Yeah, she thought you were both dead." He flipped on his blinker and slid into the next lane.

Beth gasped. "Both of us?"

"She was happy to know you were still around. But she said something bizarre the first night." The light in front of him turned yellow, and he slowed his car to a stop.

"Can this get any stranger?"

"You have no idea. She said her parents were missionaries and you all lived in Mexico for a while. Do you know where that came from?"

"Mexico. Her father and I went there for a few weeks on a business trip, but Louisa didn't go."

"That must be one of those things the doctor mentioned. He said she would remember parts and add her own details to them. She swallowed her pills without water because she'd learned how in Mexico where the water was scarce."

"She stayed with her father's cousin, Phil Jefferson. I ran into him on my cruise last month. We've been seeing each other. I can ask him—maybe he'll remember something."

"It's good that you're dating, Beth, and I'm glad it's someone you already know."

"It does make it easier."

The light turned green, and traffic surged ahead. "If you think of anything else, give me a call at the office. I need to focus on the drive now."

"I will of course call if I think of anything, but right now

I can't imagine what could have caused such a trauma in Louisa's life." Beth then assured him she would call Louisa right away.

~∞~

The living room, vacant of toys, looked like a peaceful resting place with the backdrop of the lake through the windowed wall. The honey-colored wood floors gleamed. The two-story stone fireplace begged to be lit. The cream-on-brown striped chairs beckoned her to rest and read a book. Jazz almost sighed with pleasure—everything was just as neat as it had been when she'd arrived from the hospital.

"Can you come twice a week?" she asked Joy, the woman who had worked magic on the house.

Joy peeled a yellow rubber glove off her hand. She snapped the fingers back into place before placing it into her blue plastic bucket. "Sure, we can come as often as you want to pay us."

Jazz smiled as she wrote a check to Cleaning Maniacs. She hesitated only a moment before signing the unfamiliar name Louisa Copeland on the signature line. She ripped the check from the book and handed it to the woman waiting by the door. "So I'll see you next Tuesday, Joy." Jazz inhaled the smell of the clean house.

Tim tugged on her hand. "Can I have my snack now?"

"You have to eat it in the kitchen today."

"But I always get to eat in front of the TV."

"Not anymore, bucko. Rules are a-changing around here.

This house is going to stay picked up and clean, and not by me. At least this room is." Jazz wondered what Collin would say when he walked into a picture-perfect living room. When, though, was the question. He'd come home late last night, after she already had Tim and Joey in bed.

"I don't like the new rule. It's like the old rules. Madison and Joey won't like it either."

Jazz bent down to Tim's eye level. "You don't have to like it. You just have to follow it."

"Are you going to change the lasagna rule too?"

"I called Laurie while you were upstairs, and she told me about a wonderful restaurant that delivers." After telling Jazz what she needed to know, Laurie told her to make sure no one knew she planned to order eggplant lasagna if she wanted anyone to eat it.

"Nope, I have that covered. In fact—" she checked the clock on the mantel—"dinner should be arriving from Augustino's any minute now."

"What's an 'astino'?" Tim's upturned nose made her smile.

"I'm not sure. It's a restaurant, like the Italian restaurant on the hill."

Tim's eyebrows scrunched together.

"Laurie told me about it. I don't know where the hill is either. Tim, do you think the restaurant is on top of a real hill?"

"Maybe." Tim nodded. "We could go there sometime and see."

The front door opened, splashing sunshine on the floor as Madison bounced through, her hair bobbing in time to some band playing on her iPod. Joey followed, dragging his backpack on the floor behind him.

"Stop!" Jazz pointed her finger at the two as they prepared to leave their backpacks on the floor. "Carry those to the kitchen."

"We have different rules." Tim's hands were anchored to his hips as he imitated Jazz. "We have a new mom, and she says things have to be done her way."

"Well, I'm not doing anything her way," Madison said. She stomped off to the staircase without a backward glance. As she climbed she called over her shoulder, "I'll be doing my homework in my room, not the kitchen. Do not bother me." She disappeared upstairs. Her bedroom door connected solidly with the doorframe.

At the slam of the door, Jazz grimaced. "Joey? You okay with homework in the kitchen?"

"I don't care." Joey's shoulders drooped as he made his way to the kitchen.

The realization of how difficult this must be for the kids stunned her. They missed Louisa, the mom they were used to. Shocked by the sudden pain of their hurt, she didn't know how to help them understand, not when she couldn't figure out how Louisa became Jazz. Maybe if she tried to act more like Louisa, it would help give them a sense of security. Next week at Laurie's sleepover, she planned to take a notebook, ask questions, and get this right. God had entrusted her with these lives, and she would not mess up. After all, it might be the only time in her life she would get to be a mom.

CHAPTER SEVEN

JAZZ WENT OUTSIDE to play with Tim and Cleo, or rather Jazz let them play while she watched from the fabulous deck. Tim threw a huge rope through the air, and Cleo ran after it, grasped it in her big jaws, and brought it back to Tim. She didn't drop it at his feet, though. Tim would reach for it, and Cleo would back up two steps. Eventually Tim would be lucky enough to catch the raveled ends of the thick braid and would yell, "Drop." Then Cleo would give it up, spin in circles, and the game would start over.

Even though it was fall and they'd had some cool days, today held only comforting warmth. She curled up in a chair, feeling quite satisfied that dinner waited in the oven.

She had successfully managed to get Joey and Madison to work on their homework. Motherhood wasn't as hard as it looked.

Jazz opened the browser on Louisa's cell phone. All she had to do was check Amazon for her books and google her name for a list of all the interviews she'd given. But she'd been stalling all day. Why? She didn't know—maybe she didn't want to leave this idyllic little family. She could learn a lot here; there was nothing compared to hands-on research. And having a husband that looked like Collin was a definite bonus. But then again, he wasn't really hers, was he?

Maybe she could put it off another day.

Madison screeched from inside the house. "I'm telling!"

Battle seemed to be forthcoming, and Jazz shuddered. She had no desire to have any part of it. She'd do it now. One by one, online bookstores came back with suggested titles, none of them hers. Three search engines revealed nothing, and even Wikipedia was blank. She looked up some Christian bookstores and dialed the numbers, but the response to her question, "Do you have any books by the author Jazz Sweet?" was always the same—no such person existed. Discouraged and somewhat alarmed, Jazz swallowed back tears. Maybe they didn't look hard enough. Maybe they were too busy to check the shelves or the computer. That had to be the reason they didn't know her books were there.

The next time she went to the mall, she would look for herself. *And if they aren't there? What will I do?*

Dinner and *disaster* were two words that didn't go together, but when Jazz pulled the lasagna from the oven, it was clear that tonight they would. Collin arrived home much later than he'd said, and the lasagna had shriveled in the pan. She tried cutting it into small serving pieces, thinking maybe with a salad and bread they could "make do," as her mother would say. She discovered there was no tender giving of the pasta, so she pushed down on the knife with both hands and it broke through. The eggplant had the texture of those navy Crocs Louisa seemed fond of.

Collin perched on a stool at the counter behind her, flipping through the newspaper. "It smells good. I'm sorry I'm late."

"The smell is all we're going to enjoy. I don't think even Cleo could chew this stuff." Jazz tossed the pan of food into the trash. She whirled around and flashed him a grin. "So let's get ice cream for dinner."

Collin dropped the paper to the counter. "Ice cream, for dinner?"

"Why not? It has calcium—probably more than this lasagna. And as a bonus, the kids will no doubt enjoy it more." Jazz didn't wait for him to refute her logic. She strode into the family room. "Anyone interested in a waffle cone for dinner tonight?"

Tim and Joey thundered past her to the back door, ready to leave in case grown-up minds regained their senses. Madison hunched over on the couch.

"Madison? Wouldn't you rather have ice cream than vegetable lasagna for dinner?" Jazz sat next to her on the couch.

"No. I can eat a sandwich. Can I stay home alone?" Madison looked at Jazz with the innocence of a street urchin.

Jazz could feel what she had declared her "Louisa twitch" in her eyebrow. "Not a chance, girly girl. It's ice-cream dinner for the entire Copeland family tonight. Get your shoes on and join the family."

Madison gave her a frown that would frighten a killer into confessing. "I said I don't want to go."

"Doesn't matter. It's not a choice." Jazz waited for Madison to get off the couch before she joined her. "Besides, how long can it take from your busy schedule? Those boys will down their cones fast, and you'll be back in time for whatever text-messaging event you have scheduled."

Once in the van, Jazz empathized with Madison, stuck in the back with her brothers. The van seemed much smaller with the entire family spilled across the back. Madison probably thought staying home alone sounded more appealing than an evening riding in the back with her brothers.

Maybe I should have stayed home too, she thought, *where it would have been quiet.* The noise from the back was becoming unbearable. "Are we almost there, Collin?"

"It's right around the corner. You're frowning. Does your head hurt?" Collin reached over and stroked the back of her head. "Maybe this wasn't a good idea tonight?"

She didn't want to admit it, but Collin's hand on her hair drained the tension from her. "It hurts a little, but I'll be okay. I imagine it's good for the children to do something normal."

"This isn't normal." Collin spoke so low, Jazz almost didn't hear him.

"Why isn't it?" She dropped her voice to match his level.

"I'm usually at work until seven, sometimes later." Collin parked in front of Sweet Smiles Ice Creamery.

"That's terrible. It's exactly why I never married and had children. I knew I couldn't have a career and a family."

"Good for you, but *my* family has to eat, and Louisa appreciates the chance to stay home with the kids instead of working."

"You think she doesn't work? She raises your kids alone, like a single parent. Better rethink your statement, Counselor."

"I know she works hard. I didn't mean she doesn't work; it's just that she doesn't work for a paycheck. How about you? Do you make enough in royalties that you don't have to take other types of jobs?" He grinned. "Like being a nanny?"

"Funny man. I've never been a nanny. I think—or thought—I made a lot of money, but then I couldn't find my books online. I even called some bookstores today, and they didn't have any of my books." She sighed. "But that's probably just a mistake."

"How many places did you call?"

"Five, including the ones in St. Louis County."

"That many? And you really think all the clerks in all those stores couldn't find even one of the books you've written?"

"They might not even have taken the time to look." Weariness mushroomed in her head. She was beginning to doubt she was a famous author, or an author at all, but that didn't make her Collin's wife, did it? She wrestled with that thought for a moment.

"Are we going in or not?" Madison asked with a perfect teenage attitude.

"Yes. Help Tim get out of his seat, please," Collin said. He put the van in park and turned off the engine. The doors automatically unlocked.

Jazz pushed the button to slide open the side door of the van. Warmth from outside rushed in, displacing the cool air-conditioning. "It's still great weather for ice cream. Let's go, everybody. Double scoops in waffle cones!"

Once inside, Jazz looked at the quaint interior, filled with old-fashioned ice cream tables and chairs. It looked like a place to bring a date. She wondered why Collin would want to bring her and the kids here. Why not go to the Lick and Drip in the strip mall close to their house? They'd passed right by it on their way here.

The glass-fronted freezers held an array of flavors in big tubs. Jazz pursed her lips. She didn't know which to choose. She didn't feel adventuresome today, so she would pick "old reliable," the one that had brought her through many trials.

"Ice cream parlors have such a unique smell, don't they? Like cookies and childhood rolled into one." Collin interrupted her thoughts.

Jazz inhaled. "It does smell good in here, but I'm not sure I feel the same as you. Let's see . . . I'd describe it as a place where vanilla cools the sunburn from a day at the pool."

"Not bad, pretty much what I said. You just said it more descriptively. Is butter pecan still your favorite?"

"No. I don't think so. I like mint chocolate chip." Jazz tried to read the puzzled look on Collin's face. "Let me guess. Louisa hates mint chocolate chip?"

"'Anything green and frozen can't taste right' was her phrase," said Collin.

"Fine. I'll get the butter pecan. Maybe it will bring back my other personality."

"Get whatever you want."

"Are you really going to order ice cream?" Joey tugged on her shirt hem.

"Why not? I love ice cream, don't you?"

"I like ice cream, but, Mom, you almost never get any 'cause it makes your hips big."

Jazz caught Collin's gaze on her. He was holding back a smile, or maybe a laugh; she wasn't sure. She ignored him and bent down to Joey's level. "Will you still love me if my hips get bigger?"

"Yeah."

"Then I'll have two scoops. Joey, since I'm being brave about my hips, what kinds of ice cream do you think I should get?"

"Bubble gum and cookie dough. They're the best."

"You're sure?" Jazz wondered how frozen gum could be a treat.

"Yes. Are you going to get the same ice cream as me?" Joey looked at her with awe.

Jazz stood. "I'll have one scoop of bubble gum and one of cookie dough, please, in a waffle cone," she said to the shiny-faced clerk behind the counter.

The five of them sat at one of the round tables. Jazz felt odd as the children watched her finish her ice cream right down to the last piece of the cone.

"You did it," said Joey. "Just like you said."

She blew a big bubble with the gum and let it pop. "Good choice, Joey. I didn't know those flavors would taste so good together." The small boy in front of her beamed a toothy grin that tugged at her heart.

"Jazz?" Collin leaned over with a napkin. "You have ice cream on your chin."

She leaned forward and let him wipe the spot. Her breath caught as he came in closer. Did he plan to kiss her? In front of his children? She scooted her chair away from him. "Thanks, Collin. What's next for the evening?"

Collin sat back in his chair, a frown on his face. "I guess we'd better head home. It's almost bedtime."

"Do we have to?" Madison asked.

"Is your homework finished?" Collin peered at his daughter.

Madison folded her arms in front of her and cocked her head in a don't-mess-with-me pose. "No."

"Then home we go since you didn't do your homework after school like you're supposed to."

"But, Dad, things are different." Madison pouted and then her bottom lip quivered. "Mom isn't here anymore."

"Yes she is, you dope. She's right there," said Joey.

Madison flung her chair back as she scooted away from the table. "It is not her. She just looks like Mom and talks like Mom, but she isn't Mom!" Tossing a disgusted look in Jazz's direction, she continued with a sneer. "Mom would never eat that much ice cream." Madison spun on her heel and headed for the exit.

"Madison! Sit down," said Collin to Madison's disappearing back.

With a gentle touch, Jazz put her hand on Collin's shoulder. "Let her go. This has to be confusing to her. You and I are having trouble with it. Why shouldn't she?"

"Is Madison in trouble?" Tim's worried face pierced Jazz's heart. These children shouldn't have to deal with this.

"No, she's not, Tim." Jazz folded her napkin and placed it on the orange tray resting on the table. "I think we should go home, Collin. Who wants to carry the tray to the trash can?"

"I can do it," said Joey.

"Great! I'm glad you offered, Joey." Jazz's praise lit his face.

Back in the car, Jazz opened the mirror on her visor to check for more ice cream spots. She glanced up to see Madison pouting in the backseat. She wondered what the relationship between Madison and her mother had been like. One thing was for sure: if tonight was any indication, she didn't think Louisa and Madison were good friends.

"I called your mom today after I dropped the kids off at school." Collin backed the car out of the parking space.

Collin talking to her mom. That sounded wrong when she was so sure she'd lost her mother a long time ago. She wanted to talk to her, but what would she say? *"Hi, I'm your daughter, but I don't remember you after my twelfth birthday. Do you still read true murder books and knit sweaters?"* Anxiety threaded through her fingers as she twisted her ring in circles. "What did she say?"

"She's concerned. I'm surprised she didn't call you herself today."

"Maybe she did while I was outside with Tim. So does she remember any traumas I experienced as a child?"

"None that should have made you want to forget your identity. But she did have a connection with Mexico. Your parents went on a business trip, but you stayed with a relative while they were gone."

"What relative?" The bubble-gum ice cream in her stomach felt like it expanded into one giant bubble pressing up into her throat, and it didn't feel good. She twisted the ring faster.

"Your dad's cousin. You could ask her for more details."

She pressed the button to lower the window and stuck her head outside. "Collin, can you pull over? I'm going to be sick."

Collin bumped off the pavement and onto the shoulder of the road seconds before the giant bubble of ice cream erupted from Jazz.

Louisa lay curled on the couch like an infant. Her eyes were clenched shut, and a tear leaked and ran down the bridge of her nose. Collin gently wiped it dry with his finger. She didn't move away from his touch, and that concerned him. *She must be in a lot of pain,* he thought. "I brought you an ice pack for your head. It might help the headache."

She rolled over onto her back and took it from him, then plopped it on her forehead. She winced as the cold bag touched her skin. "Thanks, it might." Her words came out with a quiver.

Collin knelt down on the floor next to her, reminding himself not to call her Louisa again. "Jazz, did you remember something? Is that what made you sick?" he pressed.

"No memory. I think it's just the ice cream." Her lips resembled a ventriloquist's as she tried not to move. "My head hurts worse than it has before."

"I'll get you a pain reliever." He stood. He didn't like how pale her skin looked. "Maybe you need the stronger stuff?"

"I think so. Get the one from the pharmacy, the good stuff," she whispered.

Feeling more in control, he bounded off to the kitchen for her medication and a glass of water. He felt hopeful even though his wife was miserable. The doctor had said the headaches would get worse as her memory returned, and he thought the conversation about her mom just might be a clue. One he would explore even if it was painful for his wife.

He brought the pain pills and water to her, expecting

her to reject the water like the last time. He felt some relief when she took it from him. She swallowed the pills with a sip from the glass.

He knelt on the floor again. "Do you realize you took your pills with water this time? Do you think your memory is coming back in small ways?"

"Collin, I feel horrible, and right now I don't want to discuss my medical condition."

He started to rise from the floor but halted when she reached out for him.

"Don't go. I just don't want to talk about me right now. Tell me about the trial you've been preparing for—or can you not talk about it?"

"I can't share details," Collin said, sinking back to the floor. He stretched his legs out in front of him. "I could tell you that my client is not guilty." He grinned. "They never are."

"Right. How do you defend someone when you think they might not be so innocent?"

"That's what I'm paid to do." He frowned. "Sometimes I don't like my job."

"So why are you doing it?"

"You know why." At the confused look on her face, he swept his hand around the room. "For this—for the kids and for you."

She rolled away from him. "Wrong answer. You're doing it for you, not for me."

He touched her shoulder. "You just said not for you—as in Jazz? Or Louisa? Is that what you meant?"

"Collin, leave me alone. You know I meant for me—Jazz. Please, I just want this headache to go away. Let me sleep."

He nodded, and even though she wasn't looking at him, he thought he might be on the right track. He would keep hounding her until her memory broke through, but maybe now wasn't a good time. He reached over her, grabbed the throw to drape it across the back of the couch, and gently spread it over her.

"Thank you," she said softly.

CHAPTER EIGHT

EXCEPT FOR THE white brick and gray siding, the house next door was a mirror image of the home Jazz had just left. Standing at the door, she paused before pushing the doorbell. Her stomach felt queasy. Maybe she should go back. Had she brought the right clothes for a sleepover? She had cotton pj's in a backpack Madison had loaned her, but maybe she should have brought that cinnamon-colored satin lounge set hanging in the closet. She didn't know.

The door opened, and Laurie's bright, whitened smile welcomed her. "You're here! Come in! I can't believe you came! We're gathering in there." She pointed to the room at the right of the doorway.

"I'm here, but you have to help me. It's going to be weird. They know me, but I don't know them." Jazz crossed the entryway and stopped, surprised at the appearance of the family room. Their homes seemed to have the same floor plan, but the house Louisa lived in had the touch of a decorator while Laurie's house seemed to have been decorated for children. The windows Jazz loved in Louisa's home were here, but they were covered in heavy fabric blocking the lake view.

"That's why I had you come early. I thought you would be more comfortable if you didn't walk into a room of women staring at you." Laurie ran a hand through her tangled curls.

"Thanks, I appreciate that. So where do I know them from?" Jazz resisted the urge to clasp her hands in front of her.

"School. We met at our kids' preschool. We started taking turns bringing all the kids home once a week." She hovered against the doorway.

"All the kids? How many are there?" Jazz made her way to a denim sofa that rested in front of a wall-size television. She sank into the cushions and wiggled between two bright-red pillows.

"Just five. Which means once in a while you get the month off."

"Five?" Jazz couldn't imagine how she would handle that many children at once. She picked at a piece of Cleo's hair embedded in her sweater. "Are they all boys?"

"Yes. It's much easier that way. They like the same activities. Besides, it's only four if you don't count Tim."

Babysitting five boys? She didn't sign up for this, but

apparently it was something Louisa did with ease, so now she was stuck with the job. "How do we get them home?" Jazz took in the crayon-colored pillows adorning most of Laurie's floor space, along with picture books. Maybe she needed to brighten Louisa's house, make it more kid-friendly.

"That's the fun part. We all meet at school and put the car seats in the van of the mom taking them home. It's quite a system, but we've managed to figure out what works the best." Laurie plunked down on the sofa next to her.

"When do I have everyone?" Did she have time to arrange the family room for the kids to play in? The basement would be ideal, but Collin had been clear that it belonged to him.

"Louisa should have a calendar somewhere with all the dates that are hers."

Jazz felt a slice of pain in her forehead. "I haven't seen a calendar."

"She has a notebook she keeps everything in. Maybe it's in the van or the kitchen desk?" Laurie jumped up from the sofa. "I have my master list. Let me get it, and then we can figure this out."

Jazz watched Laurie almost fly from the room. She didn't blame her; she'd like to fly out of this room and back into her own life. What would she do with five little boys? She would have to ask Tim to help her and hope he didn't lead her astray.

Laurie bounded back into the room, paper in hand. "You have next Tuesday."

"Tuesday? So soon?" She managed to squeak the words.

"We could trade if you want. I have the week after. Maybe you'll feel more comfortable by then."

"Or maybe Louisa will return."

Jazz noticed Laurie's discomfort at her statement. "I know I'm supposed to be Louisa, but I don't remember anything! It's frustrating to be handed a life you know nothing about and then be told to live it. It's like playing a board game, and you get the card where you have an instant family and responsibilities to fill." She sank farther into the sofa. "It's exhausting."

Laurie dropped into a chair. "I can't imagine waking up with a family to take care of. It's much easier when the kids come one at a time and you can adjust to your life changing."

The doorbell rang, cutting off any more deep conversation between the two as Laurie scurried to answer it.

Jazz listened to the lighthearted banter and giggles of the women at the door. It seemed they had all arrived together. As her foot began to tap the carpet, she squeezed her hands together, tensed her shoulders, then released the tension building inside her. Why did she care what these women thought of her?

"Now, remember, she doesn't know she's Louisa," Jazz heard Laurie explaining to the women. "So introduce yourself and make her feel welcome."

"But it's so weird." Even with the classic rock music Laurie had playing in the background, the loud whisper seemed to echo through the house.

Yet another voice drifted in. "Shh. She'll hear you. Besides, I wish I could wake up and be someone else a lot of days."

Jazz tightened her fists again and released them. She wished they would come in and get this over with. *Why wait for them?* She stood, deciding to forge ahead when she realized they must feel as strange about this as she did.

At the doorway, she paused and rested her hand on the doorframe. "So, Laurie, any food around here? Hi, everyone. I'm the strange woman who doesn't remember who she is." She grinned. "Maybe you all can fill me in on my life."

"Food! Of course. Jill, can you help me carry in the trays? Tina, you stay and get to know our new friend, Jazz." Laurie seemed relieved to give orders.

"Her gift is telling people what to do." Tina held out her hand. "I'm Tyler's mom."

Jazz shook her hand. "Nice to meet you. I'm grateful for Laurie's gift. This way I can talk to you alone for a few minutes without facing so many new people at once."

Tina's face flushed with embarrassment. "I didn't mean . . ."

"I'm sure you didn't. I didn't take it as a condemnation." Jazz smiled at her. "So we have maybe two minutes? Tell me what our friendship is like, please."

"In two minutes?" Tina laughed. "We haven't known each other long; this is my first year of being at this preschool. Louisa and I share an interest in reading."

"What do you read?" Jazz loved to read, and now she'd discovered a connection to the woman she didn't remember.

"Biographies of famous women, mostly; we call it our upper-class tabloid fix. We can't get enough of other people's lives. I just finished reading one about Jane Austen. I can loan it to you if you want to read it."

Before Jazz could respond, the other women came in bearing trays of snacks. "We have everything kids wouldn't eat and some things they love, like chocolate." Laurie set the tray on the wooden trunk that served as a coffee table.

"So what's the plan for the night, Laurie?" Tina asked. "Games, gossip, or girl time?" She turned to Jazz. "Girl time is my favorite since I have all sons."

"How many do you have?" The politeness of the conversation had driven Jazz to the edge of screaming. Instead she flopped into a chair.

"Three, and Tyler is the youngest. He's four and wants to be a meteorologist."

"Just wait until you take him for the afternoon. The other week when I took him home, I learned about cloud formations." Laurie plucked a grape from one of the bowls and popped it into her mouth.

"Isn't there supposed to be someone else here?" Jazz asked.

"Nancy. She called earlier and bailed on us. Again." Laurie dipped a cracker into the crab dip.

"We should tell her we had a great time, make up some grand thing, like . . . like . . . ," Jill said.

"Right, there isn't a 'grand thing' to make her feel like she's missed something big," Laurie sniffed. "I don't throw a fun girls' night out, I guess."

"Maybe you need to have a penalty instead. Remember

pajama parties and being afraid to go to sleep?" Jazz's mind whirled with thoughts of past pranks.

Jill gasped. "What could we do?"

"TP her house?" Jazz reached into a bowl for a miniature candy bar. She slid her nail under the foil, unwrapped it, and popped it into her mouth. Then she noticed the clarity with which she could hear every word Madonna sang in the stillness of the room. The women stared at her.

"What?"

"You ate chocolate," Laurie said.

"You never eat sweets," Jill said.

Tina bobbed her head in agreement.

"Louisa might not, but I do. What a miserable person she must be if she doesn't at least have chocolate in her life."

"But you're . . ." Jill's voice faded as if unsure what to say.

"Louisa, so they tell me." She unwrapped the gold foil on another miniature chocolate bar and popped it into her mouth as well.

"It's so weird that you don't remember." Jill crossed her legs and slid her feet under her thighs. "Maybe we can help, if you want us to. We could tell you what Louisa is like."

"I don't know if we should do that, Jill." Laurie squirmed on top of her stack of pillows.

"I think it's a great idea," Jazz said. "Collin thinks I should figure it out myself. I've been asking Tim for help. So far I know I exercise because I might get a fat fanny." She stood and tried to look behind her. "I didn't think I was in bad shape. Am I?"

"I wish I had your shape," Jill said, tossing a pillow from the couch at Jazz.

"So what is Louisa like? What does she think about Collin?"

"I'm not comfortable with this, Jazz." Laurie hopped off the cushions she sat on. "Anyone need anything from the kitchen? Another soda?"

Jazz reached out and touched Laurie's arm before she passed her. "We're fine, Laurie. I know you are Louisa's best friend. Are you thinking you'll be gossiping about her?"

"Sort of." Laurie didn't move. "It's weird."

"But it's okay because what if you didn't tell me anything, and you are holding the words to bring back Louisa's memory?" Jazz felt guilty of manipulation. Maybe she did want to snoop into someone else's life.

"You could be right." Laurie sat back down on a bright-blue pillow.

"Great!" Jazz piled a plate with dip and chips, then settled back in her chair.

Jill started the discussion. "First, Louisa would never eat that stuff you have on your plate. She gets nuts if she gains a pound because she thinks Collin will leave her."

Jazz halted the progression of chips to her mouth. "Would he?"

"I don't think so." Laurie reached across and patted Jazz's hand. "Go ahead and eat the chips. Don't worry about it because if Louisa returns, she'll work off all the calories in a day."

"What does she do for fun?" Jazz put the chip back on the plate; she didn't want to think about the workout that would be required to remove what she had eaten in the last five minutes.

"I don't think she knows how to have fun. She's never done girls' night out with us. She prefers to go to lunch because Collin isn't home then," Tina said.

"Why? Collin doesn't want her to be gone at night?" Jazz began to feel uncomfortable about leaving him with the kids for the evening.

"I don't know," Jill said.

"Louisa is a good mother, right? She seems to be super organized, right down to what they have on Friday nights for dinner."

"She's a bit controlling," Laurie said, then frowned. "Are you sure you want to hear this, Jazz?"

"Can't you find something nice to say about Louisa?" Jazz felt a pain she didn't understand, as if someone she loved had been hurt.

"Sure. I think she is an amazing cook, but she wouldn't agree." Laurie smiled. "She hosts the most incredible dinner parties for Collin's clients."

"And she has this almost magic ability to rearrange furniture. She made my living room look completely different without spending any money," Jill added.

Jazz nodded. "Thanks. I knew the house looked as if a decorator had been there. And now I know she uses all those cookbooks in the kitchen."

"She loves Collin and the kids a lot. She doesn't seem happy, though, does she, Laurie?" Jill said.

"No," Laurie answered, "she doesn't."

Jazz knew she didn't want to hear any more from Louisa's friends, not now, anyway. In fact, she felt kind of queasy, as if she had been caught looking in someone's medicine cabinet. "So where does Nancy live?" Jazz grinned as she changed the subject. "Have any extra toilet paper, Laurie?"

The van slowed to a stop in front of Nancy's house. Laurie killed the engine. "Still want to do this?"

"You bet." Jill hiccupped. "I'm a bit—*hic*—ner—*hic*—vous." Her comment brought on high-pitched laughter from the rest of them.

The side door slid open. The women stumbled from Laurie's van, giggling like teenagers.

"Shh! You have to be quiet," Jazz whispered, holding a finger to her lips. "We don't want to get caught."

They stood in a tight little group until the crickets returned to their nighttime sonnets.

"That's better," Jazz said. "Try to stay out of the beam of the streetlights, and remember not to squeal when you throw the rolls, or someone will hear us. Laurie, get the weapons."

"Aye, aye, Captain." Laurie offered a goofy salute and went to the back of the van. She opened the hatch and held out the first rolls to Tina.

"I think I'll just watch." Tina backed away.

"No way. We're all in this together. Right, Jazz?" Jill whispered.

"One for all and all that rot," Jazz said while grabbing her two rolls.

Tina stuck her hands deep in her jeans pockets and stepped back from the group. "I always tell my kids not to follow the crowd like sheep."

"Come on," Jill said. "We aren't doing any damage. Have a little fun for once, Tina."

Tina sighed and withdrew her hands. "All right, but I don't like doing this."

"Noted," Laurie said. "You can pick the next activity."

"Naysayers have to throw the first roll," Jill said.

Laurie giggled. "She means you, Tina."

"No way. I'm not going first." Tina shook her head and faltered back.

"I'll go first since it was my idea," Jazz whispered. "Line up behind me. We have to get in and get out quick."

"Let's do it all at once, and then we'll get done faster," Jill suggested. "I'm really scared now. What if we get caught?"

"She's a friend, right? We get her to laugh and tell her we'll be back in the morning to clean up the mess." Jazz began to creep toward the house. She stopped as high-pitched giggles came from behind her. She looked back at Jill and Laurie huddled on the sidewalk, encircled by the glow of a streetlight. They covered their mouths with their hands. "Remember, no noise! Just throw as high as you can to the top of the tree."

"Sorry," they said in unison.

Standing in the front yard, the women aimed the rolls of toilet paper at the top of the oak tree and tossed. The rolls spiraled out of their hands. Ribbons of tissue cascaded, draping over branches and causing them to bob.

Unable to contain their nervousness, they broke out in loud giggles. "Stop, we're going to get caught," Laurie said through a snort.

"Listen! There's a car coming up the street. Back to the van!" Jazz squealed, breaking out in a run.

Bright lights engulfed the yard before she could get to the sidewalk. The women stood still like deer caught in the beam of a spotlight.

"Hold it right there, ladies," an authoritative male voice called from beyond the light.

Adrenaline raced through Jazz. Collin wouldn't like this turn of events. Maybe she could talk her way out of this. She at least had to try. "We're sorry, Officer. We were just pulling a prank on a friend because I've lost my memory, and my friends are helping me get it back; only this friend didn't show up for the sleepover tonight. We promise we're planning to come back in the morning to clean up everything."

"Up against the car, lady." The officer shone his light over Jazz and moved closer.

"But you don't understand—this was my idea. Can you let everyone else go home?" she pleaded with the armed man. Fear built a highway through her back—this man was not Officer Friendly.

"No. I'm taking all of you in. Now, up against the car."

Jazz put her shaking hands on top of the car like she'd seen criminals do in the TV series *Cops*. Her friends followed her lead, and one by one, hands hit the police cruiser.

Tension mounted in Collin's jaw. He was thankful she had been brought to the local station and not the municipal court, where he was well-known. His eye twitched, and he felt a ping in his forehead, then wondered if he could lose his memory like his wife. His life would be so much simpler if he could. How should he play this? he wondered. Hardened lawyer or desperate husband? How did his wife end up getting arrested? Not his wife, he reminded himself—Jazz. Louisa would never be in a police station unless she was on a Scouts field trip.

He checked the watch on his wrist. Jazz had called him almost an hour ago. Since she had managed to get all her friends arrested, finding a babysitter proved to be a challenge as the other husbands had to collect their own wives. He had left Madison in charge, fully aware he could be in trouble with the law himself if anyone reported him. A law he thought should be changed. Two more years and they could leave Madison with the boys, free and clear.

He approached the khaki-clad clerk behind the glass window. "You have my wife, Louisa Copeland?"

The clerk looked at him blankly.

Collin released a heavy sigh. "Jazz Sweet?"

The clerk nodded. "Her we have. Take a seat in the lobby, and I'll send the arresting officer out to talk to you."

In the lobby, Collin paced and then sat on one of the fern-green plastic chairs. Black-and-white posters of missing children covered one wall. The parents' heartache had to tower over them every second as they wondered where their children were and if they were alive. How would he feel if it were his kids? His shoulders tensed. It was unimaginable. He stood and paced the room a few more times. He heard someone laugh behind the door where his wife was being held. He could hear the channel 2 sound bites now: *"Local lawyer's wife behind bars."* The minutes slowed. Waiting with a client had never felt like this. He'd never noticed how loud innocuous sounds could be if your nerves were in the process of unraveling—the jangle of coins in the vending machine or the sloshing of coffee as it poured from the machine into the cup. He sat back down, and his heels bounced.

"Mr. Copeland?" An officer stood in the open doorway.

Collin jumped from his chair. "Yes?"

"Come on back." The officer turned and walked down the hallway without looking to see if Collin followed.

Collin upped his stride to catch him. "Are charges being pressed?"

"By the city. There is a nuisance law. We usually have teenagers breaking this law around prom time. I think this might be a first, though—four moms on a girls' night out. Glad it's not my wife." The officer stopped in front of a closed door. "She's in here. She wouldn't sign anything until you came, said you were a lawyer?"

"I am. I'm also her husband; she just doesn't remember that."

The officer turned to face him. "She mentioned that. Didn't quite believe her, though she made a valiant effort to convince me."

"Unfortunately it's true, and living like this can make your head ache."

"Let's get this done, then. Sounds like you've had a rough time." The officer ushered him into the small room.

Jazz sat before him, her hair askew and mascara smeared under her eyes. He wondered if she had been crying, then canceled the thought as she rubbed her eyes with her hand.

"Collin! What took you so long? Everyone else already left."

Jazz gazed at him like he had climbed a stone tower to rescue her from a dragon. He stood a little taller. He couldn't help but feel good about that dewy damsel-in-distress look. But he wasn't about to let her know that.

He cleared his throat, readying it for his in-court voice. "I'm here now. So what made you TP Nancy's house?"

"We were . . . I don't know . . ." She lowered her eyes to the table in front of her. Using her fingernail, she traced a name etched by someone who had been here before her.

"Bored?"

"Not exactly—more like we were acting like teenagers at

a pajama party." Jazz flashed him a grin, seemingly pleased with her rebuttal.

The officer handed him a stack of papers. "It's good she enjoyed the experience, but I don't think she'll be laughing when she's picking up bottles, cans, and unmentionables."

"Trash?" Jazz seem puzzled.

"Yes, ma'am. You and your friends have landed yourselves a community service sentence: four hours on a Saturday morning picking up trash along the interstate. Better pray for a nice, cool, sunny day."

Collin breathed a sigh of relief. "So we don't have to go to court for this one?"

"No. We found with teenagers that having them work for the city is a greater punishment than fines."

"But I'm not a teenager! Can't we just pay a fine?" Jazz pleaded.

"Nope. You broke the law, and you have to pay the penalty."

"Collin?"

Collin knew he could force the issue, take this to court, and maybe even win, but he was tired. Jazz could just take her punishment. "I hope you look good in bright orange." He turned away from her angst-filled face and looked over the papers. "Sign these," he said as he pushed them at her, "so we can get out of here. I still have a few hours of work to do."

He refused to acknowledge the tears welling in her eyes.

CHAPTER NINE

STANDING INSIDE THE massive bedroom closet, Jazz surveyed her choices. Another day of wearing someone else's clothes. True, the clothes did fit, but they were so boring they made her yawn. There were no rainbow colors in this wardrobe, only navy, cream, and an occasional brown. Didn't Louisa have one adventuresome bone in her body?

It was a cool day, and Jazz longed for a red sweater, or something with fun trim that would shoot sparkles of color across a room, or a collar of feathers that floated around her neck.

"What are you doing?" Madison padded into the closet.

"Trying to find something fun to wear." Jazz held a cream

satin shirt to her chest—fun fabric, but still didn't come close to her style. This blouse was too dressy. She hung it back on the rod.

"Like what?"

"Anything with color or even stripes would be nice." She shoved a hanger holding a navy-blue T-shirt to the side. "Boring." Jazz sighed one more time and pulled a plain white T-shirt from the closet along with a navy skirt.

"Mom says one should always stick to buying the classics." Madison stroked the dress next to her as if appreciating the value of the designer.

Jazz stared at Madison for a moment. "You're the only one who doesn't think I'm her. I find that refreshing."

"You look like her, except . . . you smile more," Madison said, "and you look at people when you talk to them."

"I don't think I'll be smiling today." With a hand on Madison's back, she edged her from the closet and into the room. "Your dad is pretty mad at me, or he was last night." She pulled the shirt over her head, then stepped into the skirt, shimmied it up her legs, and zipped it. "What do you mean I look at people?" she said, realizing Madison had offered her a clue about Louisa's personality.

Madison flopped across the unmade bed. "I don't know. It's just different. Mom talked to lots of people, but she was always doing something else at the same time, like picking up Tim or looking for him or something. You just stop what you're doing and talk."

"I should be spending more time watching out for Tim.

That's probably a mom thing I'm supposed to know how to do." Jazz shrugged her shoulders. "Maybe someday I'll figure out how to multitask."

"Maybe," Madison agreed. "So what happened, anyway?"

"Apparently there's a Nosy Nelly across the street. She called the police."

Madison's eyes widened. "What's it like to be arrested?"

"Scary. I wouldn't recommend it."

"What did Dad say?" Madison's voice sounded a bit fearful.

Jazz sank down on the bed next to Madison. "He said I broke the law and had to pay the penalty. His mouth didn't even move, just stayed in a straight line."

"That means he's really mad. You probably shouldn't get too close to him today. That's what I do when he's mad. I stay far, far away from him," Madison said. "Sometimes it helps if you clean your room."

"That might be hard for me to do. I can't hide in the bedroom all day." She rooted through the dresser for a scarf or a belt to brighten her outfit. "And I'm not cleaning anything."

"We could go shopping," Madison said. "Then you could get some clothes you like."

"Do you know how to get to the mall?" Jazz slammed the drawer shut with her hip. Her heart pounded at the thrill of the hunt for new clothes. Clothes that shouted "Jazz."

"We could ask Laurie to go with us. But let's leave Tim and Joey home with Dad," Madison said as she tugged the hem of her nightgown over her feet.

"I think that's a great idea. We'll have ourselves a girls' day out." Jazz slid her feet into a pair of sandals. Remembering how angry Laurie was last night when the police put them in the car, she said, "I think it would be better to go to the mall by ourselves."

"If it's girls' day out, we won't get arrested, will we?" Madison asked.

"Not planning on it. I don't think your father will bail me out twice in one weekend. Go get dressed and meet me downstairs." She shooed Madison out of the room and tromped down the stairs to the kitchen. She found Collin sitting at the counter, drinking his coffee and flipping through the sports page. "Good morning, Counselor."

"Is it? At least you didn't make the newspaper." Collin picked up his cup, then set it back down. "Do you know how embarrassing this will be for me at the firm? It might hurt my chance of becoming partner."

"Just remind them I'm not really your wife and you can't control my behavior," Jazz said.

"I don't think they'll believe me." He flipped another page.

"Madison and I are going to do some shopping today." She wished he would at least look at her. *Or maybe it's better he doesn't.* His rough morning beard begged her to reach over and pat his face. What would it be like to kiss a man with a scratchy face? Would it leave marks on her skin? She felt the heat in her cheeks and was thankful Collin wasn't looking at her. *I've got to get a grip on reality. He is not my husband—he belongs to Louisa.* She grabbed a glass from the cabinet and shoved it under the filtered-water dispenser on the front of the fridge.

"What about Tim and Joey?" he asked.

Jazz took a sip of the ice-cold water and felt more in control of her feelings. She glanced over her shoulder at him. "You can watch them. Do some boy stuff, like practice casting with one of those fishing rods you have stored in the garage, or how about kicking the soccer ball around in the park?"

He peered at her over the top of the paper. "I don't take care of the kids on the weekend. Louisa always watches them so I can have some free time." He looked at her sheepishly. "She insists."

"No wonder she took a vacation from you, Collin." Her words held a touch of anger, and it surprised her. "Please, could you give me directions to the nearest retail-therapy center?" She attempted to soften her attitude with a gentle tone.

"What are you going to use for money?"

Jazz smiled her sweetest smile. "Louisa's credit card."

"Don't spend a lot on clothes. There's too many in the closet now," Collin said.

Jazz shook off his warning. What did he know about clothes and how many a woman needed, anyway? "I'll pay you back as soon—"

"—as you remember where you live. I know," Collin grumbled as he found a paper by the telephone and wrote out the directions to the mall. "Like that will ever happen."

"What?"

"Nothing. Just don't be gone all day."

"I'm sure you and the boys will be fine."

"But can you handle Madison?"

"Why couldn't I?" Jazz turned and stared at him. "I can't imagine how hard it could be to shop with her."

"She doesn't need anything," Collin said.

"Need has nothing to do with shopping, dear." Jazz cocked her head and threw him a grin as she scooped up her pass to retail heaven. "Madison, let's rock," she hollered up the stairs.

Madison came barreling down. She had parted her hair in several directions and then braided a small piece, which she'd clipped into a loop on the side.

At least Louisa's daughter had some personality. "Nice hair," Jazz said, realizing her own blonde locks lacked excitement. Apparently Louisa liked wearing her hair in a classic style to match her classic clothes.

"Thanks." Madison's mouth formed a perfect perky smile. "I think it's awesome."

"It is." Jazz paused in the open door to the garage. "Let's take the convertible." She scooped Collin's key ring off the rack, leaving Louisa's in place.

"Dad's car?" Madison spoke in a whisper.

"Yeah." Jazz loved the excitement on Madison's face.

"But we never get to go in Dad's car. He doesn't let us." Madison looked back at the kitchen with a worried expression.

"Suit yourself, but I'm going in that car. We need to leave the van in case your dad has to take the boys somewhere." Jazz opened the driver's door of the sports car and slid behind the wheel. "Coming?"

Madison's blue eyes sparkled like sapphires. "Oh yeah. This is so cool! Wait until Hannah finds out."

Jazz stuck the key in the ignition, and the engine jumped to life with the low rumble of a tiger. "It is. It's better than cool." She shifted the car into gear and backed out of the garage.

Inside the dressing room, Jazz pulled a bright red-and-orange knit dress over her head. She patted her hair into place. Then, not liking the look, she tousled it. She admired the fit from all angles. Definitely a great dress. She'd take it and the others she'd brought in with her. She couldn't wait to begin wearing these clothes. The short T-shirt made her belly look flat. All she needed was a tan and maybe a diamond in her navel. No more cream and navy for her. She sighed in happiness. She felt like herself again. Had it only been a week that she'd been living Louisa's life?

She gathered the clothes and left the dressing room to search for Madison. She found her at the jewelry rack. "Find anything?"

"Yeah, can I get my belly button pierced?" Madison looked at her expectantly.

"Um." What was she supposed to say to that? Hadn't she been considering doing that very thing in the dressing room? But she wasn't twelve, and Madison was. "Do your friends have pierced belly buttons?"

"No. I want to be the first." She held one ring in each hand, alternating them over her T-shirt where her belly button was.

"What would your dad say?" Jazz felt her foot begin to tap—a nervous habit she now recognized as a sign that she was in over her head. Or maybe it was a message from Louisa, letting her know this was unacceptable.

"Dad wouldn't care. He wouldn't even notice. We don't have to tell him, do we?" Madison pleaded with wide eyes.

"So if we don't tell him, it means he wouldn't like it, right?"

"Probably not." Madison frowned and slapped the belly button rings back on the wire hanger. The wall of jewelry trembled with her disappointment. "I knew you wouldn't let me do it. You act like you're all cool and stuff, but you're just like my mom."

"Whoa. Where did that come from?"

"Well, you weren't going to let me, were you?"

"No, but I think we can find something else to make you happy if we try." Jazz wondered just what would be appropriate for a preteen and yet acceptable to parents.

"Like what?"

"Give me some ideas, Madison. This is all foreign territory for me." Maybe she should try distraction. She'd researched that parenting tip for one of her books, but she couldn't remember if it worked or not. "I don't suppose you want to go to the bookstore?"

"No way." Madison stuck her lip into the pout position Jazz had become familiar with.

"Music?"

"A new iPod?" Madison jutted her chin a few inches higher as if to say she would bargain, but it wouldn't be cheap.

"What's wrong with yours?"

"It's not the newest one. And I want a purple one."

"We can look at them, but no promise that we'll get one." At least they had moved away from permanent alteration of Madison's body.

"But if I have it, I'll be the coolest kid at the party."

"Party?"

"I didn't ask Dad yet. I thought you could ask him for me."

"Are there going to be boys there?" Now where had that come from? She didn't think she had a parental bone in her body, but that was a parent thought if she'd ever had one. It must have been a leftover from her childhood.

Madison headed for a circle rack of hooded shirts. She gathered a hem in her hand. Her attitude screamed, *Act casual and the parent won't figure it out.* "Just a few boys. Only the cool ones are invited."

The cool ones? That sounded like trouble to Jazz. The phrase "He's such a bad boy but so desirable" came to her. Had she written that? "Whose house is it at?"

"Hannah's. Her parents will be there. She's going to be thirteen, and they said she could have a DJ. I just have to go, Jazz! You can call Hannah's mom if you want to." Madison's attitude of *It doesn't matter to me* melted into desperation. "I just have to be there!"

"When is this party?"

"In a few weeks because Hannah was born around Halloween."

"So it's a Halloween party? I don't . . ." Jazz hesitated. The idea of the mischief-making that went along with Halloween made her nervous about telling Madison she could go. She remembered the TP incident all too well. Even worse, she didn't know how Louisa felt. So for now, she didn't think a Halloween party would be a great idea.

"No, it's not! It's not going to be a costume thing or anything."

"I'll call Hannah's mom, and then we'll talk to your dad." Jazz hoped this was the right way to handle it. "Let's find something to wear to the party that doesn't put plugs in your ears. You do want to talk to people, right?"

"Yeah. I won't be able to hear anything unless I leave out one of the earbuds. Thanks!" Madison surprised Jazz with a quick impromptu hug.

"You're welcome, but we're going to the bookstore afterward." *I'm going to look for a book on adolescent behavior. There must be some kind of manual for raising teenagers.* She'd seen ones for pregnant women; surely there would be a useful one on what to do once the kids arrived. She could count it as a research book because once Louisa returned, Jazz knew she had a great story to write. *And if she doesn't return?* That thought kept nudging her more than she liked. Why couldn't she remember? Why didn't she want to? And why did it seem so important that she did?

Tim and Joey squatted on the kitchen chairs, arguing over the ketchup bottle. Collin had taken them for burgers and fries, but instead of eating at the fast-food establishment, he thought they could eat at home. Since it took them forever to eat French fries, he figured he'd have a few minutes of peace. The phone had rung the minute they walked in the door, though, so he just tossed the bags on the table for the two of them to have at it.

His mother-in-law repeated her question. "Do you think I should come and stay with you until she gets better?"

"I don't know, Beth. Let me talk to her about it when she gets home." He snapped his fingers, and when the boys looked his way, he glared at them and pointed at the ketchup bottle. They sat down in their chairs. Quite pleased with his ability to calm the sibling battle, Collin returned to the conversation. "I've been giving her things to smell, but so far no memories, good or bad, have sprung into her mind."

"I want it first!" Tim shouted

"I'm the oldest; I get it first!" Joey scrambled over the table and grabbed it from Tim.

Shocked, Collin ended his phone call with a promise to call back later. "What is wrong with the two of you?" He strode toward the table, intent on seizing the ketchup bottle.

"It's mine," Tim yelled.

Joey knocked Tim's hand to the table and planted a knee on the bottle to claim victory. Tim jerked his hand away, and Joey put enough pressure on the bottle to send a blood-red ooze shooting through the air and landing on Collin's shirt.

The boys dropped to their seats, eyes wide and open-mouthed as Collin inspected the damage to his favorite shirt.

His first impulse was to yell. Two weeks ago he would have, and he would have sentenced them to their rooms for such behavior. No, that wasn't true. Two weeks ago he wouldn't even have been spending time with the boys on a Saturday.

"Dad?" Tim's voice quivered. "Are we in big trouble?"

He didn't like the looks on his sons' faces; they knew he wasn't the fun parent. He was the parent who was all work and no play. But Jazz had shown him how to have fun again. "No, you aren't in trouble, Tim, but Joey," he said with a grin, "you are, and I'm going to get you!" His laughter was low and evil. "You have five seconds to get away."

Before he made it to two, Joey was off the table and at a run. Tim followed. Both boys were laughing as they hit the stairs.

"You can't catch us, Dad. You're too old!" Joey called from midway up the stairs.

"Old! I'm not old! You'd better run faster because I'm right behind you!" Collin double-timed it up the steps. The boys made it to Joey's room. They slammed the door behind them, and Collin heard their small bodies rasping against the door as they held it shut. He jiggled the handle. "Foiled by two small boys. Come out, little boys, come out and play."

"No!" they yelled in unison.

"We're never coming out," Tim said with a giggle.

One more jiggle of the handle and Collin grinned. "I've been beat by two boys who must have secret powers to defeat someone as strong as me. I give up." He waited.

"We aren't falling for that, Dad," Joey said. "We aren't going to open the door until you go away."

"I'm leaving right now." He stepped away from the door. "It's been a treat, but I have to change shirts." He couldn't stop the grin on his face until he entered his closet. The smell reminded him of his college dorm room. A mountain of dirty clothes littered the floor. It looked as if laundry hadn't been done since Jazz had arrived.

Collin stooped over to look for his second-favorite weekend shirt. He lifted a few of the shirts from the pile until he saw the faded image of a brown tail. He retrieved his Scooby-Doo T-shirt and sniffed under the arms. *Not too bad. Still wearable.*

He heard laughter and started to rise when he was bowled over by two tiny warriors. He wrestled with his sons on the floor until he had them pinned. "You came into the dragon's lair, you wicked urchins. Now you will pay!" He brought his hand above them and formed a claw. "Tickle Monster will now perform a symphony on two male bellies." He dropped his hand to Tim's stomach, walked the fingers to the side, and began to tickle him. Tim shrieked with laughter. Joey tried to roll over and make a getaway, but Collin stopped him with his other hand. He curled the boy to his side and began tickling him too.

"Stop, Daddy, stop!" Tim had tears coming from his eyes from laughing so hard.

Collin relented and let them both go. "The dragon is tired. I want a solemn promise to be peaceable at the kitchen table from now on. Do I have your word, small boys? Or do I need to go in for another attack?" He raised his hand.

"I promise!" Joey shouted.

"Me too!" Tim scampered far from his dad.

"Good, you may go, then." He could see the ketchup from his shirt had made an impression on theirs as well. "Change your shirts before you go back downstairs."

He pulled his own dirty shirt over his head. He glanced at the red spot smeared like a chest wound on the front. He knew he should do something so it wouldn't stain, but he wasn't sure what, so he tossed it on the pile of clothes at his feet.

His connection with his boys may have improved, but everything else seemed to be falling apart since Jazz arrived. He missed Louisa. He hadn't realized how well she had kept the house running. If only there was a way to get her back, return their life to the way it was. He craved his old routine.

"Dad, I can't find any socks," Joey said, decked out in his favorite soccer shirt. He stood in the doorway, shadowed by his brother. "And Tim doesn't have any clean shirts."

"Didn't your mother do any laundry this week?" Collin grumbled.

"Nope. We didn't have laundry day." Tim's eyes were barely visible under the visor of his prized Rams hat. "Jazz wrote me a story instead."

Great, even Tim referred to Louisa as Jazz. He had to find a way to bring her back. The kids needed her. He needed her.

"Gather your dirty clothes, boys. Take them downstairs to the laundry room, and we'll do them. I think I still know how to turn on the washing machine."

Collin watched the boys back out of the room with

wonder on their faces. Heaven knew what they were thinking. "Probably that you've lost your mind," Collin mumbled to himself as he turned back to the pile. He bent down and began to gather the stack when he noticed the closet wall seemed to have a hole in it. He bent down for another look. It wasn't a hole but rather a hidden cubby. The hem of a shirt was caught on the corner of the door. That would explain why it didn't shut. His wrestling with the boys must have pulled it the rest of the way open.

Why didn't he know about this? Did Louisa have this installed or did it come with the house? Maybe she didn't know it was there either. What was on the other side of this wall? He thought about it and remembered the shallow linen closet. That meant this hidey hole had to be a pretty good size. Good for hiding Christmas presents or valuables. That made sense; it probably came with the house. He stuck his hand inside and felt the side of a box. He slid it out onto the closet floor.

It was labeled *Private Journals*. He started to open it, then hesitated. No, he wouldn't read them. She would be angry if he did. He shoved the box back where he found it. She must have put them there to keep them out of Madison's hands. *Or mine,* he thought.

He'd leave them there. Collin had always respected Louisa's privacy. He fingered the edge of the lid and couldn't help but wonder—what had she written? How many journals could that box hold? His fingers started to lift the lid, but he pulled them back. No, he shouldn't. It wasn't like

Louisa had died, after all. She was just mentally missing, and he didn't have the right to read these without her permission. He gathered the clothes and gave the box one more thoughtful look, then slid it back into the cubbyhole and closed the door.

✑

That afternoon Jazz stood in front of the mirror over her dresser. She slid her fingers over the streaks of dark blonde and red. Now that she'd added color, she liked her hair—or most of it. She'd kept the style since she didn't want to make it any shorter. But the glasses she hated.

Madison came into her room to model her new clothes. Getting into the spirit, Jazz put on her new shirt and pants as well. When she twirled in front of the mirror, her glasses slid down her nose. Jazz pushed the black frames back in place. "I hate these things! Glasses are such a pain. They won't stay where I need them. And I used to think they were a great fashion accessory."

"You could put in contacts." Madison primped in the bedroom mirror. "You have them in the bathroom."

"I wouldn't know how to put them in. I can't imagine sticking my finger in my eye." Jazz pulled one of Madison's new earrings away from its plastic holder. "These are really cute. They'll look great with that shirt." Her eyes met Madison's in the mirror.

"Do you think so?"

"Sure, and drop earrings are the thing now."

"I know." Madison moved her fingers back and forth against a brush on the dresser. "I guess I have to tell you, or Dad will be mad."

"What?"

"Mom won't allow me to wear anything but studs until I'm sixteen."

"Seriously?"

"Are you going to make me take them back?"

Jazz held the dangling dolphin up to the light to inspect for something that would declare the wearer without virtue. The light caught the tiny blue glass eye, and it seemed like the dolphin winked at her. "I don't see anything inherently bad about these. They don't dangle like chandelier earrings, so you shouldn't get them caught on a comb or your finger. A dolphin is a friendly critter. I mean, it's not like you chose a pair with skull and crossbones. So the message you would be sending by wearing these could be nothing more than that you like intelligent sea creatures."

Madison chewed her lip. "Dolphins are my favorite. I just have to have them. They remind me of the ones we saw last summer in the Oceanarium at the Shedd Aquarium."

Jazz noticed how Madison's eyes sparkled when she talked about dolphins. "What makes them so special?"

"Did you know that every dolphin makes unique sounds like we do?" Madison warmed to her subject. "And they don't have vocal cords. They help people in the ocean sometimes too. So can I have them?"

"I proclaim this particular pair worthy of Madison

Copeland's ears." Jazz handed them to her. "Wear them and enjoy them."

"But what if you remember being Mom and you don't remember you told me I could wear these? You might ground me."

"I hadn't thought about that. What do you think we should do, just in case?"

"Maybe you could write me a permission slip."

"Excellent idea." Jazz grabbed her notebook from the nightstand and began to write. *Madison Copeland has my permission to wear her dolphin earrings whenever she desires.* With a flourish she signed her name, *Jazz Sweet, aka Louisa Copeland.* She capped her pen and tore the sheet from the spiral spine. "Here you go. Put it somewhere safe."

Madison read the note to herself. She gave Jazz a huge grin. "I'll be right back. I'm putting this in my jewelry box."

CHAPTER TEN

SOFT LIGHT BATHED JAZZ'S EYELIDS. She was so comfortable, and the bed seemed too warm and cozy to think about leaving it. Collin had pressed his back against hers, and . . . *Collin?* Jazz flung back the covers and bolted from the bed. "What . . . ?" She burst into giggles.

Cleo raised her head off the bed, and her tail thumped as if to say, *"It's just me."*

Jazz sank back onto the bed, then remembered it was Sunday. They hadn't gone to church since she'd been hurt, but she was pretty sure that was because life had been on the edge of insanity. She glanced at the clock and realized she'd almost overslept. Why was the house so quiet? Shouldn't everyone else be up and getting ready by now? They did usually go to church, didn't they?

Downstairs she found Collin still asleep on the couch. He slept on his side with his hand curled under his face. She longed to wake him with a kiss. Instead she bent down and gently pushed his shoulder. "Wake up. We'll be late."

Collin peeked at her through dark lashes. "What? Late for what?"

"Church. Come on, Collin, we have to get the kids ready. They're still sleeping."

Collin rose on one arm and then collapsed back on the sofa. "Jazz, we don't go to church unless it's Christmas or Easter, and it's neither one today. Go back to bed."

Not go to church? She glanced at the clock on the mantel. There was still time to get everyone ready. She shook Collin. "We're going to church as a family, so get up."

He smelled wonderful, like comfort, and she wondered what it was like to be surrounded with his arms. *He's not yours,* she reminded herself. She averted her eyes from the sight of his bare, masculine chest rising in front of her as he struggled to sit up on the couch.

She straightened and ran upstairs. "Time to get up," she yelled into each room. From the closet she grabbed a navy knit dress from Louisa's selection of clothes, but added a bright-red leather belt from her shopping trip.

Joey ambled into her room, sleepy-eyed. His pillow hair was flattened to the side of his head. "Why do we have to get up?"

"We're going to church." She yanked on the belt and slid it through the buckle.

"Is it Christmas?" He rubbed his eyes and yawned.

"No, it's not. But the church is open every Sunday, and we're going." How could Louisa be a good mother if she didn't take her kids to church? And Collin—he should be in charge, not her. *It's his job to get his family to church*, she fumed. She noticed Joey's expression and felt immediate guilt at the harshness of her voice. He wasn't responsible, and she shouldn't take her frustration out on him. "I'm sorry, Joey. I'm a little tired this morning. Go get dressed in something nice, okay?"

After what seemed to be a lot of arguing, Jazz assembled everyone into the minivan.

Before the garage door hit the pavement, Tim began complaining. "When do we get to eat? I'm hungry."

"After the service we will go out for breakfast," Jazz promised. "Next week we'll have to get up earlier."

"Are we going to do this *every* Sunday?" Madison moaned.

"As long as I'm here," Jazz said. *And maybe after I'm gone, if Collin understands how important this is.* That would be her prayer. It was the least she could do while taking care of Louisa's family.

All around them, other diners dressed in their Sunday best chattered over plates piled high with pancakes. Silverware clanked against china. *The church crowd*, Collin thought. He leaned back in his chair as the waitress brought a tray of plates to their table.

"Who gets the blueberry whipped cream Belgian waffle?"

"That's mine." Jazz reached for the plate. "Thank you."

The waitress handed Collin his pancake platter. "The rest are all kids' meals, so that's an easy one." She placed identical plates in front of the others at the table. "I'll be back in a bit to check on you all."

Collin scooted his chair closer to the table after the waitress left. His kids looked happy, even content, as they poured the tiny pitchers of maple syrup over their pancakes. The orange slice used for a garnish caught his attention.

He reached over and grazed the top of Jazz's hand with a gentle touch to get her attention. He put the orange slice under her nose. "Smell this."

She pushed his hand away. "No thanks, I have my own."

"I didn't say eat it; I said smell it."

She gave him a strange look and took a whiff. "I hope that made you happy."

"Did you really smell it? It smells like . . . ?" He waited for her to fill in the blank.

"Christmas?"

"Yes!" he almost shouted. "You associate oranges with Christmas." His excitement seemed to puzzle her even more.

"Doesn't everyone?"

His shoulders sank. "So no onslaught of happy memories?"

"No, sorry, Collin. It just smells like an orange with maple syrup on it."

He put the slice back on his plate and took a bite of his pancake. "This was a good idea, Jazz."

She wiped her mouth with her napkin. "Breakfast or church?"

"Church. It wasn't what I expected. It seemed more relaxed than the other times I've been there. People were friendlier too."

"Holidays are always different at church." Jazz took a sip of orange juice. "It's easier to spot the new people on a regular Sunday."

"That doesn't mean people shouldn't be friendly on Easter." Collin stabbed his fork into his pancakes.

"How do you know the person sitting next to you on Easter isn't a visitor too?" Jazz asked. She leaned in closer to him and lowered her voice. "Collin, the kids are listening to you. Learning about God is important, and they didn't mind going this morning."

He looked up to see Madison leaning in with her *Don't notice me; I'm just eavesdropping* stare. He didn't know why he wanted to argue with Jazz this morning. He had enjoyed going to the service. The youth band had surprised him with their exuberance and musical talent. Tim had joined in clapping with the congregation, and Madison had discovered two friends from school. The sermon had even spoken to his heart. Everything about it felt right. Correction: almost everything. The twenty-minute report about the church garage sale and how well the penny room did almost drove him out of the pew and sent him running for the exit.

But it wasn't just attending church that had him bothered. He could go to church every Sunday with his kids. He enjoyed eating breakfast with them at the Palace of Pancakes. What bothered him was the effect Jazz was having on him.

At first she had looked like Louisa, and it hadn't been hard to imagine she was the same person. He could even ignore the way she hired a cleaning service. He didn't mind that at all. He'd told Louisa to hire one months ago so she wouldn't have to spend so much time and energy keeping the house spotless. Even the microwave dinners Jazz had been serving were edible. At least she let him have meat instead of the tofu and soy crumbles she ate now.

What bothered him was the way Jazz smiled, the way she had pulled her hair back on the side with a huge rhinestone barrette this morning, and the new colors in her hair. He found her exciting. And she smelled so good. *She must have bought perfume at the mall yesterday.*

And then there was Madison.

Madison and Louisa never giggled with their heads together the way she and Jazz were doing right now. At the mall they'd both had their nails "airbrushed," whatever that meant. It seemed to be a big deal to Madison. They had rushed into the house yesterday to show him.

He finished his breakfast, listening to the quick-paced conversation between Jazz and his daughter about fall fashions, and wondered if maybe he should read Louisa's journals. He had to protect his Madison from the pain she would feel if Louisa returned and didn't treat her the same.

And what about Collin's own feelings? He couldn't continue to fight off his attraction toward Jazz much longer. He lowered his cup. He didn't have a choice for the well-being of his family: to him, that was a worthy excuse to breach Louisa's privacy.

❧

Curled on the couch with her feet underneath her, Jazz flipped through a photo album, searching for anything that looked familiar to her. The phone rang.

"When were you planning on informing me that you'd lost your memory?" a woman's voice asked.

"Excuse me? Who is this?" She almost hung up but realized this person must have some connection to her or she wouldn't know about the memory problem.

"Your mother, Beth Harris. Why haven't you called?"

"What would I have said? 'Hi, this is your daughter, and I don't remember you'?" Something about Beth's voice set her on edge.

"I could have been helping you remember things by now. Did Collin tell you I offered to come and stay?"

"He mentioned it, but he also said you were busy, something about a new person in your life. You really don't need to come. Other than my vacant memory, everything is okay." The coolness of her own attitude puzzled her. Why didn't she want this woman to stay with them?

"Fine, I won't come, but if you change your mind, you can call me," Beth said.

"I will, thanks." The words had barely left her mouth when she heard the click of Beth disconnecting. *Such an odd woman*, she thought. The mom she knew wouldn't have even asked to come if her baby girl was in trouble. She'd be there in a flash.

Jazz put the phone on the table beside the couch. She felt the telltale sign of the beginning of a headache as her forehead tightened. She would not let this one get out of hand. She scooted off to the kitchen for her pain reliever. After taking it, she decided she should do something to distract herself.

She wandered back to the couch and frowned at the photo albums. Distraction seemed to help keep the headaches at a level she could stand. But what could she do? Looking at photos didn't seem to help. Collin was probably in his workroom banging on something, and the boys were building a fort in Tim's room.

"Jazz?" Madison hung over the stair rail. "Can Angie come over this afternoon?"

"Sure, I suppose so. Maybe you should ask your dad because I'm not sure what you usually do on Sundays. Last Sunday wasn't a normal one."

"We don't do anything. Dad always messes around in his shop and Mom bakes," Madison said.

Jazz frowned. *Louisa bakes.* "She might as well come over, then."

Madison beamed as she continued talking to her friend, telling her what to bring with her.

Bakes? Jazz wondered what she could make for the kids to eat. Maybe Louisa had the makings for marshmallow squares. Not exactly baking, but easy and sweet. And it would be a great distraction.

Collin pulled the box from under the clothes. His heart beat faster. *It's okay,* he reassured himself. He had to find out what Louisa had written. Maybe it would help him get her back. He would take them to the workshop and read them. At least it felt like he was taking action instead of hoping every day that Louisa would be waiting when he came home, arms outstretched and eager to embrace him. Not that he wouldn't miss Jazz's fun spirit and quirky personality. He would.

He clutched the box to his chest to hide the block letters. No need to let Madison or Jazz see he was invading Louisa's private thoughts. He had a feeling neither of them would approve.

As he ran down the stairs, Jazz was coming up. Her face appeared to be dusted in light brown powder.

"What's all over you?" he asked.

"Chocolate. I thought I would try to bake something. All I could find was a cake mix."

"Did any of it make it into the bowl?" For a moment he was tempted to lick the chocolate from her cheek.

She blushed and used her sleeve to wipe her face. "Most of it. What's in the box?" she asked.

He felt the box grow heavy in his hand. Caught! What

could he say? What would squash her insatiable interest? "Financial records," he said with satisfaction. "I need to figure out where our money is going."

"Ugh, math!" Jazz moved away as if he carried toxic waste.

He smiled to put her at ease. A connection. Louisa didn't like math either—maybe he *could* find his wife again. "Then back off, lest the mere proximity of financial statements causes you great illness."

Jazz inched close to the railing. She splayed her hands across her face in fake terror. "Please, come no closer."

Easing into the role, he sucked in his stomach and attempted to broaden his shoulders. "I'll keep it contained. Careful now, I'm coming through. Don't breathe," Collin said, using his superhero voice as he brushed past her.

"Is it safe yet?" she mumbled from behind her hands.

"It's safe now for mere mortals. Hey, tell me when the cake is ready," he said on his way to the basement workshop.

"No promises on how good it will taste," Jazz called after him.

He found himself grinning at the silly exchange on the way down the stairs. Once safely behind his workroom door, Collin set the box on his bench. With great respect, he grasped the lid and set it aside. "It's now or never," he said softly to himself. He pulled the first journal from the box. It was from last year. Should he start with that one or dig deeper? Maybe if he started at the beginning, he could read what Louisa may have written about their dates. That would help him re-create those moments, he thought. Decision made, he took the box and turned it over. Now the journals should be in chronological order. He picked up the top one, written in a black and white composition book like the ones he had used in school.

Aware of the breach in privacy he was about to make, he took a deep breath and flipped open the cover with a finger. Louisa's handwriting jumped from the page. *Keep out. This is a journal of my private thoughts, not meant to share with others. If you continue to read, I will not be responsible for swelled heads or hurt feelings,* he read. He'd keep that in mind, but he didn't think his feelings would be hurt. Louisa loved him. He sat down on his stool and continued reading.

"Collin?" Jazz's voice interrupted him. How long had he been sitting down here? He glanced at his watch. Almost two hours. He went to the bottom of the stairs and stared up at the wife he'd never really known.

"What?"

"The kids are hungry."

He sighed. "Tell them to eat some cake."

"I burned it," Jazz said. "I'm shocked the smell didn't invade your kingdom down there."

Now that he was back in the present, he was surprised, too, that he hadn't noticed the acrid odor. "I'll be up in a minute. Tell the kids to get ready. We'll go out for dinner."

She smiled at him. "Terrific. They'll enjoy that, and so will I."

Collin went back to his workshop. He had to hide the journals. But where would they be safe from prying hands and eyes? Maybe he was being paranoid; no one ever came down here. Just in case, he put the journals back into the box and buried them under a pile of wood scraps.

He stood back to see if the bright yellow-and-blue box could be seen. Just a bit of color peeked through. He shifted a few of the wood scraps to cover the spot. Satisfied, he closed the shop door behind him, tested the lock, and went to collect his family.

CHAPTER ELEVEN

THE SOUND OF THE TV behind her assured Jazz that Tim was still watching his show. She chewed on the end of the pen and stared at the legal pad in front of her. Did she want to kill off this character, and why was she even considering death for him? She wrote romance, which was not a genre known for gruesome death scenes. Maybe she should think about changing her focus. A mystery might be fun and challenging to write. She snorted. She could write about her own life. It qualified as a mystery, didn't it? One woman begins to make dinner and then disappears deep inside herself to become a stranger to her and her family.

Tim climbed into the chair next to her. "Are you almost done?"

She shook her head and didn't even look up. "Not yet, kiddo. Watch something else."

"Are you writing a good story?"

"I hope so."

Tim plunked an elbow on the table and propped his chin in his hand.

Jazz could feel his quiet stare. She ignored him. She just needed a few more minutes to come up with a twist to her plot. "Aha!" she said, and her pen scratched and skittered across the paper like a match to a month-old Christmas tree.

At the chiming of the clock, Jazz looked up. It couldn't be noon! Pages of paper littered the table. Lucky for her, Tim had been independent this morning and played by himself. She hadn't even noticed when he left the table. She glanced over her shoulder at the television. The primary colors of the Cartoon Network shot across the room.

She stacked the papers together. "Tim? Are you ready to go for our walk?"

Only the chatter of animated voices answered back. "Tim?" Maybe he had fallen asleep. She couldn't tell from here, with the back of the couch facing her. If he were sleeping, she could keep writing. She slid out of her chair to avoid scooting it across the hardwood floor, tiptoed into the living room, and peeked over the edge of the couch. It was empty.

A warm breeze fluttered past, lifting papers from the table and sailing them like dandelion seeds through the air before they landed on the floor. Startled, she wondered where it had come from, and then she noticed the open French door that led to the backyard. The sunlight bounced off the lake, causing her heart to pound. Had Tim gone out without her? She walked out onto the deck and searched the yard for any sign of him. "Tim, are you out here?" When he didn't answer, she spun around and ran upstairs to his room.

"Tim! Are you hiding from me? Please come out. You're scaring me."

Once again, the only voices Jazz heard came from the television. Not even Cleo whimpered an acknowledgment. In her heart she knew Tim had gone outside, alone. She raced down the stairs. She would have to find him. But what if he'd fallen into the lake? She'd need to get help. What to do first? She hesitated by the door, then remembered Louisa's cell phone. She rushed to the counter and grabbed it.

Jazz stumbled over a pair of boots that Collin had left on the deck but caught herself before she could fall to her knees. "Father, help me find him. Please let him be safe and not . . . in the lake."

"Tim!" She ran to the boat dock. She didn't see anyone or anything. No sign of him. But if he had fallen into the water, she might not see anything. Maybe he went for a walk on the bank. She squinted in the bright light. Nothing!

Maybe Cleo was with him. The thought brought her a moment of comfort, but that passed as she remembered how easily the dog could be distracted. She clutched the phone tight in her hand. A sob broke from her. She had lost Louisa's baby.

She would have to call Collin. He had told her his cell was

number 1 on the speed dial. As she pushed it, she wondered how often Louisa had needed to call Collin for help.

Never, she thought.

The phone call came while Collin was driving to the court-house. If Jazz had called ten minutes later, she wouldn't have been able to reach him. As it was, he was only planning to observe another lawyer's courtroom delivery, so he wouldn't be missed this afternoon.

She had lost his child. Anger welled within Collin as he drove down the street. This would never have happened with Louisa. Tim had never felt the need to run away with her in charge.

The stoplight turned red, and he banged his hand on the steering wheel. He should run it. He glanced in his rearview mirror to make sure there were no police nearby nor a camera mounted on the pole. Still, he kept his foot on the brake. He couldn't break the law.

Getting to the house a minute earlier wouldn't change things, he tried to reassure himself. As he argued internally, the light turned green and he sped through the intersection. He would risk a speeding ticket. In fact, if he were pulled over, he'd enlist the help of the police in searching for Tim. He glanced in the mirror again, almost hoping to see flashing lights behind him this time. Nothing but an empty road followed him.

With great relief, Collin turned onto his street and raced

to his driveway. He hit the horn as he slowed the car to let Jazz know he was home, climbed out of his roadster, and slammed the door behind him. He could see her running to meet him as he pulled into the driveway. She was alone, and her face was streaked with tears. He bit back the angry remarks he had planned to make as she flew into his arms.

Instead, he welcomed her with a tight embrace, the comfortable fit of her body next to his giving him strength. He brushed the tears from her cheeks. "We'll find him. I promise."

"I've looked everywhere. I've called and called," Jazz said with a sob. She stepped away as if she suddenly remembered she didn't belong this close to him. "Even Cleo is missing."

He pulled her back toward him. "Jazz, don't. It's okay to accept comfort from me."

"Thank you, Collin, but finding Tim is the only comfort I need right now."

With reluctance, he let her slip away from him. Later, he reassured himself, after they found Tim, he would find a way to bring her back to him. He had a feeling the journals hidden in the basement would help him rediscover his wife and his marriage.

"I've searched everywhere I can think of," Jazz cried, her words clipped and shrill, like a high-speed gun.

"He likes to hide in closets," Collin said as he walked toward the back of the house.

"I checked all the closets. I even went to the basement. Collin, why do you lock your workroom? I couldn't open that door. I yelled, but Tim didn't answer, so I don't think he's in there."

"Power tools. I lock it so the kids don't mess with the tools while I'm not home. He can't be there. I'm the only one with a key." The worry and fear Jazz felt crawled inside his skin and gouged into his heart.

"If he's not in the house, then he went to the lake. He loves the water." Collin loosened the knot in his silk tie and pulled it off with a snap, shoving it into his pants pocket. "We've got to find him."

As he and Jazz walked along the shoreline, they took turns yelling Tim's name. Collin's throat burned and his stomach roiled from the anxiety that kept building as each moment passed. "Tim!" Again no answer; even the ducks on the lake remained silent.

"Tim!" Jazz's voice was no longer loud but more of a croak.

Collin wiped the dampness from his face. He began promising God he would be a better father if only Tim could be found unharmed. Then he switched to asking for God's guidance, realizing his promises to God meant nothing.

Jazz whispered, "Amen."

He looked at her in surprise. Had he spoken out loud? No, he thought, she was praying too. He felt comforted by that knowledge.

"Collin, I can't yell anymore," Jazz said with a hoarse voice.

"No, I suppose not." Frustrated, Collin kicked at the stones that covered the beach. "I think we need to call our friends and maybe the police. We need more help."

"I left the cell phone at the house. Do you have yours?" Jazz brushed her hair back from her face.

Collin groaned. "It's in the car. We'll have to go back to the house." Dejected, he turned and began walking back.

"Collin," Jazz called to him. "He wanted to play soldiers today. Do you think he might have gone somewhere else?"

New hope flooded Collin. "Jazz, you're brilliant. The old farm! I bet that's where he went. He likes to crawl through the ruts in the field." He began to run. "Come on, Jazz. I know where he is."

Collin looked back to find her lagging behind. He slowed, letting her catch up. "He knows he isn't supposed to go there alone."

"It's my fault, Collin. I told him I would go outside with him. He asked me several times, and I kept telling him as soon as I finished what I was working on we would go. I guess I took too long." Jazz stumbled on a clump of dirt.

Collin grabbed her so she wouldn't fall. "You can't do that to kids, Jazz. Tim, especially. He thinks he can do things on his own, like his brother."

"I'm sorry, Collin. I didn't mean to lose your son."

"I know," he said, wishing she would remember that Tim was her son too.

Collin led the way as they walked single file through the corn stubble in the field.

"It goes on forever," Jazz said. "How will we ever find him?"

"At the edge of the field there's an old tree house. Tim and Joey have decided it's their fort. They've kept it a secret from the neighborhood kids, even Madison. I'm sure he's up there."

"Did Louisa know about the fort?" The jealousy in her voice made him turn and look at her.

"Yes, she knew. She would pack them a lunch and let them spend Saturday afternoons out here while she sat on a blanket and read."

"I should have known. You should have told me, Collin. You leave me with your kids, but you don't tell me the rules."

"Tim knows he isn't supposed to come here alone, ever," Collin defended himself.

"And I bet he never did, until today, when I failed him," she said, hanging her head. "He could be hurt."

"I should have told you about the fort, but I forget what you don't know. He still shouldn't have come here alone, Jazz." Collin tilted her chin and looked into her eyes. "You'll see. He'll be fine when we find him."

Jazz followed Collin down the uneven path, glad for a reason to watch the ground rather than the muscular form in front of her. She couldn't calm her emotions, unsettled since Collin had lifted her chin and gazed into her eyes. At that moment she'd wanted to be Louisa more than anyone else, even more than Liana Desire, the top-selling romance author in America.

"There's the tree house," Collin said.

Jazz looked into the distance and saw nothing that looked like a tree house. "I don't see it."

Collin moved closer to her and pointed his finger into a grove of trees. "Right about the middle. You can't see the tree house from here; it blends in. That's what makes it so fun for the boys."

"Should you yell for him?" Jazz didn't offer to do it herself. Her throat hurt, and she was tired and didn't want to walk any farther.

"Nope, I think we'll creep up on him. Scare him a bit, you know?"

"That's mean. Why would you do that?"

"Because he isn't supposed to be here alone. Because if I scare him, maybe he'll think twice before running off again."

"But you're his father. Shouldn't you be a comforter?" Jazz was puzzled.

"Yes, but he has to learn in a safe way. What if someone else found him? I don't even want to think what might happen to him." Collin began to walk faster.

Jazz found it hard to swallow around the lump of fear stuck in her throat. "What if someone already found him? What if someone took him? What if he's hurt? Hurry, Collin!" Her heart tripled its beat. She took off at a run. Collin ran after her.

At the bottom of the tree, Jazz collapsed. Her lungs hurt and her legs ached. "Tim!" she called into the tree branches.

There wasn't an answer back.

"Tim!" The fear in Collin's voice spidered through her veins.

A sharp breeze whirled through the leaves, making the

dust sting her eyes. She blinked to clear the tears and took a gasping breath. It seemed she and Collin had been staring at the tree house without breathing for hours. In reality it had been only seconds since she had yelled for Tim and hadn't received an answer.

"I'm going up," she cried. She felt Collin's hand grab her shoulder. "Let go, Collin. I lost him. I'm responsible."

"Jazz," he whispered, the pain in his voice halting her next step. "Please let me go. You don't know what's up there."

"Maybe Tim is there. If he's not, we're losing time by arguing about who goes first." She felt Collin release her. She scrambled up the crude step boards nailed onto the trunk.

She didn't hold out much hope of finding Tim inside. He would have answered when she called, wouldn't he?

Poking her head through the door, she waited for her eyes to adjust to the shadowy light. Sunlight pushed through tiny cracks in the walls, dappling the floor.

Jazz exhaled the breath she hadn't realized she was holding. Tim lay curled up in the corner of the minuscule room, sound asleep.

She felt Collin's warm breath on the back of her neck and turned to him. "He's here, asleep." She knelt and crawled a few feet to the peaceful child. "Tim," she said softly. "Wake up!" She brushed his bangs back from his face.

His eyes fluttered open. "Mommy, I love you. I was quiet."

Tim's declaration tore at chains she hadn't realized bound her heart. "I love you too, Tiny Tim."

"What are you doing here, Tim?" Collin asked from the

doorway. He leaned into the room, unable to come into the child-size crawl space.

"Writing stories, like Mommy. I had to go somewhere quiet." Tim picked up a notebook from the floor and held it out to Jazz. "See, I wrote my story in pictures."

Jazz took the book with joy. "You wrote a story? Tim, that's great! Pictures work better than words sometimes."

"Can we read it together?" Tim asked.

"Later, big guy. After we get home and talk about why you were here all alone," Collin said.

"I'm sorry, Daddy. Mom was busy and I couldn't wait anymore. Cleo came with me."

"Where is Cleo, Tim?" Collin asked.

"I don't know. She left. I think she was hungry." Tim rubbed the sleep from his eye. "Maybe she went home."

"Let's go see, Collin. You can talk to Tim while we walk home." Jazz climbed down the tree behind Collin. She offered a silent plea that God would forgive her for ignoring this small child placed in her care, along with a prayer of thankfulness that Tim had been found unharmed.

CHAPTER TWELVE

LAURIE, TINA, AND JILL WERE huddled in the corner of the police station lobby. They looked out of place among the sullen teenagers who had already donned their bright-orange vests. A few of the teens strutted around the room as if they had been awarded high honors. Her friends' faces were not as welcoming to Jazz as they had been the night they gathered at Laurie's home. Jazz felt like she was walking through thick sand on her trip across the black-and-white tile floor. Cautiously she offered a small smile. "Hi, hope you all look good in orange."

"Not my favorite color," Laurie said without returning the smile.

The other two seemed to be studying the ceiling above Jazz's head. Almost in unison, they turned their backs to her and began talking in hushed tones to Laurie. Behind her someone popped gum in rapid succession. Several teenagers laughed. Jazz suddenly understood what it meant to be at a party where no one knew your name or cared. She didn't remember ever experiencing it before, and she didn't like it. Her new friends seemed to edge closer to the teenagers. Were they distancing themselves from her in space and friendship? She didn't think she could feel any more remorse at getting them in trouble.

The community service officer strode through the door. A hush settled over the lobby as the tall and muscular black woman with short, spiky blonde hair waited until everyone looked in her direction. "I'm Officer Georgia Warren. You may address me as Officer George. I am allowing you to do that because you aren't incarcerated. That does not mean I am your buddy. You are here because you did something to our community. Today is about you making amends to that same community.

"All right, all of you, let's get ready to go," Officer George said as she made her way past the young man with the lip piercing and through a group of bunched-up teenagers. She stopped short in front of the huddled women, towering over them. "And, ladies, listen up. Everyone has their safety vests. Get yours on, now." She turned and walked away toward the door.

Jazz let out her breath and glanced sideways at Laurie. "I'm sorry," she mouthed.

Laurie looked down at the vest in her hands, then pulled it over her head without a word.

"Line up in single file." Officer George waited until the last person took his place. "We will be boarding the prisoner van. It is just outside this door. You will not speak to anyone. You are serving your sentence—alone. You are not here on an *outing* with your friends."

Tina poked Jazz in the back the minute Officer George went out the door. "Thanks a lot," she hissed.

"I'm so embarrassed," Jill whispered. "Why did we listen to you?"

"Louisa would never have caused us this much trouble," Laurie said.

"And," Tina said with a smirk, "she wouldn't have lost her child either."

Jazz straightened her back and bit her lip. She wanted to turn around and scream at them. She wanted to tell them she hadn't lost Tim on purpose. She wanted to tell them she wished Louisa would come back because she didn't need friends like the three of them.

But she didn't. She stayed quiet, tears stinging her eyes and sadness twisting her heart. She didn't say anything because they were right. Louisa would never have convinced them to do something so childish. She shuffled into the small white van and sat in an unoccupied row. She watched the shadows of her friends' feet pass by as they found places far behind her.

The morning did not get any better. Officer George had meant it when she said no talking. She'd sent two teenagers back to the van moments after they arrived, giving them the good news that they would have to repeat their service the following weekend since they couldn't follow the rules. After that, Jazz didn't dare risk getting her friends or herself in more trouble by trying to apologize again.

Weary and hot by the end of the four-hour sentence, Jazz climbed into the van and looked for a place to sit. Not wanting to appear as alone as she felt, she parked herself in the first row next to a boy who wore pressed pants and a polo shirt. His appearance suggested he didn't belong on this punishment any more than she and her friends did. She wanted to ask him what crime he'd committed against the community, but just then Officer George stepped into the van.

"Let me remind you people, you are still under my charge. There will be no talking until you have returned your orange vests."

Hungry, Collin rushed up the stairs from the basement. He thought maybe they should go out for dinner since Jazz had suffered through community service. So far no one had called from the office to razz him. Perhaps he would come through this incident unscathed.

He expected to see Jazz playing a game with Tim and Joey. This past week, since Tim had given them a scare, Jazz had become more like a mom. He had come home early one night and found them all on the couch together. On the bookshelf, she'd discovered a book about the life of dinosaurs that was filled with detailed illustrations and a story line that interested even Madison.

Madison sat on the couch with the phone glued to her ear. Tim was at the coffee table busily drawing, making yet another book of his own. Joey lay on the floor watching Japanese cartoons.

"Joey, their mouths don't move right."

"Madison said it's called anime."

"I call it weird." Collin tossed a pillow at him.

Joey knocked it to the floor before it hit him.

"Where's Mom?" Collin surprised himself by giving Jazz that name. Even he had begun to think of her as the kids' mom.

"She's upstairs in her room," Madison said, taking a break from her conversation.

"Thanks." Collin started up the stairs, wondering just when their bedroom had become "her room." Something he would be fixing soon.

Standing at the closed door, Collin raised his hand to knock. He paused, hearing what sounded like sobbing. *Now what?* Did he burst through the door and comfort his wife or knock and give her a chance to dry her tears? He rested his hand on the doorknob when another sob tore at his heart. No matter that she didn't remember who she was; he knew who she was, he thought as he flung open the door.

"Jazz, honey, what's wrong?" Collin rushed to the bed where she lay facedown, crying into the pillow.

"Nothing," her muffled voice answered. "Go away, please."

He sat down on the bed next to her. His hand floated

above her back for a moment, and then, unable to resist offering comfort, he began to massage her shoulders. He ignored the way she stiffened under his touch—at least her crying quieted.

"Jazz, talk to me," he said.

"They hate me." She rolled over and stared at the ceiling.

Collin didn't breathe for a moment. His hand was resting on her abdomen, and she didn't push it away. It had been so long since his touch hadn't been brushed away. *Not now,* his conscience reminded him. He removed his hand.

"Who hates you?"

"Louisa's friends. They said mean things this morning."

"Didn't like community service, huh?" Collin debated whether or not to be a bad guy and point out why they wouldn't have enjoyed it. Being listed in the local paper for the community to see might be on top of the list. Then again, she didn't need any more misery from the looks of her. "Jazz, they didn't have to TP the house. They made a choice."

"I know, but they wouldn't have if I hadn't made it sound like so much fun." Her lower lip trembled.

"You know they were just angry at themselves and took it out on you."

"Yes, but you're mad at me too."

"I'm angry with them. They know you aren't yourself. They should have been better friends and persuaded you that it wasn't a good idea." She still hadn't looked him in the eyes. Good thing, too, or he knew he'd throw caution away and kiss her.

He took a deep breath. "I'm not mad anymore. You know that because I told you."

Jazz sat up on the bed, almost touching him shoulder-to-shoulder. She leaned her head on his arm. "I'm homesick, Collin. I miss the ocean. I miss my friends. It's all so crazy. I know it's all in my imagination, but it seems so real. And it hurts so much knowing that. What if I never remember being Louisa?"

"Then you don't. You have a place to live and a family that loves you." He put his arm around her.

She snuggled closer. His heart pounded as she looked up at him with her bewitching blue eyes, sparkling from the tears.

"Thank you, Collin."

He knew he shouldn't, but he couldn't stop himself. "No, thank you," he whispered and brushed his lips over hers.

For a second, Jazz didn't resist him, filling him with hope.

"Stop." She finally pushed him away and climbed off the bed. "I'm not her, Collin." Her voice could have cooled a side of beef. "I'll be fine now. Thanks for checking on me."

Collin stood, hands at his sides, feeling like a seventh grader caught sneaking a kiss behind an open locker door. "Fine, yeah, we'll all be fine someday." He strode out of the room without a look back at the woman who used to be his wife.

CHAPTER THIRTEEN

TIM HELD OUT A DAISY to Jazz. "Smell it! I picked it just for you."

Jazz took the flower. Several petals were missing, and the stem was crushed where Tim had mauled it in a tight grip. She sniffed it. "Thank you. It's very pretty, Tim."

"Now you're supposed to give me a kiss like you always do and call me 'Tim Bear.'"

Jazz loved the way he took her memory loss as a mission, determined to break through the desolate void. But she had begun to think Louisa had disappeared forever.

His big brown eyes beckoned her to do as he asked. Eyes just like his father's. She couldn't refuse Tim's innocent request. Bending over, she scooped him up in her arms. "Thank you, Tim Bear! And here's your reward." She kissed him on the cheek with a loud sucking sound, making him giggle. She put him back down.

"Did you remember?" Tim's face held nothing but expectation.

"Not yet." She held out a hand. "Let's go read a book."

With his favorite book, *All about Trucks*, in hand, Tim crawled up next to her on the couch. He snuggled under her arm. "Ready."

Jazz flipped open the book and began to read. "'This is a red truck. This truck can carry lots of things. This is a—'"

"Dump truck." Tim wiggled in closer. "Turn the page!"

By the fifth page, Tim fell asleep. She closed the book and pushed it to the end of the couch. Maybe she could squeeze out from under him. If she did it just right, he might sleep for at least an hour.

An hour she could use to write.

But she didn't move.

Somehow she knew this was a special moment, one that might never be repeated.

He made a small grunting noise and moved his hand to her lap. She traced his fingernails with her fingertip. So tiny. And so dirty. She frowned. Her heart suddenly lifted as she realized the dirt must have come from picking her the daisy from the flower bed.

Jazz leaned into the top of his head and inhaled the warm

scent of boy. The silkiness of his hair grazed her cheek. She had done this many times before.

Before?

And then she knew. Tim and Joey belonged to her.

She didn't move. Didn't dare. She didn't want to lose this precious memory ever again.

The minute Collin came home from work, Jazz told him she needed to talk. He'd finally found time to fit her into his busy schedule. She squirmed on the kitchen stool across from where he sat with a pen in his shirt pocket and a file folder full of briefs.

"So what's the news?"

"I had a moment today," she began.

"Jazz, I'm really busy here, so if all you had was a *moment*, can this wait?" He rubbed his hand across his chin.

He had dark circles under his eyes, and she knew he wasn't trying to be unkind. Still, she considered not telling him. After all, he didn't want to hear about her moment.

Tell him.

She didn't even know whose voice was in her head anymore. "I remember Tim and Joey, but that's all."

"What do you mean, you remember the boys but not Madison or me?" Collin pulled the pen from his pocket and began clicking—open, shut, open, shut.

Jazz wanted to yank it from his hand and stick it in his—well, just stick it somewhere. How dare he act like she chose whom to remember and whom to forget? Although the way he was acting, she might easily choose to forget *him*.

"Well?" The incessant clicking continued.

"You are correct, O Royal Barrister. I don't remember the two of you. I don't know why. Instead of using that trial-lawyer tone with me, maybe you should concentrate on the positive. If I remember them, how long can it be before I remember you?" She hoped that would satisfy him.

He stuck the pen back into his pocket and slid his suit jacket off his shoulders. "I'm going upstairs to take a shower. I can't believe you only remember two of us."

Jazz waited until he turned his back and started up the stairs. Then, with great drama, she stuck out her tongue and made a face. Was it all lawyers or just him? He never had a fun moment as far as she could tell. Everything needed to be serious or checked off a list or preplanned. No way could she classify him as a free and easy, let's-take-the-day-off-to-play kind of guy. *No wonder Louisa—no, not Louisa—me! I have to try and remember that. Anyway, it's no wonder I've checked out of my normal existence and into this one. At least I can make life interesting. I can cut paper for hours and arrange pictures with stickers, eyelets, and handmade embellishments. Or faux-finish an old dresser with a can of spray paint to make it look like marble. Go ahead, Collin, be your old stuffy self. But get one thing straight: I will never return to Louisa's mundane world.*

Collin didn't want to admit how much it had hurt not to be the first one Jazz remembered yesterday. He had left work early tonight thinking that maybe if he spent more time at home, her memory could return. The way he reasoned it out was that she spent more time with Tim and Joey than she did with Madison or him. Coming home early would be a surprise for the entire family. Since Jazz had arrived, family life had become more fun. Last week he'd found out he wasn't home for the pancakes shaped like clowns and root-beer-float night. No wonder they didn't miss him. All he did was work and tell them to be quiet so he could work some more.

He pulled into the garage, weary of other people's problems as well as his own. He grasped the handle of his briefcase and slid it across the seat as he climbed out of the car. Then he opened the door to the kitchen and heard a roar of laughter. They were having fun without him—*again*. He roughly plopped his briefcase on the counter. No greetings of *"Hey, Dad, you're home!"* wafted his way. They didn't even realize he had come home. *But they weren't expecting me this early.* He attempted to apply reasoning to their lack of interest in his arrival.

Over the top of the couch, he could see their heads bobbing with laughter. All three kids and Jazz were involved in an activity together. Curious, he stepped into the family room. Jazz had filled a blue wading pool with water. The kids were plinking pennies at yellow-and-pink rubber ducks, trying to get their own duck to reach the other side of the pool first. They had sandwiches on paper plates and a picnic basket filled with potato chips. Cleo stood on one side and lapped the water that splashed out of the pool. While he took in the scene before him, anger sneaked up and bit him.

"Do I need to hire a nanny to watch you *and* the children, Jazz? What were you thinking? Water on a wood floor? Do you know how much that floor cost? How many hours I had to bill to pay for it?"

Madison jumped to Jazz's defense. "Daddy, we covered the floor with plastic and then put towels under the pool to protect the floor."

He choked back a retort. "Oh. Good."

No one invited him to join in the fun. They all knew he didn't play. Work always needed to be done—never finished, just done. He'd made that clear long ago when he decided the allure of prestige and money could be his if he were chosen to be a partner.

He'd let the demands of paperwork and senior partners rule his life. But he didn't like living that way anymore.

So what did he intend to do about it? He couldn't give up his job. Or could he? What would they do for money? Where would they live? Without another word, he spun around and went back to the kitchen, unable to acknowledge the wake he'd left behind because of his own pain at being left out. He'd only desired to make Louisa happy, and now it seemed he'd never achieved that goal. And Jazz didn't appear to need his big house either.

Suddenly a more worrisome question flashed in his mind. What if Louisa returned, and like money in a teenager's hand, all the fun drained from their lives?

After making a sandwich for himself, Collin passed by the mini carnival in the family room and went to his workshop.

He found his attraction to Jazz growing stronger as each day passed. At work the phone would interrupt him, and he'd find himself hoping it was Jazz. He'd walk by someone at the courthouse and smell her perfume. He'd find himself whirling around looking for Jazz, only to find another woman. Then he'd feel disappointment, realizing she hadn't come to see him at work. Knowing she slept in his bed every night, but he didn't, tortured him. He couldn't continue to keep his relationship with her at the same level. Frustrated, he slammed the workshop door behind him and turned the key to lock it. Today he would discover the way to win back his wife—or to make Jazz love him.

He brushed aside the wood scraps hiding the forbidden box of journals. Without hesitation, he flipped the lid to the floor and pulled out a journal. He settled on the stool, propped the book on top of the workbench, and began to read.

Collin picked me up—late as usual—for dinner tonight. Mom said I should give serious thought about my marriage to him. She thinks he would be late to his own wedding. I don't think so, but I wish he could arrive when he says he would.

Collin didn't know whether to be hurt, angry, or sad that he had disappointed Louisa. He flipped through the pages until he saw *Valentine's Day* written in red ink and encircled with hearts. Feeling smug, he was sure this would be a pleasant read.

Collin took me to get ice cream tonight. I like him,
but I wish he would be a little more exciting. Oh
well, at least vanilla is predictable, and that's what I
need—safe and no surprises. I would have liked to
be a little surprised, though, maybe a hot-air balloon
ride over Forest Park.

Saddened that he had missed this side of Louisa, he almost
trashed the idea of reading more. The pain of not satisfying
her cut deep. *But she did marry me,* he thought. *That has to be
a good entry.* He knew he had asked her in March that same
year, but what was the date? In the middle, right before St.
Patrick's Day. He turned the pages until he found the entry
for March 14.

Collin asked me to marry him. I said yes. I wish I
felt like fireworks were going off overhead, or like
running down the street ringing doorbells and
shouting to everyone that Collin asked me to marry
him. I don't, though. I do know he'll be a good
father and husband. We have the same values. That's
more than most of my friends can say. Mom and
Dad are happy, and I can give up school. I never
wanted to be a legal secretary. I do love Collin, but
inside I feel frozen. I dread the wedding night.

Shocked and sickened, Collin closed the cover of the journal. He couldn't read any more. How had he missed this?

Louisa had seemed so happy to get married. She spent hours poring over all kinds of wedding magazines and searching out just the right place for the reception. She had invited two hundred people to eat the five-tier cake.

And the wedding night—he thought that had gone well. It didn't do much for his ego to think it might not have. Could that have been the beginning of the coldness between them? He didn't think he had done anything wrong, but she cried for a long time that night. She had told him she was homesick. Had she lied to him?

His confidence shredded, he tossed the book aside. He sat for a moment, unsure of what to do with the raw feelings surfing through him. He stuffed the emotions far from his heart and picked up a piece of wood he had cut earlier for a picture frame. Getting a piece of sandpaper from the workbench, he began to apply it to the coarse wood, sliding the rough paper over the grain until it polished to a silk finish. He wished he knew a way to smooth out his marriage as easily.

CHAPTER FOURTEEN

IT WAS A PERFECT MORNING for writing. All the kids were
at school, Collin was at work, and Cleo lay napping in the
morning sun that streamed through the French doors. The
only noise to bother her was the thumping of the clothes
Collin had tossed in the dryer before he left. There weren't
any distractions, and she planned to work on her new historical romance, but the words refused to come. Her outline lay
before her along with the stack of pages she'd completed for
the first two chapters, but she needed three before she could
send it to . . . to whom? That was the problem. She didn't
really have a publisher or an agent. It was a realization she was
uncomfortable with, but her heart told her to keep writing.

Jazz tapped her legal pad with a pencil. Her leg bounced under the table. Unable to concentrate, she pushed out of her chair as if she had someplace to go. She didn't. But she noticed an empty glass someone had left on the counter. She grabbed it and stuck it in the dishwasher, then opened the fridge door to get a soda, thinking the caffeine might wake up her creative mind. But there was a takeout container from three days ago in the way. That had to go, she thought. She tried to toss it in the trash, but the can was overflowing. So she gathered up the plastic edges, secured them, and headed for the garage door.

Then Jazz noticed Joey's sweatshirt puddled under its hook on the hallway floor. She bent over and scooped it up in her hand. Something in the pocket crinkled. She set the trash bag on the floor so she could investigate the noise. It was a note addressed to Louisa, asking her to send twenty-four bouncy balls to school tomorrow.

Tomorrow? Where would she get that many bouncy balls by tomorrow? Why hadn't Joey given her the note earlier?

Jazz stuck the note in her jeans pocket, snagged the trash bag, and walked to the garage. It seemed she had become more of a domestic queen lately. *More like Louisa?* Was she losing herself? Their personalities seemed to be merging.

When she came back in, the phone was ringing. Jazz listened to the audio caller ID. It was Laurie. She didn't want to answer it since Laurie hadn't made any attempt to accept the apology Jazz had left on her phone. It had been nothing but silence from the woman next door. The old Jazz would have ignored the call, but the new, evolving Jazz yanked the phone from its cradle. "Hello."

"Hi, Jazz, it's Laurie. Can we talk?"

She stood quiet for a moment, considering that this might be an attempt at being friends. She didn't feel comfortable in destroying a friendship that wasn't really hers, but Louisa's. "I'm a little busy, but I can chat for a moment."

"Good. I'm sorry—I wanted to get that in right away. I would have called you back earlier, but I had to go to my mom's. She's been ill."

Ouch. The guilt smacked Jazz in the head. Laurie hadn't been avoiding her after all. So much for the pity party she'd been holding. "Is she okay now?"

"She's better. She has pneumonia and she's worn out, so I cleaned the house and restocked her fridge, that sort of thing. Listen, I wanted to tell you this face-to-face, but since you're in a rush, I'll just tell you now. I talked to the other moms, and we decided to let you take the next month off." Laurie's rapid-fire words bounced through the telephone line.

What was Laurie talking about? Take the month off from what? She had no idea.

"We don't want you to think we're still mad about the community service thing. We kind of think it's funny now. Anyway, we decided that since you aren't quite yourself yet, it would be better if we took you out of the rotation. Wait, don't freak! Tim will still be included."

Rotation? Tim's included? She worked that puzzle in her mind.

"I know it's your day to take the kids after preschool—"

Then it hit her. That's what she was supposed to do today! Did she want to admit to Laurie that she forgot? She didn't think so, since there had been enough forgetting in her life already.

"Anyway, Jill is taking the kids today. So are you okay with that? If you're not, I guess I can call her." Laurie paused for a quick intake of air.

"I'm fine with it." Jazz's words kept pace with the rapid tone Laurie had set. "I do need to find a place to buy bouncy balls, though. Do you know where I can get some? I just found a note that Joey needs them for class tomorrow."

"The party store will have them. I don't like those surprise notes. That's why I check all pockets and backpacks the minute they come home," Laurie said with a laugh. "There is nothing like finding out you need to send thirty cupcakes the night before a party. Or worse, you need poster board for a project and the kids are already in bed. I feel much better if I've checked their bags."

Another part of mothering Jazz didn't know about. "Can you give me directions?" She chose to ignore the hidden advice in Laurie's statement. She could imagine Madison's face if she tried searching through her backpack.

"Why don't I take you? We can get lunch and talk if you like, since we are both kid-free this afternoon. I know this great little tea shop. They have the best sandwiches, and they use real plates and cloth napkins."

Jazz thought about the chapter she wanted to write, but her desire seemed to have waned. "When do you want to leave?"

"Twenty minutes? I just need to get dinner into the Crock-Pot. What are you making for dinner tonight?"

Strike two for motherhood on my part. She hadn't considered dinner. It wasn't even afternoon yet. Feeling inadequate, she said, "I think we'll order pizza tonight."

"Pizza, sure, that's a great emergency dinner. I'm sure you haven't felt like grocery shopping with all the headaches. So anyway, see you in twenty, or just come over when you're ready."

Jazz replaced the phone in its charger. Being a wife and mother was becoming more of her identity. She was losing herself, and she had a feeling it wasn't for the first time in her life.

At the tearoom Jazz felt swaddled in girl comfort. The tables were set with floral china and crystal glasses. The centerpieces were teapots filled with roses. She sighed and placed her napkin on the edge of the table. Complete calmness came over her. She had needed an outing like this. She'd missed this kind of interaction with friends.

"Isn't it heavenly?" Even Laurie seemed to have slowed her thoughts, and her curls weren't punctuating every word. Her conversation no longer centered on herself, and she now listened for answers after asking Jazz questions.

"The best. I'm glad you brought me here. Have we been here before?" Jazz relaxed back into the tapestry-upholstered chair.

"Yes, Louisa and I used to try and come once a month. You really are different from her, you know." She placed her silver fork on the empty dessert plate.

"I know. It must be confusing for everyone who knew her."

"Maybe. It's not a bad thing. I love Louisa, but I always felt like she was sad about something. She was my best friend, but I never felt like I was hers." Laurie's eyes teared.

Jazz reached across the table and patted Laurie's hand. "That can't be true. Collin told me you are Louisa's best friend, and he would know, right?"

Laurie sniffed. "I guess he would. I just wish we could be closer."

"Why do you think you aren't?"

"She's not very open about her past. It seemed like I was always telling her about the things my sister and I did when we were growing up. She never shared back. For instance, she never talked about her mom, Beth. She always changed the subject when I asked her about anything before she married Collin."

"That's interesting. I noticed when I looked through the photo albums that there are only a couple pictures of her, or rather me, when I was Madison's age. I should call Beth and ask her if she has any others."

Laurie's eyes widened. "You're calling her Beth now?"

"It feels weird to call her Mom; she doesn't feel like a mom to me."

"Did you write a lot of stories when you were young? I've

wanted to ask you that since you became Jazz. Wow, this feels like an episode of something Tom would watch on the sci-fi channel." Laurie laughed.

"It does," Jazz agreed. "Maybe I should write my life story for an original sci-fi movie." She considered Laurie's question a moment. "I did write stories, but I kept them hidden."

"Why would you do that? If one of my kids wrote stories, I'd be so excited I'd be trying to find a way to get them into a book. Do you remember what your mom did with yours?"

"No, I don't. I thought my mom and dad died when I was twelve."

"Again, *odd*. What else can be said? It's too bad you can't find the stories you wrote." She stared intently at Jazz. "But somehow, I do believe you wrote them."

Jazz walked down an aisle in the party store that offered the promise of fun times with helium balloons floating overhead. She glanced up at a silver heart-shaped balloon with legs jiggling in the current of the air-conditioning. It caught the light from the fluorescent fixture in the ceiling and sent the glare bouncing back at her. The flash sparked a sharp pain in her head. She rubbed her eyes in an attempt to erase the razor spikes from her brain. She hoped it wouldn't intensify into a daylong headache. Jazz had been having one of those at least four times a week. The doctor assured her they would dissipate when her memory returned. He'd laughed and said it was Louisa trying to get back. That statement had caused her pain again, causing her to wonder where she would go when Louisa did come back.

"Jazz, are you feeling okay?" Laurie asked with a gentle touch on her shoulder.

"Yeah, just a little pain. Where do you think the bouncy balls are in this place?" she asked.

"I'm not sure. Maybe with the birthday trinkets. I'll cruise the next aisle while you go down this one. That way we'll find them faster and get out of here." Laurie started to walk away.

"Good idea." Jazz was grateful for Laurie's company and thankful her friend had forgiven her. She turned to watch Laurie hurrying down the aisle. "Thanks, Laurie, for helping me today."

"No problem."

Jazz watched as Laurie rounded the corner before continuing her own search. She walked past sequined tiaras that caused her to wonder if Madison had tiptoed around the house with one perched on her head as a toddler. She knew she wouldn't ask her. She had noticed the hurt look on Madison's face last week when she asked something she should have known. Later this evening she would take another one of the numerous scrapbooks Louisa had made into her room. It had been odd looking at the unfolding of a life in which she had no memory of being a part.

She was now resigned to the fact that she was indeed Louisa, but that's not who she wanted to be. She liked being Jazz. Maybe that was why her old life hadn't resurfaced. It didn't matter, though; she'd decided she didn't want to return to

Louisa's life even if it meant Collin would be hers. She longed for Collin to love her for her—Jazz. She shook her head to disperse the thoughts. She couldn't allow herself to think that way, not as long as Louisa still lurked between them.

As she turned the corner, her senses were assaulted with the smell of aftershave. She felt the sweat beading on her forehead. Her stomach turned, threatening to heave. Frantic, she looked for a restroom sign. She fled toward it, barely making it before throwing up.

"Jazz!" Laurie tapped her on the shoulder with a bag of bouncy balls dangling from her hand. "I saw you run in here. What's wrong?"

"Queasy stomach." Jazz wiped her face with a damp paper towel, then washed out her mouth the best she could. "I think I should go home."

"Sure," Laurie said. "I'll just pay for these balls, then go get the car and pull up front. Just wait here for a few minutes and then come out."

"Okay." Jazz felt her legs begin to tremble. She clutched the corner of the wall as Laurie left. Something didn't feel right. Aside from one of her usual headaches, she had felt fine until she encountered that smell. Her stomach began to roil. "Forget the smell," she said to her mirror image. "It was nothing. You'll get over it." After her short pep talk, she took a deep breath and unconsciously held it as she bolted through the store into Laurie's waiting van.

"What happened in there?" Laurie shifted the van into drive.

"There was a smell, aftershave or men's cologne, I think. Anyway, it seems my stomach didn't care for it." Jazz laid her head against the cool glass of the passenger window.

"Has that happened before?"

"I don't remember." Jazz began to laugh. At Laurie's surprised expression, she laughed even harder.

"Jazz?"

"I'm sorry." Jazz tried to be serious. "This is the first lapse of memory that I'm glad about."

Laurie smiled. Her grin grew wider, and soon she joined Jazz in laughter.

CHAPTER FIFTEEN

JAZZ WANDERED into the family room. Collin sat at the desk studying some papers—trial, or new client? She wasn't interested enough to ask. There was a magazine on the coffee table. She grasped it and flipped the pages that showcased homes and more homes, each more extravagant than the last. The glossy photos didn't pique her interest either, so she let it fall back to the table.

"Collin, we have to talk about the party Madison wants to go to." *There! That ought to liven up the evening.*

"Nothing to talk about. She's not going to a party with boys until she's twenty." He stuck a paper in the shredder.

"I think you should let her go. All her friends are going. It's more of a class party."

Collin glared at her. "You think so? Have you called the mom of the party giver? Who's throwing this party, anyway?"

"Hannah. It's her birthday, and she'll be an official teenager." Jazz wanted to win this battle for Madison. It would cement their relationship. She was sure of it. "I helped her buy a cute outfit at the mall to wear."

Collin began to protest. "So you told—"

She held up her hand to stop Collin from talking. "I didn't promise her she could go. I said you had to approve."

"I don't approve."

Pulling out her best "woman moves," Jazz walked her slinky walk and stopped inches away from Collin. "It's important for a woman to feel in control of social situations. And the best way to learn how to accomplish that feeling—" she leaned over and stroked his cheek—"is in a safe environment at a young age to learn how to keep from falling into the wrong arms."

Collin's breath seemed to quicken at her touch, and his expression held that dangerous let-me-love-you-tonight look. She took a few steps back. "Do you understand what I'm saying? If she doesn't learn how to interact with boys now, she won't know how to handle men later when it's dangerous."

"Understood." Collin gave her a head-to-toe look that revved her heart rate like a finely tuned race car.

Jazz blinked and tried to distance herself from what she was feeling because *she* knew how to handle men. Didn't she? "Good, then I can tell her she can go?"

"After you call Hannah's mom and find out if they are personally going to be chaperoning this loathsome affair instead of their teenage son."

"I already called." She waited, hoping he would tell her she'd done the right thing as a parent. Though he didn't say anything about her skills, she still decided she must be doing a better job at this mom stuff. "Both parents will be there. Madison will be ecstatic when I tell her she can go."

"Tell her I said she can go if she doesn't get into any trouble before then. I'll be looking for reasons to ground her." He went back to his papers, muttering, "Think my little girl is going to learn how to be a woman at twelve? I don't think so."

"I heard that, Collin, and you can't stop her from growing up."

"I can try." He started sorting through envelopes on the desk.

"Yes, you can try." She grinned at him and started to walk away when she felt his hand on her arm.

"This one is for you. You'll have to decide what to do about it." Collin slid a thick white envelope into her hand.

"It has Louisa's name on it, not mine." She tried giving it back.

"No, it is for you. It's the invitation to your family reunion. It would be a great time for you to collect information about yourself. Might even trigger some memories."

"I'm not interested in going. I don't want to be a one-woman family-reunion freak show." She tossed the envelope onto the desk; it skidded across the pile of papers and landed on the floor.

Collin retrieved it, ripped open the edge of the envelope, and slid out the contents. "They're having it in Forest Park this year."

"This year? This is an annual event?" Jazz frowned at the thought of meeting people who knew more about her than she did.

"Unfortunately." He opened a folded piece of paper from the envelope and gave a loud laugh.

"What are you laughing at?"

"They want you to fill out this questionnaire about what you've done this past year. That should be interesting. What will you write? 'Tried out a new personality'?" He laughed harder.

Collin's laughter hurt. "Maybe. Or maybe I'll figure it out before then." She walked to the bookshelf and began loading her arms with scrapbooks and photo albums like she'd done several times before. She dropped them on the floor and plopped down, resting her back against the couch.

Jazz pulled out the album that looked older than the others—it had an eighties feel to it, with its mauve and blue design. She began flipping through the pages again. This empty past of hers was bothersome. What she'd discovered inside this album hadn't brought answers, only more questions. Louisa looked about Madison's age in a few of these photos, but she didn't smile in many of them. Jazz still couldn't figure out why. Maybe she had grown bored with the camera, or maybe she had been in an ugly-duckling stage.

In contrast, the albums with photos of Madison and the boys were delightful, each child hamming in front of the camera, trying to outdo the others.

And Louisa? No personality. *Lifeless* even came to mind as she examined the monotone clothing. If Louisa were trying to blend in, she had managed as well as any American soldier in the desert.

Collin tapped another date on his BlackBerry calendar, then another. Every day seemed to have a court date or a deposition that needed to be done. He would have to find a way to clear his calendar.

Maybe he could turn over the Esmonde deposition on Friday to Robert. He felt sure it would be a simple one and wouldn't take long. If Robert would do it, then Collin could leave the office early. He'd be able to get home about the time the kids arrived from school. He clicked the New Message icon in his e-mail account and wrote a short note to Robert. Satisfied with his request, he clicked Send.

Within seconds Robert e-mailed back, and the deal was made. They had traded work, leaving Collin free for the entire weekend. Now all he had to do was pick up a few supplies and a tent. His family would be bonding this weekend in the great outdoors at Rend Lake. He'd show Jazz how exciting he could be. This would give them a chance to get to know each other as a family. He could picture it now. A hot, blazing fire; the kids asleep in the tent; and he and Jazz sitting outside in chairs, gazing at stars and getting reacquainted.

Feeling pleased at taking action to pull his family together, he called Jazz, anticipating her response.

"We're going to sleep in a tent? Outside?" Jazz didn't say anything else for a moment. He let her digest the information, hoping she'd warm up to the idea. "Outside? Do I like that?"

"I don't know if you like it, Jazz." Her confusion amused him.

"Did Louisa?"

"I don't know. We never went camping. It will be fun. Think marshmallows, graham crackers, and chocolate, like when you were a kid."

"That sounds like an interesting combination." Her voice hesitated. "Am I supposed to know about this kind of food?"

"S'mores. That's what they're called. Trust me. I've seen you eat, and you'll like this."

"The boys will like the idea, but I'm not sure about Madison," Jazz said.

"She'll be fine once she gets over the shock that there won't be any instant messaging for an entire weekend."

"Maybe we can let her take a friend along?"

"No. I want this weekend to be about the kids and being a family." Collin paused. He wanted to add, *"and about you falling in love with me again,"* but he didn't. He knew she still held on to the belief that Louisa would return soon. But he hoped if and when she did return, she would keep Jazz alive.

When he looked at her, he saw Louisa's face, but the smile, warmth, energy, and enthusiasm for life belonged to Jazz.

"Collin? Are you still there?" Jazz interrupted his thoughts.

"Yeah, just thinking about what we might need to take along."

"A Scrabble board, I hope."

"Good idea. Can you get the games together? I'll take care of the equipment. I have a friend who might loan me his camping gear." He suddenly remembered Jazz's inability to cook, even in their fifty-thousand-dollar kitchen. "I'll get the food too."

Collin plopped three pizza boxes onto the table. "Let's eat," he yelled. "Pizza's here." Tim and Joey were the first to climb into their chairs. Madison took her time to get settled. Jazz brought liter bottles of soda over and set them on the table. Collin couldn't wait any longer. He had finally come up with a family activity, and he knew the kids were going to love it. "Guess what?"

"You won't be home next week because you'll be involved in a trial," Madison guessed. "That's nothing new, Dad. You're gone all the time." She pulled a slice of cheese pizza from one of the boxes.

"That's not it." Collin grinned. This was going to be good. He could almost hear the whoops of joy when he told them. He looked at Jazz and winked to let her know he appreciated her letting him tell the kids.

"What is it, Dad?" Joey stuffed a hunk of pepperoni in his mouth.

"We're going camping this weekend!" Collin almost shouted the words. He sat back and waited for the information to sink in.

"Camping? Dad, I am not sleeping in a tent!" Madison tossed her napkin onto the table. She shoved her chair back and stood. "You can't make me go!" She burst into tears and ran upstairs. Just in case he might mistake her tears for joy, she slammed her door hard enough to correct his erroneous thinking.

Joey scowled at him. "Dad, I have soccer practice."

"Do we have to eat outside with the bugs? I don't want to eat with bugs." Tim grabbed another slice of pizza. "I'd better eat a lot now so I don't have to eat with dirty, disgusting flies."

Collin was truly surprised at the reaction from his kids. He thought they would be delighted at the prospect of a weekend family camping trip. Maybe not Madison, but the boys should have been eager to camp. Nope, this hadn't gone the way he had planned at all. Not one happy face beamed at him from across the table. Not even Jazz looked happy, and she was always ready for adventure.

Collin sought cover in his workshop. He looked at the unfinished picture frame on the workbench. He picked up the cordless drill, pressed the on switch, and let it run in the air for a minute before setting it back down. He didn't feel like working on the frame right now.

Unable to stay away from Louisa's journals, he lifted the

box onto the bench and pulled out a stack of papers that had been stapled at the corner. A title splashed across the first page: *The Model and the Taxi Driver*, by Jazz Sweet. Startled, he wondered how Jazz had found a way into his workshop. Then he realized it was Louisa's handwriting, and the air thickened in his throat. He had found it! The connection to Louisa—she really had written a book. He sat down to read.

Annette Richmond yanked the door handle of the yellow cab. She tossed her leather backpack onto the floor of the taxi and slid onto the worn cloth seat.

"Twelfth and Oak," she said to the back of the driver's head as she slammed the door. Exhausted from hunger, she lay back in the seat. Her stomach growled. She patted it gently as a pregnant woman might to reassure an unsettled child. But no amount of rubbing seemed to calm the stabbing hunger pangs. She made good money, but none of it went for food. She couldn't afford to eat much, only what would keep her alive and walking down the runway. Some days she came close to spending her money on drugs to curb her appetite. Many of her friends urged her to try some new designer pill. Even Kate, her best friend, had folded, and now she swore she never needed to eat.

"Miss?"

She looked into the rearview mirror, where brown eyes reflected back at her. "What?"

"There isn't a Twelfth and Oak." His Southern accent brought her into the world she had given up—no, the world she had fled—twelve months ago.

"You're right," she stuttered, her own accent creeping past her lips. "Ah meant Twelfth and Pine."

Collin adjusted the papers in his hand and leaned against the wall. He continued to read. As he flipped the pages, he realized his wife had a gift. One that she'd kept hidden for a long time. He wanted to run upstairs and tell her how well she wrote; he wanted to tell everyone his wife was Jazz. That Louisa was a figment of the world's imagination, a star peg trying to fit into a square hole. But he couldn't let her know about the journals because she didn't remember them. If he told her he had them and hadn't shown them to her, well, it was just too complicated. For a little longer he would keep the evidence of her previous life to himself.

Collin looked around his workshop. His getaway-from-the-world place. Jazz needed someplace like this, he thought. And then he had an idea. It would take some time to implement, but it could be done. He sat up straighter, proud that he had thought of something he could do to encourage his wife. He would start today. Collin tossed the stack of papers back into the box and covered it.

He surveyed the room. He would hire someone while they were gone this weekend to clean out his tools and paint the room. That brought the first problem to mind: what to do with his tools? He couldn't put them in the garage because that would mess up the surprise. And he wanted this to shock his wife to the core. Maybe he could build a workshop next to the garage. He'd wanted to do that for a long time. *Focus, Copeland. This is about Louisa, not you.* For now, to keep this project a surprise, he could rent a storage place. After he gave the room to Jazz, he could put his tools in the garage.

Walking past the MP3 player, he flipped the off switch before closing the door behind him. He was on a mission, one that would bring a smile to Jazz's face.

The evenings were getting cooler, and the breeze off the lake chilled Jazz. She zipped her red plaid jacket and plopped down on the deck steps while waiting for Cleo to finish her business so they could go back inside. Her mind was restless. Laurie had tweaked something when she asked about the stories Jazz had written as a child. If she had written stories, wouldn't Beth—her mother—have brought it up? It seemed logical to Jazz. If Madison had lost her memory and thought she was a writer, at least Jazz could say, *"No, you like to draw things, not write."* And she could show her all the sketches she'd piled in a box. Why didn't Beth say it made sense that Jazz thought she was a writer because she'd written stories as a child? She didn't know but intended to find out.

She called Cleo, and the dog bounded across the lawn, her tongue swinging freely from her mouth. "Let's go inside, girl. You probably need a cool drink of water, and I need to make a phone call."

Inside the house, she took off her jacket and placed it on the hook by the others. It felt good to see it there as part of a coat family, like she was now—part of something bigger than she remembered. She grasped the phone and dialed. Beth answered on the first ring, and after a few minutes of niceties, Jazz went to the subject that was bothering her.

"Can you tell me about the stories I wrote as a kid?" Her throat tightened as anxiety rippled through her.

"Stories? Oh, those little make-believe things you wrote?" Beth asked.

"Do you have them stored somewhere?" A flow of excitement knocked out the anxious feelings as she pictured boxes of short stories that only she would probably appreciate. She wondered if she wrote animal stories or stories about people, maybe about her best friends.

"No, I didn't keep those. If I remember right, it seemed you were always bothering us with some kind of outlandish problem or idea."

Her joyful spirit fizzled. No record of her early work, no books currently in bookstores, and only two chapters written of her new book.

Maybe she could still get some of the blanks of her life filled in, at least. "When did I write them? How old was I?"

"You were writing cute little stories before we went to Mexico, but when we came back, you were . . ." Beth stopped.

"What? What was I writing when you came back?" Jazz pounced through the phone line with her words.

"You started writing dark stories about people being killed

and children being kidnapped. It was upsetting to your father and me, and we asked you to stop writing them."

"Who did I write about? What did I say?" Her curiosity increased her heart rate.

"I don't remember now." Beth sighed.

"Do you remember if I stopped writing when you asked?" Puzzled, Jazz tried to glean some meaning from this information.

"Of course you did, dear. You were always a good girl." She could hear the pride in Beth's voice.

Jazz hung up the phone, and her stomach churned. Something felt wrong. She didn't know what, but the cramps in her stomach insisted she needed to figure it out, and she didn't think they were from the dinner she'd eaten.

CHAPTER SIXTEEN

IN THE DISTANCE small motorboats raced across the lake, leaving wide wakes that bounced against the shoreline. Jazz felt soothed by the rhythm. The lake didn't have the color or smell of her beloved ocean, but it was water. The campsite Collin had reserved jutted into the rocky beach. A host of scraggly pines and ash trees with their bright-yellow leaves separated their space from the rest of the campground, giving them privacy. She let the warm rays of sun massage her shoulders. Collin had said it might be the last of the warm weather.

Jazz swatted at a fly as she stood in the doorway of the unzipped tent. Five sleeping bags lay in a row across the floor.

The army-green edges of blow-up mattresses peeked between the plaid bags and blue flooring, mocking her with pretend comfort. "I'm not sleeping here," she said under her breath.

She jumped at the touch of Collin's hand on the small of her back.

"Why not? It's perfect. We aren't sleeping together." He pointed to one end of the line. "That's your bed, and I'm over there." He swept his hand to the other end. "The kids are between us. See, I'm following your rules."

She placed one foot on the nylon floor.

"Stop! You have to take your shoes off and leave them on this rug." Collin pointed at the rough welcome mat. "It keeps the tent cleaner."

Grasping the pole that held the awning upright, she started to balance on one foot to remove her shoe.

"No! You'll yank down the entire tent. Look . . ." He collapsed onto the floor of the tent with his legs sticking straight out the door. Bending his knee, he yanked off one sneaker and then the other. "That's how you do it."

"Terrific. I get to practice yoga while camping." But she followed his example. Once her feet would no longer endanger the tent floor, she swung them inside and stood. "There isn't any room."

"Enough space for all of us to sleep comfortably," Collin said.

"Couldn't we have a girls' tent?" she pleaded, offering her best beguiling smile. "Like down the road at the Sleep Inn, Sleep Tight?"

"No, come on, Jazz. Give this a chance. It's a great way for a family to bond."

"In these quarters you don't have a choice, do you? I mean, it's like a slapstick comedy in here: if one person rolls over, everyone has to roll." Jazz sank down on her appointed bed, or tried to. She bounced, then slid to the side. "This isn't going to work."

Collin took her hand. "Please, Jazz, try it—for the kids, for us?"

His touch sent ripples of heat through her. She wanted to please him, to say yes to anything he asked, but he wasn't hers.

"Jazz?"

It would help if his voice didn't soothe her like hot fudge on a sundae. "One night. If I don't like it, I can leave?"

He considered her offer and then smiled. "Deal."

She realized he still held her hand and began to pull away.

He held on tighter and leaned in to kiss her.

She didn't move. Her heart beat faster. Her mind screamed *"run,"* but her lips said *"yes."*

The kiss lasted only a second. Jazz couldn't remember another time when a kiss had felt so wonderful. Dazed, she shook her head to wake up from the dreamlike trance she'd fallen into.

Collin brushed her cheek with his hand and stood. "Thank you for not rejecting me," he said over his shoulder as he pushed through the loose screen door.

Jazz lay back on her sleeping bag, hugging the feeling of being wanted. She savored the feel of that kiss. If she were

Louisa, she could have Collin's kisses anytime she wished. *Please, God, let me remember this part of me if I turn into Louisa,* she prayed.

Slapping at mosquitoes hours later, Jazz couldn't imagine why she would ever want to be Louisa. "Tell me again why you didn't bring any repellent?" She winced as she hit her thigh again, missing the offending insect. The bite marks on her legs told her who was winning this war.

"I told you I'm sorry." Collin tossed more dead leaves into the fire.

"Does smoke really keep them away, Collin, or do people die from lack of air so they don't know they're still having their blood sucked from their bodies?" Jazz waved the offending smoke away.

Madison giggled. "Yeah, Dad, does it work?"

"Maybe it has something to do with what you burn," Collin replied.

Joey threw a potato chip into the fire. He and Tim scooted closer to watch it burn.

"Back up, boys. You won't have any eyebrows left if you get too close. The fire will melt them off your faces." Collin stood, ready to pull them away from the fire. He relaxed when they moved back.

"That's okay. We don't need them," said Tim. "Mom's always pulling hers out with tweezers. I don't want to do that when I get old."

"Don't be stupid, Tim. Women do it to make us look good," said Madison. "Bushy eyebrows scare men off."

"You aren't a woman, so how do you know?" Joey asked.

"Stop. She knows, Joey, and she'll be a woman soon," Jazz said. "Tim, you need some eyebrows to help protect your eyes, so don't be burning them off."

Thwack. *Missed another one.* Her leg, where she had been repeatedly defending it, glowed bright red in the firelight. "I think I'll go to bed. At least it will be bug-free in there."

"Me too." Madison unfolded her colt-like legs and stood, ready to follow.

"I think it's time we all went inside," Collin said.

Thunder woke Jazz. She struggled to loosen herself from the sleeping bag as lightning lit the inside of the tent. "Collin!"

"It's just a storm, Jazz. Don't scare the kids," he muttered as he flung his arm over his eyes to block the lightning flashes.

"Dad? I'm getting wet," Madison said as she scooted off her mattress and onto Tim's. "Move over."

Tim didn't move, so Madison pushed him. "Dad?"

Only a snore from Collin answered back.

"Madison, want to make a run for the van?" Jazz whispered.

"It won't be comfortable," Madison whined.

"At least it won't be wet inside." She wasn't about to stay in the tent any longer. Madison could stay and fight off the puddles that were forming by the bed if she wanted to.

"We could recline the seats," Madison suggested, seeming more willing to run for it.

"Grab your pillow." Jazz fought her way to the end of the makeshift bed and felt around for her shoes.

"I'm ready," Madison said. "Should we tell Dad we're going?"

"I don't think he'll hear you if you try," Jazz said as Collin began to snore louder.

"What time is it, anyway?" Madison asked.

Jazz pushed the button on her watch and groaned. "It's a little after twelve." She thought about spending at least six hours in the van with the windows rolled up. It would be stifling.

Jazz felt around on the floor until she found the jeans Collin had been wearing. Locating the pocket, she retrieved the keys and pushed the Unlock button. "Go get in the van, Madison."

The zipper pull clicked as the teeth separated, allowing Madison to squeeze through and run to the van.

Using her hands to feel in front of her for wet spots, Jazz crept to Collin's side. She shook his shoulder and whispered, "I tried. I can't do this. Madison and I will be back in the morning." She waited to see if he responded.

He didn't. She pushed the button on her watch next to his face to see if he responded to the light. He rolled away from her.

At the doorway she whispered, "Bye, boys. Enjoy the night."

Collin woke from the best sleep he'd had in a long time. The diffused light coming from outside the tent made him wish he could wake this way every morning. His stomach growled. He'd be making scrambled eggs, toast, and coffee over an open fire. *Just a few minutes more,* he thought as he sank back into sleep.

He dreamed of living on a mountain with Jazz by his side. They had a log cabin, no electricity or water. They were a mountain couple, not needing more than each other to survive. Jazz whispered something—did she say she loved him? He felt her touch his face.

"Daddy, wake up." Tim poked him in the ear with a finger. "I'm hungry."

"Me too," Joey said. "Where's Madison and Jazz?"

The dream popped from Collin's mind, but the after-effects stuck to his memory like gum in his hair. He pushed Tim's hand away from his head. "Maybe they're outside."

"It's raining, and the van is gone. Did they go to get us breakfast?" Joey asked. "I wish they would have taken us with them. I'm cold."

Collin raised himself up on his arm and looked over to where Jazz should have been sleeping. Her pillow was gone, and so was Madison's. Little rivers of water ran down the side of the tent next to Joey's bed. The corner of his sleeping bag had sucked the water like an absorbent paper towel, spreading it across the bottom of the bag. No wonder he was cold. Collin scratched his head. Where did Jazz go?

"Well, boys, let's get dressed and make a fire. I'm sure they will be back soon."

Tim and Joey bumped into each other as they tried to pull on shorts and socks.

"Where's my shoes?" Tim yelled, flipping his brother's T-shirt into a puddle on the tent floor.

"Where did you leave them?" Collin asked while tying his sneakers.

Joey grabbed his shirt and smacked Tim on the head. "We left them in the van, remember?"

"Oh, yeah."

Collin sighed. The weather report had been warm and sunny all weekend. This trip was not turning out like he'd planned. "Stay in the tent until I get a fire going, and then you can sit there until Jazz and Madison get back." *And it better be soon,* he thought.

The cold rain soaked through the back of his shirt while he huddled under a tree. No food, no matches, and no cell phone. They were all in the back of the van. He had left everything locked safely inside, away from the morning dew. Jazz had taken everything with her. His earlier dream of living like a mountain family seemed more torturous than idyllic.

Poking his head through the tent door, he saw two uncomfortable boys huddled together. "I have bad news, boys. We're not going to have breakfast or heat until Mom and Madison return."

"Are they bringing doughnuts?" Tim asked.

"When are they coming back? I'm hungry," Joey said.

"I don't know. Want to play cards while we wait?" Collin

stepped inside and rummaged through his duffel bag. "I'm sure I have some in here."

Tim peered over his shoulder. "Do you have any candy in there?"

"I don't think so, Tim Bear, but I do feel something." He pulled out an unopened chocolate-peanut-butter-with-cranberries energy bar. "What do you say, guys? We'll split it three ways."

Tim wrinkled his nose. "No thanks."

"Me neither. How old is that? You should check the expiration date," Joey said.

"It's been in there a long time. It's probably older than you." Collin tossed the bar back to the bottom of the bag. "We'll leave it until we're almost unable to move from hunger." As the first wafts of breakfast smells from the other campsites entered their tent, he added, "And that might not be as long as we think."

CHAPTER SEVENTEEN

Pipes knocked in the wall behind Jazz's bed as the occupant in the next room turned on the shower. Jazz awakened with a leisurely stretch and flung off the heavy comforter. It felt early, but the line of bright sunlight sliding through the curtains let her know it wasn't. She climbed out of the comfortable bed. In the bed next to her, the only thing visible was a strand of Madison's blonde hair. She gently shook Madison's shoulder. "Wake up. It's late."

Madison groaned and rolled away from Jazz. "Just a few more minutes?"

"No, we can't. I planned for us to be back before the boys woke, but it's almost ten." Jazz walked to the bathroom. "As soon as I'm out, you're in, all right? So don't go back into a deep sleep, Madison Girl." Not receiving any indication that Madison had heard her, Jazz flipped on the television. She surfed the channels until she found cartoon robots. She had discovered how much Madison hated cartoons and hoped the screeching voices would wake her. She smiled when Madison popped up from the bed.

"I hate that show."

"I know." Jazz grinned. "Call your dad on his cell phone and tell him we're leaving soon. I don't know where my phone went."

When Jazz came back from washing her face, Madison had dressed in her jeans and T-shirt. "Is Collin mad?"

"Beats me. My phone is dead." Madison pushed past Jazz. Just as she entered the bathroom, she called out, "Besides, didn't he put his phone in the van with the food to keep it safe?"

Jazz felt the blood rush from her head to her feet. "I didn't see him do that. Hurry, Madison, we have to get back."

She gathered the pillows they had brought along, collected the books they had been reading, and had the keys in her hand when Madison came strutting out the bathroom door, hands full of tiny bottles.

"I'm taking these. They'll be cool to take when I go to a sleepover. Can we stop in the lobby downstairs and get breakfast?" Madison asked.

"I don't think we better. I imagine there are going to be some very hungry males waiting for us." Her foot tapped as she waited for Madison to tie her shoes.

"Then we'd better bring them food so they don't have to cook," Madison said. "They can stuff their mouths and won't be able to yell at us."

"Good idea. We'll stop for doughnuts. Now let's get going." Jazz guided Madison out the door. "I've got all our stuff, and I used the video checkout system. All we have to do is find the best doughnut shop in the universe."

At the campsite, Collin attempted to make a fire using matches and dry kindling from a neighboring camper. He was worried. Their neighbors had offered the use of their cell phone, but when he tried calling Jazz, she didn't pick up, and Madison's phone went straight to voice mail. He didn't want to call his friends and admit his crazy wife had taken his daughter and left him and the boys. They had to return soon. *Madison probably insisted on stopping for some important hair item,* he tried to reassure himself. He would continue to treat this as a fun challenge for his sons.

"Now remember, boys, when Mom and Madison get back, you have to pretend you're really hungry." Collin paced in front of the two sitting on the concrete table. "We'll tell them later about how we found neighbors to give us food."

"It was fun begging for food." Tim grinned. "I'm going to try that when we get home."

"No, you're not. I told you this was an exception." Collin frowned and stopped in front of his son. With his finger under Tim's chin, he tilted the boy's head. "Right? No begging at home."

"Okay. But it was fun." Tim's lower lip trembled. "Is Mom coming soon?"

"I'm sure she'll be here in a few minutes." Collin looked up as he heard a car coming slowly down the blacktopped street. He scowled. "That better be them."

It wasn't. The glum faces of his sons looked at him for reassurance, if not answers. He needed to turn this back into an adventure, fast. "Let's go for a hike, men. There's a little store down the road. Who wants a candy bar?" He was thankful Jazz had not taken his wallet along with her.

"Me! Me!" the boys yelled. Tim and Joey slid off the picnic table, big toothy grins splashed across their faces as they followed their dad.

Jazz pushed the accelerator harder. "I can't believe it took us so long to get these doughnuts. Hand me my cup?"

Madison reached across the van and held out the coffee. "Careful, it's hot."

The tire fell into a pothole. Jazz bumped the cup with her hand, and the hot liquid spilled onto her lap. "Ouch!" She glanced down at her leg.

"Watch out!" Madison cried.

Jazz looked up to see the van shooting straight at a pine tree. She didn't have time to react, and the front of the van struck the trunk. Both air bags shot from the dashboard with a loud bang. For a second the world turned white and silent. Then a hiss began as her bag deflated into her lap.

Stunned, Jazz gasped. "Madison, tell me you're okay." She reached across the seat and touched Madison's face. "No blood or cuts."

"I'm okay. Are you?"

Jazz grimaced. "I think so." As a mother, she still wasn't doing well. Twice now she had failed. Losing Tim and now involving Madison in an accident. What if the third thing killed one of the kids? *Be quiet,* she told the voice in her head. *You're just saying that because you're a writer and you always wonder, "What if?" It doesn't mean it will happen.*

Jazz wrinkled her nose. "Stinks in here." She opened the van door and stepped out. Seeing the front of the van mashed by the tree, she said, "I'm toast. Collin is going to kill me."

Madison came around the other side of the van, wiping dust from her face.

"We're miles from town, but not too far from the campground. Think you can walk about a mile?"

"Do I have a choice?" Madison said.

Jazz held back the smile of relief at Madison's sarcastic tone. At least she knew Madison was normal. "No, not really. We could wait and see if someone comes along, but it's almost lunchtime."

"Dad is going to be so mad." Madison zipped her jacket. "How are you going to explain this?"

"I don't know. The truth, I guess." Collin *would* be mad.

Her rating as a wife had to be around a zero. First jail and now this.

"How are we going to get back home?" Madison asked.

The road stretched far into the distance. "Let's just walk. Maybe some answers will miraculously come to me." Jazz reached into the car, grabbed her purse and keys, and locked the van.

Madison fell into step next to her. "Did you hit your head hard?"

"I don't remember; I don't think so, why?"

"You have blood," Madison said, "on the side of your face."

Jazz raised her hand and touched the spot. Sticky. "Is it bleeding a lot?"

"No, some of it's dried already. I was wondering since you hit your head again if you're Jazz or Mom?"

Madison's hopeful face peered at her. "It doesn't work that way in real life." Jazz wished she knew what answer Madison wanted to hear, but she only had one to give. "I'm still Jazz."

"Okay, then." Madison turned away, and Jazz couldn't read her expression. The flat tone in her voice gave no indication.

What seemed like hours passed by before Jazz saw the little hut where the park attendant kept wait for new arrivals. Her feet hurt. Her ears buzzed from listening to Madison's relentless litany of how her life couldn't get any worse. Her only hope right now consisted of a ride from the front of the park to their campsite. Beyond that, she didn't care anymore.

She should have cared.

She should have been praying, Jazz realized as she saw Collin pacing the campground. The ranger pulled into the small gravel driveway next to the tent.

"Thank you for the ride," she said as she and Madison climbed out of the golf cart.

"No problem," the ranger said as he turned off the engine.

Collin walked over. "What happened?" He grabbed Jazz into an embrace and inspected her face.

"She's still Jazz, Dad." Madison pushed past him. "By the way, I'm okay too."

Collin released Jazz and reached out to snag Madison by the arm. He pulled her close. "I'm glad you're safe, too, pumpkin." He gave her a quick kiss on the forehead and let her go.

"The van hit a tree," Jazz said. "The airbags came out, and we walked back to the park. We had doughnuts for you and the boys. They're still in the van, though."

"Excuse me," the ranger interrupted. "Is there someone I can call for you?"

"I have a phone. Did you bring it with you, Jazz?"

"No." She sighed and leaned against the side of the golf cart. "It's still in the van."

Collin frowned. "Everything is in the van, Jazz, including the boy's shoes."

"Sir, your wife thinks the car is about a mile from the park entrance. I can give you a ride in my car, and we'll pick up the kids' shoes and your phone."

"Thanks. I can call someone for help then, along with the insurance agent." Collin hopped into the golf cart.

Collin finished packing the last of the camping equipment into the rental van. He looked up to see Jazz watching him. As soon as she noticed his gaze, she dropped her stare. He thought if it were possible, she would curl up on the ground and cover herself with a blanket in an effort to be invisible.

He didn't know what to say to her. He had handled everything wrong in his marriage. At least he felt that way after reading some of Louisa's journals. He knew Jazz was fragile, and he couldn't express the anger he felt.

He slammed the back door of the van. "Everyone in?" he asked Jazz as a way to start the conversation.

"Yes," came the quiet response.

"Let's go, then." He held out his hand as an offering of forgiveness. She hesitated, then took it. He gave it a gentle squeeze. "It will be okay."

She smiled a half smile at him. "It will be more work for you. I'm sorry."

"I know."

"I feel bad the camping adventure turned out all wrong."

"It's a trip we won't forget though, will we?" Collin leaned over and kissed her forehead. She didn't back away from him this time. Instead, she tipped her head and brushed his lips with hers. His heart pounded. This kiss made the problems of the weekend seem small. Could it be possible she was beginning to accept him as her husband?

CHAPTER EIGHTEEN

Settling back into his leather office chair, Collin held one of Louisa's stories in his lap. His tuna sandwich remained untouched as he munched barbeque chips. As he continued reading, he felt he had made the right decision to build Jazz an office. When they'd returned from the memory-making camping trip, he'd checked out the work that had been done while they were gone. The transformation from workshop to office was well on its way. The walls were painted a nice butter yellow, and the plush, sandy-colored carpet had replaced the workshop atmosphere.

At the end of the chapter, he set the pages aside and took a bite of his sandwich. Glancing at the clock on his desk, he decided he had enough time to read a few pages of Louisa's journal. Not that he wanted to. Almost every page drew blood with the sharp words of disappointment in their marriage. He discovered Louisa thought taking out the trash was equal to hugs and kisses. One day he had driven the soccer car pool, and she had written three pages on how wonderful it had been to have time alone to write.

He picked up the journal and then set it back down. He couldn't do it. He didn't want to read about his old life. Now he had Jazz to love. His heart quickened as he realized what he had never admitted. Could it be possible Jazz was easier to love than Louisa? He wanted to know everything about Jazz: Why did she stare off into space and then jump when he touched her arm? Why did she dissect movies when she watched them? That's it. He would learn all her secrets.

After a few moments he decided to take her away for a romantic getaway—no kids, no tents, and if it rained, it wouldn't matter. He pulled out his BlackBerry and opened the calendar to check when he could leave. He couldn't go on Friday, but if they left after lunch this Saturday, he wouldn't have to be back until court Monday afternoon. He had heard his secretary talking about a quaint little town not too far away—*R*-something? He grasped the phone on his desk and asked his secretary to come in.

Hail crashed against the window, waking Jazz. The lightning flashed repeatedly. She pulled the blanket over her head to block the irritating light. Inside, a headache kept time with the rolling thunder.

She flung back the covers and fumbled for the bedside light. The switch clicked in her hand. Nothing. The clock next to the light no longer gave off its familiar eerie green glow. The air stilled, and for a second, the house seemed to have no life. The ceiling fan no longer turned; the vents didn't send out air. Just stillness, then thunder, louder than before. She clutched her head between her hands in an attempt to stop the pain. The ibuprofen was downstairs in the kitchen.

The lightning flashed again, sending a fresh wave of pain through her. She had to get relief. She shivered and tugged one of Collin's shirts over her tank top and boxer shorts. At the top of the stairs, she peeked over the railing. The storm sent a flash and briefly lit the room. Collin's shape didn't seem to be moving on the couch. She crept down the stairs, praying she wouldn't wake him. He needed his sleep.

Jazz made it to the kitchen. She stood in front of the open cabinet, ready to cry in frustration. Darkness made it impossible for her to know which bottle contained the ibuprofen. She found two bottles that felt right in her hand. But which one was it? One of them had to be Cleo's heartworm medication. She set them on the counter, reluctant to take a chance. She had made the trip for nothing.

"Jazz?" Collin's whisper made her jump. "What are you doing?"

She turned and reached out to grasp his arm. He stilled beneath her hand. His stillness electrified her feelings. She could hear his breath in the darkness and wanted to crawl into his arms. Did he have to smell so good? Her defenses were down, and she knew it. The headaches seemed to make her vulnerable to a strong desire for him.

Pulling away, she said, "Headache. I'm sorry I woke you." The words rushed from her mouth. "Where's a flashlight? The power is out."

"There's one in the basket on top of the fridge." He brushed past her close enough for her to feel his warmth on her back. "I'll get it."

She could hear him fumbling in the basket, and was grateful for the distraction and the darkness. She knew she had to make a choice soon. Either be Collin's wife or not. It was that simple. Or at least it sounded easy.

"Got it." The click of a button seemed to flood the room with light. "I'll hold it while you open the bottle."

"Thanks, but you could set it on the counter and go back to sleep. I know you need to be at the office early."

"No, it's okay. I'm not sleeping well. I keep expecting the storm to wake one of the kids."

Guilt flooded her. "The kids. I didn't even think about them. Should we check on them?"

"You have a headache, and you aren't used to checking on them. If they were awake and scared, you would know it." Collin's words reassured her that she hadn't made another mistake. "Jazz, will you go away with me for a weekend? Just the two of us? No kids?"

Stunned at his request, she didn't answer. Thoughts,

bouncing as fast as popcorn in a microwave, burst in her mind. *A weekend alone, in the same room?* A choice had to be made.

"We'll have your mom stay with the kids," Collin said. "I'm sure she'd be happy to watch them. She hasn't been here in a while."

"I don't know, Collin. I don't think I'm ready to take that step." She couldn't, not yet. Not until she felt comfortable being—that's just it, being who?

"No steps, Jazz. Just a chance to rediscover—discover each other. I can't keep living like this. I want you for my wife, and I intend to do what I can to make that happen."

Her heart thudded with the realization that "discover each other" didn't mean finding out who her favorite singer was when she was thirteen.

"If you go with me, I'll buy you a laptop."

"A bribe, Collin?"

"If that's what it takes." He pulled her close and kissed her. "That's a bribe to go with me, not to sleep with me."

She backed away and bumped into the counter. "Do I have to tell you tonight?"

"No, but I wish you would."

She thought about what he was asking of her. In her heart, she felt God would want her to go—not for the computer, but to get to know Collin. Didn't she just pray about what choice to make? She didn't expect to have to make it in the middle of a thunderstorm, though.

"Jazz, are you going to say anything?"

"I don't know what to say. If I say yes, then I feel like a bought woman because of the computer. If I say no, then I have to keep sharing with the kids. I think I would like to go with you, but now I'm confused."

"Forget the computer, then. I've already bought it. I just wanted to give it to you at the right time." He paused and ran his hands through his hair. "I shouldn't have tried to bribe you."

"You bought me a laptop? Can I have it now?"

"It's not here yet. I ordered it."

She rushed into him and hugged him tight. "Thank you! You do believe in me." She reached up and kissed him. Fighting the urge to hold on, she let go. "Good night." She sped through the room as a round of lightning flooded through the windows. Halting a safe distance away, she looked back in the darkened room at his silhouette. "Thank you."

Jazz eased the bedroom door closed behind her and rested her back against the six-panel door. She hadn't given him an answer. Could she do it? Spend a weekend alone with Collin? The thought sent shivers through her. And they weren't the tingles of joy she had expected.

CHAPTER NINETEEN

COLLIN OPENED THE DOOR to his old workshop. He stepped inside and locked the door. Reaching under his striped T-shirt, he removed a copy of *From the Inside Out*, by Susan May Warren and Rachel Hauck. Late at night last week he had wandered into a chat room full of romance writers and asked for recommendations. This book topped everyone's list.

He rubbed his hand over the smooth oak bookshelves he had installed along one wall. Proud of his handiwork, he placed the book next to a new shrink-wrapped dictionary. There should be more books or something else on the shelves, maybe some seashells, but he didn't have any. He didn't want to put any of Louisa's collections in the room.

Somehow he didn't think Jazz would appreciate that touch. And he wanted her appreciation. More than wanted it—he craved it.

The yellow paint on the walls caught the light from the ceiling and bounced a sunny glow over the room. The ocean mural on the back wall made the room uniquely Jazz's. It had to be his favorite part. Jazz wanted an ocean, and he had found one. He beat his fists against his chest, then looked around, embarrassed and glad no one could see him strutting around like a big bad rooster. He imagined her sitting in the wicker rocker reading over her day's writing and gazing out into the mural's horizon, or perhaps inviting him to sit with her while she read her work aloud to him. The mural looked real, or it did if you squinted and didn't focus on the seam lines. All the room needed for ambience was the sound of waves crashing against the shoreline. He could do that with a sound machine. Madison would know where to find one, but then he'd have to tell her about the room. No, he didn't want any chance of this secret getting out until he was ready. He'd find one himself.

As he continued to survey his handiwork, he could picture Jazz's face shining in excitement. Then Jazz turned back into Louisa, her hair pulled back, her face accusing. He could almost hear her ask why he hadn't loved her this much.

With a leaden heart, he left the workshop, asking God to ease his guilt and make sense of the conflict he felt about his wife's two personalities. And while he was asking, could God make his life normal again, but with a mix of Louisa and Jazz?

At a rapid clip, Jazz charged down the basement stairs, followed by Cleo. "Collin!" She banged on the workshop door. "You can't stay down here anymore."

He opened the door a crack, and she tried to peer around him. "You're always down here when you're home. What are you doing, anyway?"

"Nothing. Just stuff."

"Stuff and nothing? Then you won't mind climbing those stairs and separating your children from each other's throats and walking that beast." She pointed her finger toward the stairs, where Cleo sat panting and watching them. "Now!" She spun on her heel and headed back upstairs, not even checking to see if he was following her demands.

"Louisa?" Collin whispered after her.

At the name, her feet stopped, and a chill settled within her. "No," she said, almost not breathing. "Did I sound like her?"

"A little."

"I'm sorry." Jazz turned to face him, unsure what sounding like Louisa would mean to him—to them.

"It's not a bad thing to sound like her, Jazz. You are her."

"In theory." She looked down at the carpeted stairs. Time to face the fact that she may never return to being Louisa, and if she was truthful, she didn't want to. She liked who she was even if her past didn't hold a single strand of truth. She wanted to be Collin's wife and best friend. She wanted to wake up next to him every morning. Odd as it sounded, Louisa never needed to return—but if she didn't, Jazz would have to get past the creepy crawlies in her stomach when she thought of sleeping with him. She looked up to find Collin staring at her.

"What are you thinking about?" His face reflected the caring he seemed to have for her.

"Dinner. I thought I could cook something—tuna casserole." She hoped to distract him. Food seemed to be a passion for him.

"No. I don't think that's what you're thinking about. You never think about what to cook." Collin squinted one eye and cocked his head. "I think you're thinking about us." He took a step toward her.

She gasped. He had read her that well? It wasn't fair that he knew all of Louisa's habits and traits and could apply them to her, Jazz. Not when she didn't know him as well. Maybe she should go away with him and take a notebook. She could write down all of his quirks and put them on a spreadsheet.

Collin reached his hand toward her. "Come here."

Jazz found her feet moving on their own in obedience to his order. She chastised herself for not stopping or at least taking her time as she sidled close.

His arms wrapped around her, enveloping her in calmness and security. "So have you decided to go away with me?"

"Yes," she said, knowing that one word had propelled her relationship into a marriage with Collin. She felt his arms tighten. Feeling suffocated, she pushed him away with force. "I'll go. Don't make a big deal out of this, okay? It's only a weekend away. A long extended date, really."

"If that's how you want it, Jazz." His husky voice sent shivers through her. Collin took a step back. "I'll get the kids and take them for ice cream. You can come along if you like or stay here and relax."

"I'll stay here alone."

Collin stared, then shrugged his shoulders. "We'll be back in an hour." He brushed his hand against her cheek. "Enjoy your time," he said as he turned away.

Jazz blinked back tears and followed him up the stairs. He had to be as confused as she. Would she ever understand her hot and cold nature? Why did she continue to push him away when he was so easy to love?

As they reached the top of the stairs, she asked, "Collin? When are we going?"

"This Saturday. I made reservations yesterday. I had a feeling you would go with me."

"So soon?" She hadn't expected him to be that prepared. But maybe it would be better to go quickly before she had time to consider the ramifications of her decision and change her mind.

"Not soon enough," he replied, so low she almost didn't hear him.

She reached up to brush a swatch of hair from her face.

Collin grabbed her hand. "Why is your wedding ring on your right hand?"

Jazz took her hand back and extended it. The light bounced from the six diamonds stacked two deep across the platinum band. "I'm using it as my right-hand ring."

"Your what?"

"It's kind of a new thing. Women are taking charge of their own happiness. Instead of waiting for a husband or boyfriend to surprise them with a diamond ring, they buy one for themselves."

"But that's your wedding ring."

"No. It's Louisa's, not mine."

The traffic began to creep forward inches at a time. Collin couldn't wait to get out of the car. This part of the road trip wasn't going the way he'd planned. Since Jazz had opened her computer, she'd said very little. He'd tried to ask her questions about what she was writing, but all he received for an answer was a stare that could have shrunk him to Tim's size.

Had they been in this car for only three hours? Impossible! It had to be longer. His idea of driving with the top down hadn't lasted more than thirty miles before Jazz demanded he pull into a rest stop and put it up. The sun was glaring on her screen, she'd said, and she couldn't see. He glanced over to see that her fingers were still flying.

"Jazz, I think we're almost there. Want to help me look for signs?"

She stared back at him. The same look he'd witnessed on a client's face who had been convicted of murder. "Sorry." He began to wish he hadn't bought the computer for her. He knew he regretted giving it to her right before they left. And what made him think giving it to her with a power cord for the car was a good thing?

Keys continued to click, the repetitive sound making him edgy. He liked the song on the satellite station. Who was singing? He looked down at the screen for the artist's name.

"Watch out. Stay in your lane." Jazz's excited voice startled him, and he corrected the car.

"I was in my lane. I'm surprised you even know you're in a car. You could be on a cruise and wouldn't know it."

Collin heard a snap as she closed the screen. He breathed a sigh of relief. Now maybe they could spend some time talking. He blinked. Talking? He wanted to talk? Would his life ever get back to conversations about baseball?

"There, turn there!" Jazz pointed to a street as it went by. She settled back in her seat and gave him a disgusted look. "You passed it. Didn't you see the sign, 'Turn here for Rocheport'?"

"You distracted me." He gripped the steering wheel tighter.

"Now we'll have to turn around and be even later checking in."

Was she smiling? Collin couldn't tell without stopping the car to look at her. She seemed to be, though. It saddened him that the thought of being alone with him scared her. He reached over and grasped her hand to give it a gentle squeeze before releasing it.

A sign for a gas station peeked above the tree line. He rounded the corner, and there stood the abandoned gas station. Weeds poked through the cracks in the cement.

A crooked overhang looked lonely, standing sentinel over rusty gas pumps. *A reflection of my marriage.* He whipped the car through the lot and back onto the two-lane road.

Collin tightened his grip on the handle of the duffel bag and yanked it out. He set it next to Jazz's on the parking lot and slammed the trunk. The trip to Rocheport had taken longer than he had expected. When he printed out directions, the suggested travel time didn't include construction slowdowns.

Jazz stood motionless next to the car.

"Jazz? What do you think?"

"It's so quaint," Jazz said as she turned slowly in circles, taking in their surroundings. "They call it the Schoolhouse Bed and Breakfast Inn. Do you think it was? A schoolhouse, I mean?"

Collin stared at the redbrick building, three stories high with six long and wide windows across the top. "It looks like an old grade school to me. I'm sure they'll tell us the history when we register."

He picked up the luggage and began walking to the door, then noticed Jazz wasn't following him. He stopped. She no longer stood in front of the car. He scanned the parking lot. No Jazz. Where did she go? Her red dress peeked out from a green bush and caught his attention. "Jazz, are you coming?"

"Collin, you have to see this." She poked her head out from behind the bush. "It's an old school bell."

"Later. I want to get settled in first before we explore." Collin turned and began walking up the sidewalk to the steps.

Jazz rushed up behind him and touched his arm. "Can we put our stuff away and explore the area?"

"Sure." A nice walk would be great. At least she couldn't take her computer along with them. Maybe being married to a writer wouldn't be as fun as he originally thought.

Jazz raced ahead of him. She waited at the top of the stairs with a huge smile that made him feel guilty about being grumpy. She held open the door, and he caught a hint of her perfume as he passed. The woman smelled great, and he couldn't wait to get her into their room.

Inside, the foyer light from the doors and transom sparkled against the cream walls. A child's rocking horse sat at the top of the stairs. Just off the lobby, an older man perched behind a dark wood desk. "Welcome to our inn. I'm Gary."

Collin reached out and accepted Gary's outstretched hand. "Collin Copeland, and this is my wife, Jazz."

"We've been expecting you. Traffic bad today? Kind of thought you'd have been here a few hours ago." He pushed a book toward Collin. "Please sign our guest book."

Collin motioned for Jazz to sign the book. "You write better."

Jazz picked up the pen next to the book and signed. Collin read over her shoulder and winced as she wrote his name, followed by *Jazz Sweet*.

"You two have one of the nicest rooms. It's meant for couples." Gary winked at Collin. "It's on the second floor.

We call it the Show-and-Tell room. It comes with a large Jacuzzi."

Collin felt Jazz's retreat before he saw her move. *Don't leave,* he commanded her in his mind. He breathed a sigh of relief as she nudged him aside.

"I want my own room, please. I plan to be up late at night working, and I don't want to disturb Collin—my husband."

Her china-doll smile would have fooled anyone, but he knew she was running away from her feelings and from him.

Gary rubbed his chin. "Well, I don't know. We didn't plan for the extra room. It says here on the reservation you're on a weekend getaway?"

"Sort of, but it would be better this way, please," Jazz said. "It doesn't have to be big."

The change in plans caused obvious confusion for Gary. He looked at Collin with questions on his face.

Collin stiffly nodded his approval. He'd take this matter up with Jazz in private.

Gary flipped through his reservation book. "I suppose I could put you in Miss Edna's room. She never married, you know. She taught school here for many years. It's small, though. It doesn't have a shower, just a tub. You wouldn't even be on the same floor."

"Perfect!" Jazz grinned.

"Yeah, perfect," Collin muttered under his breath.

CHAPTER TWENTY

FOLLOWING COLLIN UPSTAIRS, Jazz forced a smile in case he turned around to look at her. He wouldn't, though; she knew him well enough by now to know when he was angry. He stood straighter, his back almost rigid—right now, there wasn't a curve anywhere in the plaid pattern of his shirt.

He stopped at the second-floor landing. "Do you want to come see the room we were supposed to share?"

The terse question pained her. She avoided his gaze by inspecting the well-worn path on the wooden floor. "Maybe later. I think I'll go upstairs and check out my room. I'll knock on your door in an hour, if that's okay?" She held out her hand for her luggage.

Without a word, Collin shifted her bag off his shoulder to her. He turned to leave, then stopped. "An hour will be fine," he said, and without looking back he strode down the hall.

Heartsick, she climbed the stairs with the knowledge that this time together would hold nothing but explosive emotions for the both of them. Collin never took Louisa away without the children. That thrilled her and made her angry at the same time. One moment she felt like a satisfied only child, and in the next moment jealousy leaked from her pores. How was she supposed to deal with those kinds of feelings?

By the time she reached the door with Miss Edna's name engraved on a pewter plaque, she regretted bringing along so many books. The shoulder strap bit into her skin. She knew if she looked, it would be raw skin and quite possibly bloody, which could lead to an infection. Maybe she would lose her arm, and then how would Collin feel? She gave her head a shake to erase the thought. *Stop being a writer for a minute, will you? Your shoulder isn't bleeding, and gangrene won't happen.*

Jazz slid the key into the lock and turned it. Stepping into the room, she sighed with pleasure. Oak bookshelves lined the walls, and they were filled with books! A white iron daybed topped with fluffy pillows rested against the wall under a dormer window. The walls were covered in wallpaper graced with tiny pink rosebuds. A perfect writing haven, and it was all hers for the weekend! She stopped just short of twirling for joy as she remembered her original intention of being here. It wasn't about writing; it was about becoming Collin's wife.

"Enough. It isn't going to work out this weekend, so I might as well make use of this room in a way that would please Miss Edna." Her laptop case thumped as she slid it on top of the small white desk by the door. She dropped her other bag on the floor, not in the least concerned about unpacking her clothes. All she wanted to do was set her computer free of its case, curl up on the bed, and write until dark.

Collin paced his room like a hound roped to his doghouse. He'd unpacked his clothes, called home to check on the kids, and regretted more than once that the room came without normal hotel amenities like a television and a fridge full of drinks.

Collin checked his watch for the third time. Where was she? Five more minutes, and he was climbing the stairs and banging on her door. It had been more than an hour. *You shouldn't have trusted her, Copeland. She's probably got that laptop plugged in already and found some creative way to use it.* He had a feeling this weekend would be tougher than he'd imagined. Spending time alone with Jazz would be fun; spending time with Jazz and her computer wouldn't be.

At least the kids were in good hands. Beth could handle anything Madison threw at her. He guessed experience raising a daughter helped with a granddaughter. He did wish Beth and Jazz could have had more time together. Maybe something would have connected in her memory. The odd thing was the distant way Jazz had greeted her mom. True,

Jazz didn't remember her, and Beth seemed preoccupied these days. That didn't seem right to him. Beth only lived about an hour away, but she hadn't driven in to see Jazz when she heard about the accident, and that wore on his mind. Collin figured Beth was probably caught up in her new relationship with Phil. He knew she'd been lonely these last two years since her husband had died, and Phil had to be a welcome change from a quiet house. He'd taken her to Hermann, Missouri, to tour the wineries, and they'd biked part of the Katy Trail. Still, he suspected Beth might have the key to Jazz's memory problem. Why wasn't she trying harder to help her daughter? But maybe he was being unfair. He did tend to suspect the worst in people sometimes.

Collin checked his watch again. Why wait for her? She wasn't coming. He would have to go get her. He thought about calling her but didn't want to talk to the front-desk guy again. He was still reeling from the humiliation of having his wife ask for a separate room. She'd given up a room with sloped ceilings, a giant tub, and a feather bed covered with intricate woven lace just so she wouldn't have to sleep in the bed with him. He didn't even get the chance to be a gentleman and offer to take the smaller room. No, his wife pounced like a kitten at the chance to stay in the old schoolmarm's room. *The unmarried schoolmarm,* he added.

Angry now at being made to wait, he grabbed his keys off the old dresser. In seconds he had closed the door and started up the steps. He wasn't sure how he would pull her away from her new friend if she were involved with it. But he would. Yes, he would, and he wouldn't hesitate to take it away from her if he had to. After another flight of stairs, his temper began to cool and logic took over. Maybe he should just stay in her room and let her work while he rested. Then he could take the computer later.

Collin arrived at her door winded. He knocked.

No answer.

He knocked a little louder.

Still no answer.

He put his ear on the door and listened. Maybe she was taking a bath, but he didn't hear water splashing. Frustration mounted as he realized she must be ignoring him. He wouldn't wait for her anymore. He would at least enjoy the small town. The time off from work could still be a good thing; he could focus on the upcoming week, maybe plan next year's goals or relax by himself if that's how Jazz wanted the weekend to be. He didn't need her. He thundered back down the stairs.

He reached the common room and stopped in his tracks. Her blonde hair was twisted and tied with a colorful scarf, her ponytail bounced, and her hands waved while she talked. Jazz. She hadn't stopped for him; instead she came down without him. At least she wasn't upstairs ignoring him.

Collin strode into the common room where Jazz was apparently holding court with the other B&B-ers. What is she doing? She held a pad of paper on her lap and her pen moved across it. He couldn't believe it. She was interviewing the other guests! He should halt this procedure, but it didn't appear that anyone minded talking to her. He stopped to listen for a moment.

"When and how did you meet?" she asked the couple holding hands on a purple velvet couch.

"It was the oddest thing. I was doing my laundry, and so was he. We started talking and discovered we knew the same people, but we'd never met each other." The woman's skin crinkled with joy as she smiled at the man next to her.

"Where was your first date?" Jazz didn't look up from her notes.

"We went to the fair," the woman said. "It was a great time, fireworks and watermelon under the stars. We sat on a quilt your grandmother made, remember?"

"The fair." Jazz wrote on the paper some more.

"No, we didn't. I took you to the movies."

Jazz scratched out what she'd written.

"That wasn't me. That was Helen Darcy, not me." The woman pulled her hand out of the man's.

"Are you sure? I thought it was you I took to see that film. What was the name of it? You cried all over my shirt."

"That wasn't me. I never cried on your shirt." The woman moved over an inch.

Collin thought he'd better step in and break up this interview before Jazz caused the couple to argue all weekend. "Jazz, there you are. I was waiting for you."

"I'm sorry, Collin. I just thought I'd look around before coming upstairs. But then I started talking to the Shatzes. This is Carrie, and this is her husband, Rick."

He shook hands with Rick and gave a nod to Carrie. "Nice to meet you." Then he turned back to Jazz. "I thought we would explore the town and get a snack. Maybe we can rent a bike and ride the trail for a while."

"Sounds like fun. I can't remember when I rode a bike last," Jazz said.

"No doubt it was in India or on the coast of Alaska," he grumbled. Jazz gave him a look that had belonged to Louisa, and he began to wonder if all women were born with the innate skill to freeze a man in his tracks.

"Don't be mean, Collin. I'll talk to the two of you later," she said to the Shatzes. "Thank you for sharing your story with me."

Collin and Jazz left the couple still arguing about their first date. He hoped Rick could sort it out. If not, Collin would offer to share his room with him. He wondered if Jazz even realized she may have ruined that couple's weekend getaway. Not likely. She often seemed oblivious to the small fires she started around her.

The sidewalk was old and bowed. They watched their step to keep from tripping on a jutting piece of concrete that was being evicted by tree roots. Ahead of them, a bush laden with tiny pale-yellow flowers wound over and through an iron fence. It swayed in the gentle fall breeze. When they reached the bush, Collin plucked one of the flowers and held it out to Jazz. Louisa loved them; maybe they would trigger a memory. "Smell it."

She took it and put the flower to her nose. "I love the fragrance. It's a clean smell, isn't it? Not all perfume and show like the rose tries to be."

"So you recognize the smell?" *Always playing the optimist,* he thought.

"Sure. It used to grow in our backyard. I like the smell, but there always seemed to be bees buzzing around it, so I stayed away from it most of the time."

It surprised Collin to discover it didn't bother him that the honeysuckle didn't trigger what he'd come to call the "big memory." Again guilt attacked from beneath his heart—he should want his wife back to normal and healthy.

They walked past a few stores that were closed, and one of them was a small publisher. Collin took a mental note of the name. An idea occurred to him, and he planned to follow up on it when he returned home.

They found the wooden shed where bikes were rented by the hour or the day. Collin sent Jazz to pick out helmets while he paid the bike attendant for the rental of a bicycle built for two. He wasn't sure how Jazz would feel about riding with him, but he personally thought it was romantic. It would be similar to the kind of trust exercises he had to do in youth group when he was younger. Who knew those were going to come in handy on a date with his wife?

He pushed the bike from the lean-to and rolled to a stop in front of Jazz. She stood open-mouthed and speechless.

"You can be in front or back—your choice."

"I've never ridden one of these before." Jazz circled the metal beast as if it were a tiger in the zoo. "If I take the back, I give up control of where we're going. But on the back—" she looked up and flashed him a charming smile—"you won't know if I'm not pedaling. I'll take the back."

"You have to pedal. It's a partnership, like marriage. You have to work together or it will all fall on the other person's shoulders." *Like our marriage now.* He realized he was being unfair to Jazz, but it was true. He felt like he had to take care of everyone in the family right now without a break—ever. Even when things seemed to be going well, Jazz would do something crazy, and he'd have to pick up the pieces all over again and try to reassemble them.

"What are you thinking, Collin? That I won't hold up my end of the work?" She frowned at him. "Or maybe you think I'm not doing my share at home?"

He almost flinched. How did she know what he had been thinking? Louisa would have known, but Jazz hadn't been able to figure him out yet. He took the helmet from her and stuck it on his head. Pulling the strap tight, he climbed on the bike. "Let's just ride. There's supposed to be a tunnel if we go to the right."

Jazz slid the helmet on top of her head, adjusting her ponytail so it would fit underneath. After her strap was tight, she placed her hand on the bicycle seat and heaved her leg over the bar. "Didn't they have girls' bikes?"

"I'm not riding a girls' bike. It's not manly," Collin said. "Are you ready to try this?"

"Which foot should we push off with? Left?"

"Right."

"Right. Wait, am I starting with my foot on the right or left pedal?"

"Push with the left foot." He hoped their communication would improve as they rode down the gravel bike path, or they might be picking stones from their hands and knees.

They rode off in silence as they tried adjusting to each other's balance.

"Collin, you're drifting to the right. We're going to run off the path." Jazz squealed like a teenage girl.

"No, I'm not. You're shifting your weight, and it's throwing me off." Collin thought for a moment. "Try watching my back, leaning the way I do. Maybe we can learn to balance together that way."

"Sorry, it's this seat. It hurts my behind. It doesn't have any give to it at all. In fact, it feels like I'm riding on a brick."

"How many bricks have you ridden on in your life, Jazz?" Collin agreed with her on the pain from the seat, but he had a feeling that if he admitted it out loud, she would want to go back to the bed and breakfast. Once there, he wouldn't see her again until it was time to eat. Again he regretted ever buying her that computer. No, not buying it, but giving it to her before they left.

"I can't see anything except the back of your head, Collin. Is the tunnel close?"

"It's after the bridge, and I can see the bridge. Quit trying to look around me; it's messing us up and we're going to crash." Why did he ever think this was going to work?

"Can we stop at the bridge?" she pleaded.

"Will you get back on the bike after you get off?" He had a feeling he knew the answer because he wasn't quite sure he wanted to remount either.

"Of course. How else will I get back?"

Her answer surprised him. He thought she would take the easy way back. "You could walk."

"Don't think so, darlin'. It's wheels for me, not feet." Her voice had acquired a Southern accent.

"*Darlin'*? Did you just call me *darlin'*?"

"Yes, I guess I did. Sorry. I've been working on this story, and the heroine, Kelly Rose, calls her beau *darlin'*. It just slipped out."

"I kind of like it. I could get used to you calling me that."

"Kelly Rose calls her beau that. Didn't you hear me?"

"Well, you be Kelly Rose today, and I'll be her beau." Why did he say that? Maybe he was losing his mind along with Jazz.

"Seriously?"

Now he wasn't sure what to say. He didn't think she would really want to do it. "Well, maybe. What's the guy's name?"

"*Beau*, not *guy*."

"No way am I doing this if the beau's not a guy."

"Well, he is a guy, but they didn't call them that in the 1800s."

"So what's his name?"

"Jackson."

"Nope, no way am I going to be a Jackson, not even for a day."

After Jazz quit laughing, she said, "It's Dylan. Will that work for you?"

"Dylan." He sat straighter on the bike. "I like that name. What kind of work does Dylan do? Is he a doctor, a vet?"

"No, he's a funeral director."

"Funny. He is not."

"Yeah, you're right—too hard to make that into a romantic role for mainstream America. He's a lumber baron."

"So he's rich?" This was appealing, a man who worked with wood and a rich one. Not a bad life.

"Very."

"How 'very'?"

"He has his own shipping line."

Collin sat even straighter. "Now that's more like it. Kelly Rose?"

"Darlin'?"

"Let's stop at the bridge and admire the outcropping of stone; maybe one of my ships will come downriver."

It seemed to Collin that Jazz may have started pedaling as their speed seemed to increase the closer they came to the bridge. He chose not to mention it since he didn't mind the help. Or arriving more quickly at the place where he could get off this hard bike seat.

They reached the bridge and hopped off the bike. Jazz

yanked off her helmet and freed her ponytail from its rubber band. "These things are hot and uncomfortable."

"Not the best-looking hats either." Collin hung his helmet from the bicycle's handlebar.

They found a place under a willow tree where someone had placed a park bench perfect for resting. Jazz collapsed onto it. "Ouch. Another hard surface."

Collin slid in next to her. "Riding a bike is much harder than I remember."

"Want to walk back?" Jazz rubbed her legs.

"I'm not giving up. The tunnel has to be around the corner. Besides, I'm enjoying the view. The river flowing next to us and the bluffs on the side of us. It's serene."

"Collin? Do you think I'll ever remember being Louisa?"

He looked at her. Her head hung low and her hair had swung over so he couldn't see her face. "Jazz." He lifted her hair and leaned down to whisper in her ear. "You will someday. Until then, we're doing okay."

"What if I don't, though? What if I stay Jazz forever?"

"Then I'll love Jazz like I loved Louisa."

"But you don't even know me. What if I'm not a person you want to live with? We already know I'm not good at being a mother, and the wife thing . . . well, I don't know anything about being a wife."

"You could learn."

"I don't know if I want to learn, Collin. It doesn't look like much fun to have to do laundry and make dinners and grocery shop."

"What do you think it should be like, Jazz?"

"That's just it—I don't know. I write the books, but after my characters get married, the bedroom door closes and the story is over. Does that mean the romance is over—the flowers, the phone calls during the day, the surprise getaways?"

"It doesn't have to be that way. It depends on who you're married to. And we're on a surprise getaway, aren't we?"

"I guess we are. What was it like for you and Louisa? What kind of places did you go together?"

Collin removed his arm from her shoulders and brought it back to his side. He thought about the last few months before the accident. He came home late almost every evening, and he couldn't remember the last time he had sent Louisa flowers, if he didn't count the ones sent in apology. Had he even said thank you for all the nights she kept his dinner warm? He didn't want to go back to that complacency, that world of taking someone for granted and not even remembering if he had kissed his wife good-bye before he left for work. "No, it's more like you feared. We had become comfortable with each other, and I had begun to depend on her for everything I didn't want to do."

"So how do you know it won't happen again?" Her eyes locked with his.

He wanted to give the right answer. He didn't want to disappoint her. "Because I've learned how wrong I was. I've learned how valuable a good wife is—worth more than treasure."

"So I'm not doing so well; I'm not a treasure. I'll never

figure out all that needs to be done." She slid her feet to the bench and propped her head on her knees in a sign of defeat.

"Yes, you will, Jazz. You will because I'll help you find your way. We'll ask for God's help, and everything will work out."

"It won't be the same for you. Not like it was with Louisa."

"Jazz, it's okay if it isn't. I love Louisa, and if she returns, I am going to do things differently. And that's because of what you've taught me. If you stay Jazz, I will love you."

"This must be weird for you. Like having two wives."

"Yeah. It is." Collin patted her leg. "Ready to ride?"

Jazz stood, rubbed her thighs, and groaned. "I can't believe how much I hurt."

"We've only ridden a few miles too," Collin said. The sun rested on Jazz's hair, giving it a glow. His heart yearned for his partner. With an idea forming in his mind, he leaned close to her face. "Kelly Rose?"

"Yes, darlin'?" She fell back into the game with him.

"Do I ever get to kiss you?" He stroked her cheek with a finger.

"Oh, why, I'm sure Daddy wouldn't like that without knowing your intentions."

"Daddy's not here, Kelly Rose. And my intention is—" Collin tipped her face to his and skimmed his lips over hers—"to kiss you more than once."

Jazz made the trip back to the bed and breakfast in a dream-world. She trembled, remembering the kiss Collin had bestowed upon her lips. She tried to write the feeling down but found herself staring into space, reliving the sensation over and over. Collin kissed like no other man had ever kissed her. Gentle yet strong, full of passion yet somehow respectful. Very much the way any hero would kiss his girl.

She placed her fingers on the keyboard and began typing.

Kelly Rose had defied her daddy's wishes. She had allowed Dylan to be alone with her, and if Daddy found out, she would be sent to Boston to live with old Aunt Sue. She couldn't allow that to happen. If it did, she would never again experience another kiss like the one Dylan had placed on her lips not more than an hour ago.

Ten pages later, she paused and shrugged her shoulders to relieve the tension gathered there. She didn't know what would come next in Kelly Rose's story, but she was eager to find out. A quick glance at the small alarm clock by her bed told her she wouldn't have time to write any more. Collin would be waiting for her in the lobby soon. She'd rather stay in her room and write than eat dinner, but she didn't think he would understand that desire. Frowning, she started to save her document. *Just one more sentence,* she thought as her fingers began to fly across the keyboard, making the sound of music in her ears. Done. She shut the laptop cover and scooped up her door key, ready to meet Collin in the lobby.

CHAPTER TWENTY-ONE

THEY WERE BACK to ordinary life, and the weekend seemed a distant memory already. It was one she would replay in her mind for many months. Such romance! She hadn't known Collin could be so kind, caring, and loving. The best part was that he respected her decision to wait yet a little longer to become his wife physically. She didn't know why, but there was something keeping her from taking that step, and that something was major. Jazz peeked over the couch to see why Madison had been so quiet. "What's up?"

Madison jumped and slammed the book shut she'd been reading. She hunkered over and held it close to her chest, arms crossed to protect it. The only thing visible was the dolphin's head on Madison's T-shirt peeking over the top of the book. "It's nothing. Just a book I found that my mom wrote."

"A book or a journal?" Excitement flooded Jazz.

"Maybe." Madison stood and walked past Jazz. At the bottom of the stairs she turned. "Yes, it is my mom's journal." She took off running to her room.

Shocked, Jazz charged up the stairs two at a time after her. She jumped on the bed, landing in front of Madison. Answers to her questions may be just a notebook away. "Give it to me."

"No." Madison frowned at her and clutched the book tight against her chest.

Jazz tried to wiggle her hand under Madison's clenched arms.

Madison scooted away, pressing her back into the headboard. "It's not yours. You have no right to read it."

"Neither do you. It belongs to your mother, and maybe she doesn't want you to read about her innermost thoughts."

"Are you going to read it if I give it to you?"

Jazz stopped wrestling with Madison. "I want to. Maybe it will help me get my memory back."

"But you keep saying you aren't really my mom."

How could she explain her own confusion to a twelve-year-old? How could she make the facts add up when she woke every morning and wondered how she had gotten to this place? In her mind she knew her name wasn't Jazz, but Louisa. But in her heart, deep inside, she felt like Jazz. All the photos in the world of her as Louisa had not brought her back. That was why she needed this journal. Maybe reading the words Louisa had written would help unite her two personalities.

Using her most authoritative voice, she demanded Madison give it to her. "Now hand it over."

"No."

"Then you can't leave this room all day."

"But you promised to take me to the mall with Angie."

"I'm changing my mind. If you don't give me what I want, then you don't get what you want," Jazz said. "It's a two-way street here, sister."

Madison's face flushed with anger as she thrust the book at Jazz. "I hate you. I wish my mom would come back. She was never mean to me the way you are."

Jazz sat open-mouthed at Madison's outburst as she watched her flounce out the bedroom door.

With Madison out of the room and the journal now in her possession, Jazz hesitated. Did she really want to know what words flowed across these pages? She traced the letters written in gold, sparkly ink on the cover: *Louisa's Journal*. She checked her watch to see if she had time to read before taking Madison to the mall. She wouldn't have long, so maybe she should put it away until tonight after everyone had gone to bed.

She needed to hide it somewhere Madison wouldn't find it. She didn't want to go through that trauma again, and she had a feeling once Madison returned from the mall, she wouldn't be able to get it away from her a second time.

Madison appeared in the open doorway dressed in a different outfit. "So are we leaving now or not?"

Jazz felt a moment of pride as she did a mother thing, checking Madison's attire to see if it was appropriate. *Don't be too proud,* she told herself. *This girl has given you plenty of practice in this area. You've learned by survival.* "Madison, you look nice. That blue shirt brings out the sapphire in your eyes."

Madison gave her a wicked grin. "My name isn't Madison. Not anymore. If you can be someone else, so can I. Call me Summer."

As she watched "Summer" leave the room, she knew something had to be done about her own identity, and soon.

Knowing Louisa's journal waited for her at home made it difficult to shop with the girls. When the newly named Summer began insisting on henna tattoos, Jazz lost her cool-mom status. After a brief argument that would probably be followed with weeks of silent warfare, they left the endless miles of looking at clothes that only a stripper would wear.

Back at home she locked the bedroom door and pulled out the book from the nightstand. Getting comfortable, she snuggled into the tower of pillows and flipped open the journal cover. It was inscribed with a date and *Book 7—If you are reading this, you are invading my privacy and deserve to be upset if you read something you don't like.*

Book 7? That meant there were six that came before this one—and what about after? Could there be more?

Jazz jumped from the bed and ran to the closet to search. Nothing. She tore into the dresser drawers and the armoire. Still she came up with nothing. Where would Louisa hide her journals? In her heart she knew they were the key to regaining her memory.

Collin went to investigate the noise coming from his old bedroom. It sounded like Jazz was moving furniture. He didn't expect to see drawers open, some with clothes and socks dripping over the sides and others empty, their contents in a heap on the floor. "What are you doing in here?"

"Journals. Louisa kept journals, and I'm trying to find them. Do you know where they are?" Jazz spun from the armoire with her hand on her hip. "Do you?"

"The journals?" Collin hadn't expected to be nailed on those before he showed her the office and explained his reason for hiding them.

"Yes, as in more than one." She grabbed the one now on the dresser and flashed it at him. "This is number seven. That means there are more. Do you know where they are?"

"Where did you get this one?" How was he going to explain this? The fury in Jazz's face was a force he didn't want to play with. How could he tell her he had them?

"Madison had it." Did she know what he'd done downstairs too? Had Madison found the secret stash of journals?

"Summer! My name is Summer!" Madison yelled from her room as she slammed her door.

Collin's mind raced, trying to connect Madison's new edict with the journal. And where or when did she find the journal? Confusion won. "Why is her name Summer?"

Jazz glared at him. "Because I pulled the mom card and took this—" she waved the journal in his face—"away from her."

"And that's why she calls herself Summer?"

"No. It's because she decided if Louisa could be someone else, so could she. I have to know where the rest of these journals are, Collin. They hold the secret of who I am."

Collin sank back against the wall and scratched his chin with the palm of his hand. "I have them."

"What?" She couldn't believe he had the possible key to her memories.

"I found them a few weeks ago, and I thought by reading them, I could help you regain your memory."

"That's pretty selfish, Collin. Don't you think that if I read them, it would have been more helpful?" Jazz thrust a pile of clothes back into a drawer and slammed it shut.

"I know it was wrong, but when the doctor suggested I might be able to help you by re-creating events from our past, I thought this would be the best way to do it accurately."

"Well, it didn't work your way, so why don't you get them for me now?" She stood with both hands on her hips.

He held out his hand to her. "Come with me. There is something else I want to show you."

"I'm not taking your hand, Collin. Right now I'd rather bite it than hold it."

"They're downstairs." He turned away. "Please try to refrain from kicking me down the stairs. I know I deserve it."

He stopped in front of the workshop door. "Please forgive me, Jazz, but I was only trying to solve this mystery."

"Just give them to me." She placed her hand on the door. "So that's why you've been down here locked away from us all these nights? Spying on Louisa's life?"

"Not exactly." He tilted his head back and searched for the correct answer, one that would help her understand that his desire had been to help, not pry into her secrets. Expelling a deep breath, he grasped her hand and held it tight as she tried to pull away. "Listen to me. Since you've been here, I've learned more about my wife and what I've missed with her—with you. I only wanted us to be happy, and by reading those journals I discovered how unhappy I've made you."

Jazz started to say something, but he touched her lips with his fingers. "Shh. Let me finish. You have every right to be angry, but I hope when I open this door, you'll forgive me." He took a key from his pocket and inserted it into the lock. With a quick turn of the handle, he opened the door, reached in, and flipped a switch. The sound of the ocean drifted through the doorway. "This is for you."

He watched her face as she stepped through the doorway. Her lips parted as a little-girl whisper drifted out in a soft *oh*. "Collin, it's the ocean! You've given me back my home." She ran her hand against the spines of the books on the shelf. She seemed to sink into the sand on the mural, and for a moment he felt he'd lost her. She turned then, and her eyes were damp with tears. "Is this really for me?"

Excited by her reaction, he grasped her hand. "I know the bookshelves are pretty empty now. I've set up an account for you so you can buy what you need. And see these frames? I know they're empty right now too, but since I'm convinced you will be published soon, these are to hold your book covers. And when we were in Rocheport, I stopped at the printers', and they are printing copies of the stories you've already written."

She sucked in a breath. "You mean . . ."

"Yes, Jazz Sweet, you are real. The journals hold more than details of your life; they have stories—great ones—that you've written." He moved her into the chair. It sat in front of the mural that included a beach-house porch. "Here you can sit and read and edit. I kind of hope you'll let me sit here with you sometimes."

"Collin, I don't know what to say."

"That's okay. I just want you to know you are Louisa, but all the stories you've written have been penned by Jazz Sweet." He opened one of the cabinet doors on the bottom of the bookcase. "The journals are all here—except for the one Madison found."

"Thank you." Jazz wiped a tear from her eye. "Thank you for giving up your space for me."

"I wanted it to be different. I wanted to surprise you, but not this way." He leaned against the desk.

"It's okay that it's different, though. Nothing about my

life these past few weeks has been normal, so why shouldn't this be a golden moment in the middle of a battle?" She jumped out of the chair and embraced him. "I am so blessed to have you." The corners of her lips twitched as she trailed her hand over the stack of journals in the cabinet. "But could you leave now so I can catch up on my reading?"

CHAPTER TWENTY-TWO

Jazz marked her place in Louisa's journal with the color-ful bookmark Tim had made for her and then set it on the bedside table. So far she'd discovered that Louisa had dripped unhappiness. She had so much, but her heart had holes that leaked the joy from her life. She seemed to be searching for who she was between the covers of her journals, unable to experience the fullness of the life before her.

She'd read all the journals at least once, but her memory still evaded her, teasing her with flashes of the past, like the style of a dress she'd worn or the flavor of her mother's carrot cake on Easter. She wasn't sure if it was because she realized what a miserable person she had been and didn't want to be like that anymore, or if she truly would never remember. The headaches had to be a sure sign of Louisa trying to press through . . . and Jazz struggling to keep her out.

Jazz didn't want to go back to being a pseudonym who came to life between the covers of a composition book or a computer file. She liked who she was, and after reading the journals, she didn't care for Louisa and her sniveling. Why she'd never stood up for herself, Jazz couldn't understand. What kept her—*or me,* she realized—from being the person she was now? The riddle plagued her, and the more she thought about it, the more her head hurt.

"Jazz, are you ready?" Collin's voice drifted up from the downstairs hall.

Yes, she was ready—dressed for the reunion even though the headache she'd been trying to ease since morning still banged its sonata against her skull. "Coming."

She checked her appearance in the mirror. She looked normal in dark-wash jeans and a silky coral shirt. She loosened a few strands of hair from the gold and coral headband to soften her hairline. Still, the fear of relatives gawking at her and thinking of her as the crazy one, or maybe even quizzing her in fun, weighed heavy on her. If the kids weren't so excited about being able to see their cousins, she would beg Collin to let her stay home. He'd probably be willing to take the kids by himself. Since he'd been caught with the journals, he'd done anything she asked of him. She slid her feet into a pair of open-toed shoes embellished with big jewels.

No, she would go. This could be the very thing to make

her remember everything. Maybe that's why she felt like she was on her way to a funeral instead of a fun family reunion.

"You look nice," Collin said when she joined him downstairs. "We should get going if we want to get there in time for the good food. I sent the kids to the van. Still have a headache?"

"Yes. I'm sorry, Collin. I know I haven't been helpful or even fun the last few days." She picked up the plastic container of gooey butter cookies she'd bought at the store. At least they were a specialty item from the local bakery. Maybe no one would mind that she hadn't made them.

"We don't have to go." Collin tipped her chin in his hand. "Just say you want to stay home. I'll drop the kids off, and your mom can watch them."

"I can't explain it, Collin, but I think I need to go today." She swallowed. "I'm scared. I think I'm going to remember soon. That should make me happy, but instead it frightens me."

"Darlin', that's okay. Whatever happens, I'll be here for you and so will the kids. We're a team, no matter what." Collin took the cookies from her hand and scooped up a folded blanket that sat on a counter stool. "Come on, let's get this over with."

The moment Collin parked the van, the kids seemed to fly from it, scattering across the vast lawn in search of favorite cousins. Jazz, not quite so eager, took her time to climb the hill.

Collin stayed by her side while she put the cookies on a

long table that already bulged with food covered in plastic wrap. No one paid any attention to their arrival. Relieved that there wasn't a volley of questions, she followed Collin to a shady spot under a tree, where he spread out the blanket.

"You can hide out here. Let them come to you. If you lean up against the tree, you can close your eyes and pretend you're napping." He grinned. "Maybe you should have worn one of those floppy hats and sunglasses like your great-aunt Becca."

Jazz followed his gaze and saw the woman he was talking about. She seemed to be sleeping, but every few moments the hat would tip up. It was obvious Great-Aunt Becca was eavesdropping on conversations as people went by.

Tim and Joey, twin-like in their Rams jerseys and sulking faces, plopped on the blanket on either side of Jazz. "What's wrong with you guys?"

"Grandma brought a man," Joey said. "I don't like him."

"They were holding hands." Tim screwed his nose in disgust.

"Give him a chance, boys," Collin warned.

"Are we going to eat soon?" Tim fidgeted with his shoelace.

A cowbell rang. "There's your answer. That's the signal they use every year. Someday I'm going to ring that bell," Collin joked. "Let's find a place in line, boys."

Joey popped off the blanket. "I'm ready."

"I can get my own hot dog." Tim took off running to get in line.

"Eat some vegetables," Jazz called after him.

"Don't worry. I'll watch him." Joey squared his shoulders, preparing to be the older brother, the one in charge.

"They're growing up so fast." Collin held out his hand to Jazz and helped her stand.

"I don't think there will be one serving of vegetables or fruit on their plates." She smoothed the back of her shirt with her hand.

"It's a party. Let them have fun." Collin kept step with her.

"Why not?" Her feet stalled as Beth approached. Collin's hand brushed against her fingers. Unaware, she twined her hand in his.

"There you are. I'm glad you came. I was afraid you would have another one of your headaches and stay home," Beth said.

"Hi, Mom." The word felt awkward on her tongue, but she said it out of respect.

"Did you see your cousin Amy? She was asking about you. She owns some organizing company now."

"No, I haven't seen her yet." Jazz felt a flash of memory. *The shoes at the hospital!* Amy did give her hand-me-down shoes when she was little. "That sounds like an interesting career. So who's the new guy in your life?"

"Why, he's not new at all, Louisa. You know him, or you used to. It's so hard to keep track of what you remember and what you don't."

Jazz's stomach whipped against her ribs. Was that her mother's new perfume? Something smelled odd. "What's his name?"

"Phil. You have to remember Phil. He's your dad's cousin. You stayed with him while Daddy and I went to Mexico."

"No, the name isn't familiar." Her hand tightened in Collin's.

Beth looked to the right as if searching for him. "It's a shame you don't remember him."

"Where's Madison?" Her mouth went dry and adrenaline pumped through her, but Jazz didn't understand its meaning.

"She went with Phil. He seems to be fond of her already. She has on that dolphin shirt, and he asked her about it. The next thing you know, he's agreed to take her across the street to the zoo to look at some real live dolphins. He said to tell you not to worry; he'll take good care of her."

"Take care of her?" She swam in uncertainty. Something didn't feel right.

"He paid you a very nice compliment. He said to tell you Madison is as beautiful as you were at that age."

"He took Madison away?" Her breathing swelled in her chest, pushing through her throat like something wanting to be born.

"He didn't take her away; she went willingly—to the zoo. Now you're starting to sound like the old Louisa."

"How come I've never met him, Beth?" Collin asked.

Jazz turned in a slow circle, scanning the crowd for Madison amid a sea of jeans and bright shirts.

"He's been living in Utah. Not long after the Mexico trip, he moved and we lost touch. This summer I ran into him on that senior cruise. He asked about you, Louisa—Jazz.

I still can't seem to call you by that name. I know after the Tim incident, you worry, but Madison couldn't contain her excitement at seeing a dolphin. They'll be back soon. Phil is harmless as a teddy bear, so there's no need to worry that you've done something wrong." Her mom held out her arms. "Aren't you going to give me a hello hug?"

Jazz reluctantly embraced her but then pushed her away. The smell of aftershave on her mother's shirt sent her spiraling into the past, dizzy with fear. She felt herself falling to the ground and her world blackened, but she wasn't going down without a fight. She went into a kneeling position and bowed her head to keep from passing out.

Collin was beside her. She could sense him, feel his touch, but he remained invisible.

"Jazz, what is it?" His worried tone yanked her out of the darkness.

"We have to find them. Now!" She swallowed bitter bile that rose in the back of her throat. "I remember, Collin. I remember everything."

"What do you remember, dear?" her mother asked.

"Get away from me! You and Daddy left me with that man! And now my daughter is with him. Your granddaughter." Jazz's body tensed like a jungle cat ready to kill. "Get away from me!" she repeated.

"Louisa, what did he do to you? Why didn't you tell me?" Her mother's hands balled into fists. "I'll kill him!"

"We have to find her, Mom. That's what's important now." She spun around, searching the area and hoping to spot the top of her daughter's head. "Madison! Has anyone seen her?" she yelled. She took off in the direction of the zoo.

Collin caught up to her and pulled her to a stop. "Wait a minute. Let's think before running. Am I right? Jazz, did he do something to you? Do you think Maddie is in danger?"

"Yes." The word hissed from her mouth, a vile secret hidden for years, now exposed in the light. "We have to find her."

Fire burned in Collin's eyes. "We will. But I don't think he went to the zoo." He spun around, facing the thick grove of trees behind them. "It's secluded over there. That's the first place to look for them."

"Let's go."

"Wait." Collin slapped his cell phone into her hand. "Call the police and give them a description. Tell them about the dolphins, too, in case they did go to the zoo. I'm going in the woods. You follow as soon as you've told them what's going on."

She fought the impulse to argue with him, knowing he was right. There might not be reception in the trees, and if Phil . . . No, she couldn't think it. "Go, Collin. Hurry!" She punched 911 while she watched him sprint faster than she could have to save their daughter. "I have an emergency!"

A few feet into the woods, Collin halted. He tried to still his breathing so he could listen. At first there wasn't anything, but then he thought he heard a small squeal. He took off in the direction of the sound, ignoring the branches smacking his face and body. "Madison! I'm coming!"

He crashed through a row of low bushes, into a clearing, and stopped short at the scene before him. His little girl pounded Phil's stomach with her fists as she tried to twist away from him. Phil tugged at the hem of Madison's shirt. With a roar, Collin flew across the distance and knocked Phil off his daughter and onto the ground. He flattened the deviant and pummeled him with his fists until the man lay unconscious.

At Madison's voice, he looked away from his daughter's abuser.

"Daddy, I'm sorry." Her whisper broke into a sob.

Peeling himself away from the scum beneath him, he rushed to Madison's side. Her teeth banged together and her shoulders shook. Collin held her against him, trying to warm her, make her feel secure again. "Shh, baby girl. This isn't your fault. You didn't do anything wrong."

"Collin! Madison!" Jazz screamed from somewhere in the woods.

"Over here!" Collin yelled. "I've got her."

Jazz broke into the clearing at a run. She slid to a stop next to Madison and hit the ground, tears pouring down her cheeks. "Maddie, oh, Maddie, I'm sorry I didn't remember sooner. Did he touch you?"

"He said—" Madison hiccupped through a sob—"he thought I had a tick under my shirt and wanted to get it out."

"Oh, baby, he's a wicked, wicked man, and you're a good girl." She gathered her closer, running her hand over Madison's hair to calm her like she'd done so many times before.

"Daddy hit him and hit him and hit him. I didn't want him to stop." Madison curled like a kitten in her mother's arms and looked up. "Does that make me a bad person?"

Jazz squeezed her daughter closer. "No, baby. It doesn't make you bad. He did an evil thing to you, and you should be angry."

Phil groaned as police sirens sounded close by. Collin jumped from the ground and whipped off his belt. He rolled Phil onto his stomach, looped the belt around Phil's wrists, then pulled tight. "He's not going anywhere until the police get here."

"Mom? You called me Maddie."

"Yeah, I did."

"Do you remember me now?" Joy filled Madison's face.

"I do. And I'll never forget you again. I promise."

"Do you remember everything? Even Dad?"

"Even Dad."

Collin whistled to alert the search party where they were. He placed his foot solidly on the belt in case Phil became more active.

A team of two policemen burst through the brush with their radios squawking on their belts.

"We found them," one of the officers reported to his commander.

The other one slapped handcuffs on Phil's wrists. Together they helped him stand.

Blood trickled from Phil's nose. He sneered at Louisa. "She's so much like you. Your mom told me you were remembering things, and I knew it wouldn't be long. I had to have her today or I would miss my chance."

Adrenaline erupted in Collin, and he sprang across the ankle-high grass. His hands reached for Phil's throat.

One of the officers pulled him away. "I can't let you do that, sir. I'd like to, but I can't. You bring your daughter to the station and file charges. He'll get what he deserves in prison."

Collin reluctantly backed away, his animal anger barely controlled. He felt his breath coming in short huffs. "We'll be there as soon as EMS checks out my daughter."

They walked out of the woods with Madison between them, holding their hands. "Everyone okay here?" Collin asked.

"Mom remembers us, Dad."

"I know, babycakes, and we'll make sure she remembers us from now on."

"So everything will be like it used to be, Daddy?"

"I doubt life in the Copeland home will ever be the same. We've learned to work together as a family, you're almost a teenager, and everything has changed. Your mom is back with us, but I suspect she's going to be a combination of the old mom and the new one. What do you think? Can we get through this together?" He glanced at Jazz.

"Yes, we can," she said with a small smile.

It was late by the time they arrived home from the police station, and later still before everyone was calm enough to send to bed. Madison told her brothers the shocking tale of her attacker and her savior. She left out the part about Phil's intentions.

Their daughter glowed with love as she told Tim and Joey about how Collin saved her life. Joey proclaimed he'd known Phil was a bad man from the moment he'd met him. Tim held Madison's hand so she wouldn't be scared anymore and offered to sleep in her room in his sleeping bag. Surprising everyone, she said he could.

Now the moment had come that Louisa dreaded—telling Collin about the past. They had settled in her new office. It seemed appropriate since that's where Collin had read about her past. Or some of it, at least. Those pages hadn't told him what had been buried deep within her, the shame and humiliation she'd kept locked away because she thought no one would believe her.

"Can you tell me what happened to you?" He swiveled the chair side to side.

"It's not a pretty story, Collin, but I will tell you. Just let me talk without interruption; then maybe I can get through it." Her feet pushed the wicker rocker she sat in, and it protested the motion much like her emotions resisted the telling of her secret.

"I can do that," he said. The corners of his mouth suggested a smile of encouragement.

The chair rocked faster as she rubbed her shoulder with a hand as if the motion would help her release the misery inside. "My parents left me with Phil while they went to Mexico. He thought it would be fun for us to have a vacation too. So we went to a hotel that had a pool." She stopped, not wanting to continue, but realized that would give Phil power over her again.

Spurred on by her anger, she rushed through the memories as the movie played in her mind. "He told me the bathroom was broken. I was twelve, and I believed him. I took off my clothes to put on my swimsuit. I had my back to him because I was embarrassed. He said he wouldn't look." She took a ragged breath. Collin left the chair and squatted next to her. He took her hand in his. True to his word, he didn't say anything but remained still, his fingers tense against her own as he waited for her to continue.

"Stop. Never mind, you don't have to tell me any more. I love you and I believe you. You don't have to relive this for me." His forehead furrowed as pain etched his face.

"No, I want to say it once and for all and be done with it. I wanted to tell my parents, but they liked Phil so much, and I didn't want to disappoint them. I was only twelve." She could feel her nose dripping but didn't have the strength to get a tissue. "I was their perfect child."

"Louisa, you don't have to be perfect for me." His words, soft and strong, healed part of her heart.

She slid out of the chair and into his arms and let him hold her while she cried for the little girl she used to be. And for her precious daughter, Madison, and the fears she would have to overcome.

EPILOGUE

On the deck, Louisa relaxed in the thick padded wicker swing. She'd need to take the cushions in tomorrow since it was getting too cold to sit out here at night much longer. Most of the leaves had fallen, providing an unhampered view of the sky. The stars were plentiful and mirrored on the lake, appearing to be even more magnificent. Tim and Joey had been tucked into bed with a good-night story. Madison was in her room, either listening to her new purple iPod or talking on the phone with Hannah.

Louisa's eyes welled. She stretched the cuffs of her sweater over her hands to warm them. Her daughter almost had to live through the same horror she had lived through at twelve.

The counselor Maddie was seeing felt she would recover and become even stronger. *Thank you, God, for that miracle,* she thought. Phil was in jail without bond, and Collin's firm was representing Madison.

Since she had hidden her own shame so deeply inside all these years, her healing would take longer. It would require a lot of work for her emotions to realize she wasn't responsible for what had happened to her as a child. At least she felt better knowing someone believed her now.

Conversations with her mother had been awkward at first. Louisa explained how she'd tried to tell her about the abuse, but she'd always thought her mother would be angry that her good daughter wasn't perfect anymore. Her mom had crumbled like ancient text and begged Louisa's forgiveness. It hadn't been easy, but working with her therapist, Louisa had begun to travel the bumpy part of the forgiveness road. But the forgetting part of forgiveness would be the mountain climb of her life. She was beginning to understand that her mom couldn't truly fathom the thought of what happened or the reality that she hadn't caught the clues Louisa offered. If she faced the facts, the guilt would be too heavy for her to bear. As a mother, Louisa understood the need to remember the past in the very best light because only the present could be changed.

The door to the deck swished open behind her. Collin's heavy footsteps were comforting. Watching his protectiveness for both Madison and her had provided a real sense of safety. She regretted not telling him what had happened earlier. He would have believed her, and their marriage would have been so much richer without the destructive secret.

"Hey, brought you something." Collin handed her a cup of hot chocolate. The swing swayed as he sat beside her. "Are you okay? You seem to be thinking hard."

"Thanks." She grasped the warm cup. "Sure, and yes, I've been thinking. I want to thank you for my office and tell you I'm no longer mad that you kept the journals from me."

"They weren't always fun to read. I'm sorry I wasn't a better husband to you."

"Collin, you're the best husband I've ever had." Anticipating his reply, she tried not to grin.

"Humph. I'm the only husband you've ever had," he said.

She laughed. "That makes you the best." She sipped the chocolate, enjoying the taste, never mind the calories. She'd made a vow not to worry about such things again. "I've made some decisions I hope you won't mind."

"Like what?" The swing moved sideways as he leaned in to hear her answer.

"I feel it's important to continue taking our family to church. Collin, there is so much for us to gain—"

"Shh." He put a finger to her lips. "I agree. At first I didn't want to lose my Sunday mornings sitting in a pew, but now I'm beginning to see the value. I've always had faith, but I didn't realize how much I missed by not belonging to a community of believers."

She blinked back the tears that nipped at the corners of

her eyes. This man was the man she wanted in her life forever. "Thank you, Collin."

"That's one decision. You said 'some,' so what are the others?" He gave the swing a shove with his foot.

"I want to try to have a career as a writer." The words were tentative, but the intent was not. She would write, even if Collin didn't agree.

"That's good, and have you considered—"

She stopped his oration with a firm grip on his thigh. "Before you say anything more, I need to know if you'll support me in this." She inhaled deeply before sharing her dream. "I want to go to conferences and learn how to do this the right way. I won't always be available to host parties for your firm. Collin, I want to be me, not just your wife."

"I'm relieved to hear you say that, Louisa. I wanted to tell you that I've been thinking of giving up the race for a partnership. I'd like to spend more time with our family too. You and the kids are too important, but we may have to change our style of living."

"Would I have to give up that fantastic office you made for me?"

"Are you kidding? I see a vacation house up in the Rockies in our future with the money you'll make writing as Jazz Sweet."

She winced at the name. "Collin, I don't want to be Jazz Sweet ever again."

His foot stopped the movement of the swing. "Who do you want to be?"

"Your wife. Louisa Copeland, with Jazz's attitude for life, but unafraid to touch you and love you in every way." She rose and stood in front of him. The moonlight danced across his face, highlighting the love in his eyes. "Collin Copeland, will you give up sleeping on the couch and take me to our room?"

He sprang from the swing. It swooshed into the back of the deck with a crack. He pulled her into his arms and then led her back into the house, his gaze never leaving hers. "Welcome home, Louisa," he whispered.

Later that week, Louisa sat in her new office, amazed at how much thought and detail Collin had put into building it for her, right down to a pail of white sand to trail her fingers through. She swiveled in her office chair and reached for a fresh journal on the shelf. She opened it to the first page and began to write. *A Journey*, by Louisa Copeland . . .

Turn the page for a preview of
Stealing Jake by
PAM HILLMAN

"[Hillman is] gifted with
a true talent for vivid
imagery, heart-tugging
romance, and a feel for
the Old West that will
jangle your spurs."

JULIE LESSMAN, *author of the
Daughters of Boston series*

PROLOGUE

"Where's my little brother?" Luke glared at the man with the jagged scar on his right cheek.

"You do as I say, kid, and he'll be along shortly." Pale-blue eyes, harder than the cobblestone streets of Chicago, bored into his. "Otherwise, I'll kill him. Understand?"

Luke stood his ground, memorizing the face of the man who'd paid off the coppers.

"Get in." The man motioned to a wooden crate not much bigger than an overturned outhouse.

Luke crammed in, the three other boys squeezing

together, making room. Nobody said a word. Nobody cried. They didn't dare. Scarface would kill them if they disobeyed.

Luke knew he'd been stupid. He'd tried to teach Mark the art of picking pockets, and they'd gotten caught. But instead of going to jail as expected, money had changed hands, and they'd been handed off to the man with the scar.

And now Luke would be shipped out of Chicago. Without Mark.

He pulled his thin coat tight around him and curled into a ball for warmth.

Bam! Bam! Bam!

Luke shuddered with every slam of the hammer against the nails. He drew his knees to his chest, shivering. This time not from the cold.

Bam! Bam!

He pinched his eyes closed, fighting the urge to throw up.

His heart raced faster than the first time he'd picked a pocket.

Where was Mark?

CHAPTER ONE

CHESTNUT, ILLINOIS

NOVEMBER 1874

The ill-dressed, grimy child jostled a broad-shouldered cow-boy, palming the man's pocket watch. Gold flashed as the thief discreetly handed his prize to another youngster shuf-fling along the boardwalk toward Livy O'Brien.

Livy didn't miss a thing—not the slick movements, not the tag-team approach. None of it.

Neither boy paid her any attention. And why should they? To them she was no more than a farmer's wife on her way home from the mercantile or maybe one of the workers over at the new glove factory.

If they only knew.

Her gaze cut to the man's back. When he patted down his pockets and his stride faltered, she made a split-second decision. As the thin boy with the timepiece passed, she knocked him into a pile of snow shoveled to the side of the wooden walkway. She reached out, pulled the child to his feet, and dusted him off so fast he didn't have time to move, let alone squirm away. She straightened his threadbare coat, two sizes too big and much too thin for an icebound Illinois winter. "Oh, I'm so sorry. Did I hurt you?"

Fathomless dark eyes stared at her from a hollow face. Eyes that reminded her of her own in the not-so-distant past. She wanted to hug him, take him home with her.

"No, ma'am." The words came out high-pitched and breathless.

"Hey, you!" The man hurried toward them.

Fear shuddered across the boy's face, and he jerked free of her grasp and darted down a nearby alley.

Livy let him go and stepped into the man's path, bracing herself as he slammed into her. The impact sent both of them hurtling toward the snowbank. The stranger wrapped his arms around her and took the brunt of the fall, expelling a soft grunt as Livy landed on top of him. Her gaze tripped off the end of her gloved fingers and collided with a pair of intense jade-green eyes. She stared, mesmerized by long, dark lashes and tiny lines that fanned out from the corners of his eyes. A hint of a smile lifted one corner of his mouth.

A slamming door jerked Livy back to reality.

Heat rushed to her face, and she rolled sideways, scrambling to untangle herself. What would Mrs. Brooks think of such an unladylike display?

"Ma'am?" Large, gloved hands grabbed her shoulders and pulled her to her feet. "Are you all right?"

"I'm fine."

"Those kids stole my watch." A muscle jumped in his jaw.

"Are you sure?" Remorse smote her with the same force as that of the stranger's body knocking her into the snow. She'd reacted, making a split-second decision that could have resulted in catastrophe.

"Yes, ma'am." He patted his sheepskin coat again. Suddenly he stilled and removed the watch from his pocket. "Well, I'll be. I could've sworn . . ." He gave her a sheepish look. "Sorry for running into you like that, ma'am."

Livy breathed a sigh and pulled her cloak tight against the cold. Disaster averted. *Forgive me, Lord. I hope I did the right thing.* "That's all right. No harm done."

The stranger pushed his hat back, releasing a tuft of dark, wavy hair over his forehead. "I don't believe we've met. Jake Russell."

Her gaze flickered toward the alley that had swallowed up the boy. She didn't make a habit of introducing herself to strangers, but revealing her name might keep Mr. Russell's mind off the boys who'd waylaid him. "Livy O'Brien."

"It's a pleasure to meet you, Mrs. O'Brien."

"*Miss* O'Brien," she said. At least the gathering twilight masked the flush she could feel stealing across her cheeks.

Was it her imagination, or did the grin on Jake Russell's face grow wider?

"Pleased to meet you, Miss O'Brien. May I escort you to wherever you're going?" His eyes twinkled. "It'll be dark soon, and a lady shouldn't be out alone after dark."

Livy sobered. She'd never claimed to be a lady. The tiny glow inside her faded with the setting sun. Mr. Russell would never be interested in Light-Fingered Livy O'Brien. "No thank you, Mr. Russell. I'm not going far. I'll be fine."

"I'd feel better, ma'am." He gestured toward the alley. "Especially after what happened."

He held out his arm, one eyebrow cocked in invitation. Her emotions warred with her head. She shouldn't allow such liberties, but what harm would it do to let him escort her home?

Just once.

She placed her hand in the crook of his arm. "Very well. Thank you, Mr. Russell."

"Call me Jake."

Livy's heart gave a nervous flutter. Did Mr. Russell mask his intentions behind a gentlemanly face and kindly words? A common enough practice where she came from. "I'm afraid using your given name would be a little too familiar. I don't know anything about you."

"Well, I can remedy that. What do you want to know?"

Livy shook her head, softening her refusal with a smile. It wouldn't do to ask the man questions about himself. If she did, then he'd feel at liberty to ask questions of his own. Questions she didn't want to answer.

He chuckled. "You sure are a shy little thing, Miss O'Brien."

Better to let him think her bashful than know the truth. A couple of years ago, she might have spun a yarn or two to keep him entertained, but no longer. If she couldn't speak the truth, she'd say nothing at all.

Her silence didn't stop him. "You must be new around here. I don't remember seeing you before."

"I arrived in Chestnut about two months ago."

"That explains it. I've only been back in town a few weeks myself."

Livy darted a glance from the corner of her eye to study him. Discreetly, of course—she'd at least learned *something* from Mrs. Brooks. The top of her head barely reached his chin, and broad shoulders filled out his coat. A late-afternoon shadow dusted his firm jawline.

He stepped off the boardwalk and helped her across a patch of ice. Her stomach flopped when his green eyes connected with hers, and she blurted out the first thing that popped into her mind. "Oh? Where've you been?"

She could've bitten her tongue. She shouldn't have asked, but curiosity had gotten the best of her. What made her want to know more about Jake Russell? Mercy, why should she even wonder about the man? He wasn't anyone she should worry with.

If only her foolish girl's heart would listen to reason.

"Taking care of some business in Missouri. It's good to be home, though."

They ambled in silence past the Misses Huff Millinery Shop and the recently opened Chinese laundry. The scent of green lumber tickled Livy's nose, bringing forth the image of the fresh sprig of mistletoe hung over the door of the orphanage.

The boardwalk ended just past the laundry. Livy gestured into the gathering darkness. "It's a little farther down this way."

"I don't mind."

The snow-covered ground lay frozen, Livy's footprints from when she'd trekked into town the only evidence of anyone being out and about on this frigid day.

They rounded the bend, and Livy eased her hand from the warmth of Jake's arm when they came within sight of the rambling two-story house nestled under a grove of cottonwoods. "Thank you, Mr. Russell. This is where I live."

❋   ❋   ❋

Jake studied the building before returning his attention to the petite lady at his side. He'd known the moment he laid eyes on her that they hadn't met. He would have remembered. "This is the new orphanage, isn't it?"

"Yes. That's right."

"I heard someone opened one up. 'Bout time. Lots of young'uns needing a place to stay these days."

"We already have five children in our care."

They stepped onto the porch, and she pushed the hood of

her cape back. Light from inside the house shot fire through reddish-brown curls and revealed a smattering of freckles across a pert nose.

She'd knocked the wind out of him earlier, and the feeling came back full force now.

Whoa.

Jake stepped back, putting some distance between them. He didn't have the time or the energy to be thinking about a girl, no matter how pretty she might be. His days and nights were chock-full as it was. He tipped his hat. "Good night, Miss O'Brien."

Her smile lit up the dreary winter landscape. "Thank you for escorting me home, Mr. Russell. Good night."

He headed back toward town, rehashing the brief conversation he'd had with Livy O'Brien. She'd sure seemed reluctant to talk about herself. Come to think of it, she hadn't told him much of anything.

Did he make her nervous? He should have told her who he was, but the thought hadn't crossed his mind. Knowing he was a sheriff's deputy would have put her at ease, but she hadn't seemed the least bit interested in who he was or what he did for a living.

He continued his rounds, confident he'd find out more about Miss Livy O'Brien soon enough. It was part of his job, plain and simple. He chuckled. He didn't remember anything in his job description that said he needed to investigate every beautiful lady he ran across. Still, it was his job to protect the town, and the more he knew about its inhabitants, the better.

Not that Chestnut needed protection from Livy O'Brien. A pretty little filly like her wouldn't hurt a fly.

His steps faltered when he stuffed his hands in his pockets and his fingers slid over the cool, polished surface of his father's gold watch. Not prone to jump to conclusions or get easily flustered, he'd been certain those kids had lifted his timepiece. How could he have been so mistaken?

Good thing he'd bumped into Miss O'Brien, or he would have had a hard time explaining why he'd chased an innocent kid down the street.

Still, he had reason to be suspicious. There'd been reports of scruffy young boys like the two tonight roaming the streets of Chestnut. Urchins from back East, Sheriff Carter said. Run out of Chicago, they rode the train to the nearest town large enough to provide easy pickings.

He settled his hat more firmly on his head. Those ragamuffins didn't know it yet, but they shouldn't have stopped in Chestnut. The town wasn't big enough for thieves and robbers to hide out for long.

Jake clomped along the boardwalk, part of his thoughts on the youngsters, part on the girl he'd left at the orphanage, and part registering the sights and sounds of merchants shutting down for the night.

He hesitated as he spied Paul Stillman locking up the bank. An urge to turn down the nearest alley assaulted him, but he doggedly stayed his course.

The banker lifted a hand. "Jake. Wait up a minute."

A knot twisted in Jake's gut. Would Stillman call in his loan today?

The portly man hurried toward him, his hand outstretched, a wide smile on his florid face. "Jake. How're things going?"

"Fine." Jake shook the banker's hand, the knot intensifying. Mr. Stillman's continued grace made him feel worse than if the banker had demanded payment on the spot.

"And your mother?" His concern poured salt on Jake's unease.

"She's doing well."

"That's good. I should be going, then. I just wanted to check on the family."

Jake rubbed his jaw. "Look, Mr. Stillman, I appreciate all you've done for my family, but I'm going to pay off that loan. Every penny of it."

The banker sobered. "I know you will, Jake. I never doubted it for a minute. The last couple of years have been tough for you and Mrs. Russell."

"Pa wouldn't have borrowed money against the farm if he'd known. . . ." Jake's throat closed. "If the crops hadn't failed the last two summers, I could've made the payments."

The banker took off his glasses and rubbed them with a white handkerchief. His eyes pinned Jake, razor sharp in intensity. "That investor is still interested in buying your father's share of the Black Gold mine, you know."

"The answer is no. I'm not selling." Jake clenched his jaw. He wouldn't be party to more death and destruction.

"That's what I thought you'd say." Stillman sighed.

"I admire your determination to protect miners by not selling, but as much as I'd like to, I can't carry that loan forever."

Jake shifted his weight, forcing his muscles to relax. It wasn't the banker's fault that life had dealt him a losing hand. "I know. This summer will be better."

"We'll see." Mr. Stillman stuffed the cloth in his pocket, settled his glasses on his nose, and tugged his coat close against the biting wind. "I'd better get on home. This weather is going to be the death of me. Say hello to your mother for me, will you?"

"I'll do that. Good night."

The banker waved a hand over his shoulder and hurried away. Jake stared after him. Would this summer be any different from last year? It would take a miracle to bring in enough from the farm to pay off the loan against the defunct mine.

A sharp blast rent the air, signaling the evening shift change at the mines. Jake turned northward. The low hills sat shrouded in a blanket of pure, white snow. Peaceful.

An illusion. The mines beneath the ground held anything but purity. Coal dust, death, and destruction existed there.

Along with enough coal to pay off the loan.

Jake turned his back on the mine and walked away.

*   *   *

Mrs. Brooks glanced up from the coal-burning stove when Livy entered the kitchen. "How'd it go?"

Livy took off her cloak and hung it on a nail along with several threadbare coats in varying sizes before moving to warm her hands over the stovetop. She closed her eyes and breathed deep. The aroma of vegetable soup simmering on the stove and baking bread welcomed her home. "Nobody's hiring. Not even the glove factory."

Mrs. Brooks sank into an old rocker. The runners creaked as she set the chair in motion. "What are we going to do?"

Worry lines knit the older woman's brow, and Livy turned away. She rubbed the tips of her fingers together. How easy it would be to obtain the money needed to keep them afloat. Livy had visited half a dozen shops today, all of them easy pickings.

She slammed a lid on the shameful images. Those thoughts should be long gone, but they snuck up on her when she was most vulnerable. When Mrs. Brooks's faith wavered, Livy's hit rock bottom.

She balled her hands into fists and squeezed her eyes shut. *Lord, I don't want to go back to that life. Ever.*

Livy forced herself to relax and turned to face Mrs. Brooks. "Maybe the citizens of Chestnut will help."

"I've tried, Livy. A few have helped us out, mostly by donating clothes their own children have outgrown. And I'm more than thankful. But money to keep up with the payments on this old place? And food?" Her gaze strayed toward the bucket of coal. "Except for our guardian angel who keeps the coal bin full, most everybody is in about as bad a shape as we are. They don't have much of anything to give."

"Don't worry, ma'am." Livy patted the older woman's

shoulder, desperate to hear the ironclad faith ring in her voice. "You keep telling me the Lord will provide."

Mrs. Brooks smiled. "You're right, dear. He will. I've told you time and again that we should pray for what we need, and here I am, doubting the goodness of God. Let's pray, child. The Lord hasn't let me down yet, and I'm confident He never will."

The rocker stopped, and Mrs. Brooks took Livy's hand in hers and closed her eyes. "Lord, You know the situation here. We've got a lot of mouths to feed and not much in the pantry. Livy is doing all she can, and I thank You for her every day. We're asking You to look down on us and see our need. These children are Yours, Lord, and we need help in providing food for them and keeping a roof over their heads. In Jesus' name we pray. Amen." She heaved herself out of the rocker and headed to the stove, a new resolve in her step. "Call the children, Livy. It's almost time for supper."

Livy trudged down the hall to the parlor. The short prayer had cheered Mrs. Brooks but hadn't done much to ease Livy's worry. She'd have to find some way to bring in a few extra dollars if they were to make it to spring. Otherwise, she and Mrs. Brooks and the small brood of children they'd taken in would be on the streets of Chestnut before winter's end. The elderly woman would never survive if that happened.

A wave of panic washed over her like fire sweeping through the slums of Chicago. Livy couldn't have another life on her conscience. She took a deep breath. They weren't on the streets yet. And as long as they had a roof over their heads and food on the table, there was hope.

She stepped into the parlor. Mary, the eldest child at twelve, kept the younger ones occupied on a quilt set up in the corner. The two boys, Seth and Georgie, stacked small wooden blocks, then howled with laughter when they knocked the tower down, only to start the process again.

"Libby! Libby!" a sweet voice trilled.

Livy held out her arms as Mary's little sister, Grace, toddled to her. "Hello, sweetheart."

The toddler patted her cheeks. "Libby's home! Libby's home!"

Livy nuzzled the child's neck, inhaling her sweet baby scent. Grace giggled.

"Yes, Libby's home." Livy glanced at Mary and the other children. "It's almost time for supper. Go wash up now."

Against her better judgment, Livy's mind conjured up flashing green eyes as she wiped Grace's face and hands. Would Jake Russell call on her? Why would such a thought even occur to her? What man who could have his pick of women would call on a girl who lived in an orphanage, a girl who came from a questionable background and didn't have a penny to her name?

And one who'd sprawled all over him like a strumpet.

Mercy! What if Miss Maisie or Miss Janie, the Huff sisters, had witnessed such an unladylike display? Her reputation would be in tatters. Not that she'd brought much of a reputation with her to Chestnut, but Mrs. Brooks had insisted she could start over here. There was no need to air her past like a stained quilt on a sunny day.

Maybe she wouldn't see Jake again. Or maybe she would. Chestnut wasn't that big.

More importantly, did she want to see him?

She didn't have any interest in courting, falling in love, and certainly no interest in marriage and childbirth. She knew firsthand where that could lead. Rescuing children from the streets fulfilled her desire for a family, and she'd do well to remember that.

Georgie shoved ahead of Seth. Livy snagged the child and tucked him back in line. "Don't push. You'll have your turn."

When all hands were clean, Livy led the way to the kitchen. A scramble ensued as the children jockeyed for position at the long trestle table.

Mrs. Brooks clapped her hands. "All right, everyone, it's time to say the blessing." Her firm but gentle voice calmed the chaos, and the children settled down. "Thank You, Lord, for the food we are about to partake. Bless each one at this table, and keep us safe from harm. Amen."

The children dug in with relish, and Livy took Grace from Mary's arms. "Here; I'll feed her. Enjoy your supper."

Livy mashed a small helping of vegetables in a saucer and let them cool.

"Grace do it," the child demanded.

"All right, but be careful." Livy concentrated on helping the child feed herself without making too much of a mess.

Thwack! Thwack! Thwack!

Livy jumped as loud knocking reverberated throughout the house.

"I wonder who that could be?" Mrs. Brooks folded her napkin.

"I'll get it." Livy stepped into the foyer. Resting her hand on the knob, she called out, "Who's there?"

"Sheriff Carter, ma'am."

Livy's hands grew damp, but she resisted the urge to bolt. The sheriff didn't have reason to question her or to haul her off to jail. Jesus had washed away her sins and made her a new creature. She wasn't the person she'd been two years ago. She prayed every day she wouldn't let Him down.

Some days were harder than others.

She took a deep breath and opened the door, a smile plastered on her face. "Good evening, Sheriff. May I help you?"

The aged sheriff touched his fingers to his hat. "Evening, ma'am. Sorry to bother you, but we've got a problem."

"Yes?"

The sheriff glanced toward the street, and for the first time, Livy noticed a wagon and the silhouettes of several people.

Mrs. Brooks appeared behind her. "What is it, Livy?"

Sheriff Carter spoke up. "There's been a wagon accident. A family passing through on the outskirts of town. Their horses bolted. I'm sad to say the driver—a man—was killed, leaving three children."

Livy peered into the darkness, her heart going out to the little ones. "Are the children out there? Are they hurt?"

"They're fine. Nary a scratch as far as we can tell. We thought the orphanage might take them."

"Of course." Mrs. Brooks took charge. "Bring them in out of the cold. Livy, go fetch some blankets. The poor dears are probably frozen with cold and fear."

Livy ran, her mind flying as fast as her feet. Less than an hour before, they'd prayed for help to feed the children already in their care. How could they manage three more? Of course they couldn't turn them away. They'd never do that. But would she be forced to do something drastic to feed them all?

Lord, don't make me choose. I'm not strong enough.

Heart heavy, she found three worn blankets and carried them downstairs.

Mrs. Brooks met her in the hallway. "They're in the kitchen. Mary's already taken the other children to the parlor."

Her arms laden with the blankets, Livy followed Mrs. Brooks. Two girls huddled together on the bench at the table, their eyes wide and frightened. Poor things. If only she could take them in her arms and tell them everything would be all right. It must be. She'd beg in the streets before she'd let them all starve.

She searched the room for the third child. Her gaze landed on a tall, broad-shouldered man with a tiny dark-haired child nestled snugly inside his sheepskin coat. The man lifted his head, and Livy came face-to-face with Jake Russell. She saw a fierce protectiveness in his haunted eyes.

"I don't believe you've met my deputy, Jake Russell." Sheriff Carter waved in Jake's direction.

Dread pooled in the pit of Livy's stomach, and for the space of a heartbeat, she stared.

"Pleased to meet you, Deputy Russell," Mrs. Brooks said, her attention already on the two little girls at the table. "I'm Mrs. Brooks, and this is Livy O'Brien."

Livy jerked her head in a stiff nod. For a few moments tonight she'd let her imagination run away with her, thinking maybe Jake Russell would call on her, that he might want to court her, that maybe he thought she was pretty.

And maybe he would. Maybe he did.

But it didn't matter. It *couldn't* matter.

Jake Russell was an officer of the law, and Livy had spent her entire life running from the law.

TURN THE PAGE FOR A PREVIEW OF

Where Treasure Hides

BY JOHNNIE ALEXANDER

WINNER OF THE

Genesis Award in Historical Fiction

AVAILABLE IN STORES
AND ONLINE

CHAPTER
One

AUGUST 1939

The stringed notes of "Rule, Britannia!" grew louder as the crowd quieted, eyes and ears straining in their search for the violin soloist. The patriotic anthem echoed through Waterloo Station's concourse, and as the second chorus began, sporadic voices sang the lyrics. Travel-weary Brits stood a little straighter, chins lifted, as the violinist completed the impromptu performance, the last note sounding long after the strings were silenced.

Alison Schuyler gripped her leather bag and threaded her way through the crowd toward the source of the music. As

309

the final note faded inside the hushed terminal, she squeezed between a sailor and his girl, murmuring an apology at forcing them to part, and stepped onto a bench to see over the crowd. A dark-haired boy, no more than seven or eight, held the violin close to his anemic frame. His jacket, made of a finely woven cloth, hung loosely on his thin shoulders. The matching trousers would have slipped down his hips if not for his hand-tooled leather belt.

Either the boy had lost weight or his parents had purposely provided him clothes to grow into. Alison hoped for the latter, though from the rumors she'd heard, her first assumption was all too likely. She stared at the cardboard square, secured by a thick length of twine, that the boy wore as a cheap necklace. The penciled writing on the square numbered the boy as *127*.

Other children crowded near the young musician, each one dressed in their fine traveling clothes, each one labeled with cardboard and twine. Germany's castaways, transported to England for their own safety while their desperate parents paced the floors at home and vainly wished for an end to these troublesome days.

"Now will you allow him to keep his violin?" A man's voice, pleasant but firm, broke the spell cast over the station. The children fidgeted and a low murmur rumbled through the crowd. The speaker, dressed in the khaki uniform of a British Army officer, ignored them, his gaze intent on the railroad official overseeing the children.

"He better," said a woman standing near Alison. "Never

heard anything so lovely. And the lad not even one of the king's subjects. I'd take him home myself—yes, I would—if I'd a bed to spare."

Alison mentally sketched the tableau before her, pinning the details into her memory. The officer's hand resting on the boy's shoulder; the official, a whistle around his neck, restlessly tapping his clipboard with his pencil; the dread and hope in the boy's eyes as he clutched his prized instrument. The jagged square that tagged his identity.

The travelers at the edge of the children's irregular circle collectively held their breaths, waiting for the official's reply. He shifted his glance from the nervous boy to the expectant passengers, reminding Alison of a gopher she had once seen trapped between two growling mongrels. The memory caused her to shudder.

"He might as well. Don't know what to do with it if he left it behind." The official waved a plump hand in a dismissive gesture. He certainly hadn't missed many meals. He blew his whistle, longer than necessary, and Alison flinched at its shriek.

"Get organized now. Numbers one through fifty right here. Fifty-one through a hundred there. The rest of you . . ."

The show over and the hero having won, the onlookers dispersed, their chatter drowning out the official's instructions to his refugees.

Alison remained standing on the bench, studying the man and the boy. They knelt next to each other, and the boy carefully laid the violin into the dark-blue velvet interior of its case. His slender fingers caressed the polished wood before he shut the lid. The man said something too softly for her to hear, and the boy laughed.

The spark flickered inside her, tingling her fingers, and she *knew*. This glimpse of a paused moment would haunt her dreams. It rarely occurred so strongly, her overwhelming desire to capture time, to freeze others within movement. She quickly pulled a sketch pad and pencil from her bag. Her fingers flowed lightly over the paper, moving to a rhythm that even she didn't understand. Tilting her head, she imagined the notes of the violin soaring near the high ceiling, swooping among the arches.

Her pencil danced as she added determination to the man's jawline and copied the two diamond-shaped stars on his collar. She highlighted the trace of anxiety in the boy's eyes, so at odds with his endearing smile. What had he left behind? Where he was going? She drew the cardboard square and printed the last detail: *127*.

The man clicked shut the brass hinges on the violin case and, taking the boy's hand, approached the station official. Alison hopped down from the bench and followed behind them, awkwardly balancing the pad, pencil, and her bag.

The brown hair beneath the officer's military cap had been recently trimmed. A pale sliver, like a chalk line, bordered the inch or so of recently sunburned neck above his crisp collar. Alison guessed he was in his midtwenties, a little older than she. Identifying him, from his bearing and speech, as gentry, she positioned herself near enough to discreetly eavesdrop.

"Where is young Josef here going?" asked the soldier. "Has he been assigned a home?"

The official gave an exaggerated sigh at the interruption. He lifted the cardboard square with his pencil. "Let me see . . . number 127." He flipped the pages on his clipboard.

"His name is Josef Talbert."

"Yes, of course, they all have names. I have a name, you have a name, she has a name." He pointed the eraser end of his pencil, in turn, to himself, to the soldier, and to Alison.

The soldier looked at her, puzzled, and she flushed as their eyes met. Flecks of gold beckoned her into a calm presence, sending a strange shiver along her spine. She turned to leave, but her stylish black pumps seemed to stick to the pavement. She willed her feet to move, to no avail.

When the soldier turned back to the official, Alison thought the spell would break. She needed to go, to forget she had ever felt the pull of his calm determination, to erase those mesmerizing eyes from her memory. But it was too late. The Van Schuyler fate had descended upon her, and she was lost in its clutches. Her heart turned to mush when the soldier spoke.

"My *name* is Ian Devlin of Kenniston Hall, Somerset. This lad's *name*, as I said, is Josef Talbert, recently come from Dresden. That's in Germany." He stressed each syllable of the country. "And your *name*, sir, is . . . ?"

The official scowled and pointed to his badge. "Mr. Randall Hargrove. Just like it says right here."

Ian nodded in a curt bow and Josef, copying him, did the same. Alison giggled, once more drawing Ian's attention.

"Miss?"

She flushed again and almost choked as she suppressed the nervous laughter that bubbled within her. "So sorry. My *name* is Alison Schuyler."

"You're an American," said Ian, more as a statement than a question.

"Born in Chicago." She bobbed a quick curtsey. "But now living in Rotterdam, as I descend from a long and distinguished line of Dutch Van Schuylers." Her fake haughtiness elicited an amused smile from Ian.

Mr. Hargrove was not impressed. "Now that we're all acquainted, I need to get back to sorting out these children."

Ian's smile faded. "Mr. Hargrove, please be so kind as to tell me: where are you sending Josef?"

"Says here he's going to York." Mr. Hargrove pointed at a line on his sheaf of papers. "He's got an uncle there who has agreed to take him in."

Ian knelt beside Josef. "Is that right? You're going to family?"

"*Ja,*" Josef said, then switched to English, though he struggled to pronounce the words. "My father's brother."

"All right, then." Ian patted the boy's shoulder. "Keep tight hold of that violin, okay?"

Josef nodded and threw his arms around Ian's neck, almost knocking him off balance. "*Danke. Tausend dank.*"

"You're welcome," Ian whispered back.

Alison signed and dated her sketch, then held it out to Josef. "This is for you. If you'd like to have it."

Josef studied the drawing. "Is this really me?"

"*Ja,*" Alison said, smiling.

Josef offered the sketch to Ian. "Please. Write your name?"

Ian glanced at Alison, then put his hand on Josef's shoulder. "I don't think I should—"

"I don't mind," she said.

"You're sure?"

"For him." She whispered the words and tilted her head toward Josef.

Borrowing Alison's pencil, Ian printed his name beside his likeness. He returned the sketch to Josef and tousled the boy's dark hair. Ian opened his mouth to say something else just as another long blast from the official's whistle assaulted their ears. They turned toward the sound and the official motioned to Josef.

"Time to board," he shouted. "Numbers 119 to 133, follow me." He blew the whistle again as several children separated from the larger group and joined him.

"Go now, Josef," Ian urged. "May God keep you."

Josef quickly opened his violin case and laid the sketch on top. He hugged Ian again, hesitated, then hugged Alison. They both watched as he lugged the violin case toward the platform and got in the queue to board the train. He turned around once and waved, then disappeared, one small refugee among too many.

316 WHERE TREASURE HIDES

At just over six feet in height, Ian was used to seeing over most people's heads. But he couldn't keep track of little Josef once the boy boarded the train. *Watch over him, Father. May his family be good to him.*

"I hope he'll be all right," said Alison.

"I hope so too."

"So many of them." She gestured toward the remaining children who waited their turn to board.

Ian scanned the young faces, wishing he could do something to take away the fear in their anxious eyes. "Their families are doing what they think best."

"Sending them away from their homes?"

"Removing them from Hitler's reach." Ian turned his attention to the American artist. He could detect her Dutch heritage in her features. Neither tall nor slender enough to be called statuesque, she wore her impeccably tailored crimson suit with a quiet and attractive poise.

"It's called the *Kindertransport.*"

"I've heard of it. Are they all from Germany?"

"A few come from Austria. Or what used to be Austria before the *Anschluss*. The lucky ones have relatives here. The rest are placed in foster homes."

"Jewish children."

"Most of them."

While he spoke, he held Alison's gaze. She reminded him of a summer day at the seashore. Her blonde hair, crowned with a black, narrow-brimmed hat, fell in golden waves below her shoulders. Her pale complexion possessed the translucent quality of a seashell's pearl interior. The gray-blue of her eyes sparkled like the glint of the sun on the deep waves.

"Josef played beautifully." Even her voice felt warm and bright. "He's very talented."

"So are you. Your sketch was skillfully done."

"That's kind of you to say." A charming smile lit up her face. "At least I'm good enough to know how good I'm not."

Ian took a moment to puzzle that out and chuckled. "You made me better-looking than I am, and I appreciate that. For Josef's sake, of course."

"I assure you, Mr. Devlin, there was no flattery."

Ian smiled at her American accent and tapped his insignia. "Lieutenant. But please, call me Ian."

"Ian." Alison tucked away her pad and pencil. "I suppose I should go now."

Her words burrowed into Ian's gut. He couldn't let her leave, not yet. "To Rotterdam? Or Chicago?"

She glanced at her watch. "Apparently neither. I found myself so inspired by a young boy and his violin that I missed my train."

Ian felt as if he'd been handed a gift. Or had he? Suddenly aware of an absence, he looked around expectantly. "Are you traveling alone?"

A twinge of her apparent impropriety tensed Alison's mouth and chin but didn't dim the sparkle of her clear eyes. "Quite modern of me, don't you think?"

"Rather foolish," Ian began, but stopped himself. "Though it's not for me to say."

"You're perfectly right, of course. My great-aunt accompanied me to Paris, but she became ill and I couldn't stay away any longer. So I left her to recuperate within walking distance of all the best dress shops on the Champs-Élysées, and *voilà!* Here I am. Alone and unchaperoned."

Ian drew back in surprise and raised a quizzical eyebrow. "Wait a minute. You're traveling from Paris to Rotterdam via London? Most people take the shortcut through Belgium."

"Yes, I suppose it is a bit of a roundabout way." She avoided his gaze, and the awkward moment pressed between them.

"It's really none of my business."

"Perhaps not. But there's a simple explanation." Her voice sounded too bright, and Ian sensed the nervousness she failed to hide. "I had a . . . a commission. A portrait."

Her expressive eyes begged him to believe the lie they both knew she had just told. With the slightest nod, Ian agreed, though he was curious to know her secrets. He suddenly pictured the two of them wandering the fields and woods on his family estate, talking about everything and nothing, Ian capturing her every word and safeguarding it deep within himself. But he doubted a woman who traveled alone across northern Europe, especially in these unsettled times, would enjoy the quiet boredom of country life.

He had tired of the unchanging rhythms of village traditions himself in his teen years. But after several months of combat drills and facing an uncertain future, he had been looking forward to a few days of idleness and local gossip.

Until now.

"I feel somewhat responsible," he said.

"That I missed my train?" She shrugged. "A small inconvenience. I'll leave early in the morning and be home in time for supper."

"What about supper tonight?"

Alison chuckled. "It's too early for supper."

Ian glanced at his watch. "Though not too early for tea. A British tradition, you know."

Conflict flitted across her features. She wanted to say yes, but something held her back.

"I'm not exactly a damsel in distress."

"It's only tea."

"May I ask you something?"

"Please do."

"Would you have taken Josef to, what was it? Kenniston Hall? If he hadn't had an uncle waiting for him?"

Ian hesitated, not wanting to tell this beautiful woman how his father would have reacted if he had arrived home with the young Jewish boy. True, he could have made up some story to explain the boy's need for a place to stay. Even if his father suspected the truth, he'd have the story to tell those neighbors whose thinly veiled anti-Semitism skewed their view of what was happening in Germany. As he so often did, Ian wondered how long the blindness would last. What would Hitler have to do before his insatiable thirst for power was clear for all to see? "I don't know."

"He played that piece so magnificently. No one who heard it will ever forget this day."

"I don't think Mr. Randall Hargrove was too happy about it. But at least Josef got to keep his violin."

"Why wouldn't he?"

"Hargrove wanted to confiscate it. He insinuated Josef had stolen it, that it was 'too fine an instrument' for a child like him to have in his possession."

"So you stood up for him."

Ian flushed with sudden embarrassment, but smiled at the memory. "I asked the lad if he could play. And he did."

"You are a chivalrous knight, Lieutenant Devlin. I will never forget you."

"That sounds too much like a good-bye."

"Just because I missed my train doesn't mean you should miss yours."

"My train doesn't leave till late this evening."

"But I thought—"

"I only arrived in time to see Hargrove making a ninny of himself."

"Surely there's a train you could take without waiting till this evening."

Ian glanced around as if to be sure no one was paying attention to them and leaned forward. "True," he said in a conspiratorial whisper. "But my commanding officer entrusted me with a secret commission. I'm to deliver an important message to a lovely young woman who lives in the West End." With a flourish, he pulled a pale-blue envelope from his jacket pocket and handed it to Alison.

❖   ❖   ❖

The thick envelope, made from high-quality paper, had been sealed with gold wax and embossed with two *M*s entwined in a scripted design. Alison guessed that the stationery inside would be of similar color and quality. The commanding officer was evidently a man of good breeding and taste. She turned the envelope over and read the broad black strokes written on its face: *To My Darling Trish*.

"His girlfriend?"

"His wife," Ian whispered with a furtive glance around them.

Alison played along. "Your commanding officer must think quite highly of you to trust you with such an important mission."

He slipped the envelope back into his pocket with a slight shrug of his shoulders. "He knows I wouldn't pass through London without seeing Trish."

"Oh?" A slight tremor in the simple syllable betrayed her interest.

"I loved her first, you see."

A thousand questions raced through her mind. But it didn't matter. After today, she would never see him again. His past didn't matter. Whom he loved didn't matter.

Except that it did.

Aware that the man who had unwittingly, almost neg-
ligently, captured her heart couldn't seem to take his eyes
off her, Alison found one safe response. "But she chose him
instead."

Realizing her failure to achieve just the right amount of
nonchalance and pity, she tried again and found herself asking the very question she wanted to avoid. "Did she break
your heart?"

Again, Ian leaned forward as if divulging a great secret,
and Alison bent her head toward his so as not to miss a
word. "Something so personal shouldn't be discussed in the
midst of Waterloo Station. But there's a little place near the
Westminster Bridge that serves the most delicious cherry
scones you'll ever eat."

"You mean Minivers?"

"You know it?"

"My father took me there for my sixteenth birthday. He
ordered a cherry scone for each of us and stuck a pink candle
in mine. Then he sang 'Happy Birthday' to me." She remembered closing her eyes before she blew out the candle and
wishing that every birthday, every holiday, could be spent
with her father. That he and her grandfather would make up
their quarrels so that she no longer had to choose between
them. But she had hugged the futile wish to herself, telling
it to no one, and laughed at her father's clumsiness with the
dainty teacups and miniature pastries. The cheerful memory
felt as perfect, yet fragile, as the pristine white linens and
delicate china that graced Minivers' cozy tables.

"He felt awkward there, I think. It's not exactly a gentleman's place of choice, is it?"

"The scones are worth a bit of discomfort."

"What about your secret mission?"

His eyes twinkled. "Trish isn't expecting me, so she won't know if I'm late."

The corners of Alison's mouth twitched and she turned from Ian's hopeful smile toward the entrance of the station. She couldn't see the telegram office from where she stood, but it was there, looming before her like a scolding parent. Missing the train had been foolish, but spending the rest of the afternoon with Ian was sheer stupidity. He was a soldier on the eve of war. That was reason enough to guard against any romantic entanglements.

But worse, she was a Schuyler. He couldn't know how his warm hazel eyes affected her, how drawn she was to his confident demeanor and gallant charm. Or the sting of jealous curiosity she endured when he spoke of this other woman. Though she felt his mutual attraction, it was better that he never know that he already held her heart in his hands. The Van Schuyler fate may have destined him to linger forever within her, but she could still make her own decisions.

She squared her shoulders and faced him.

His smile charmed her as he offered his arm in a boyish gesture. "Shall we?"

Alison hesitated, then tucked her hand within the crook of his elbow. "I should exchange my ticket first."

TURN THE PAGE FOR A PREVIEW OF ANOTHER NOVEL BY PAM HILLMAN.

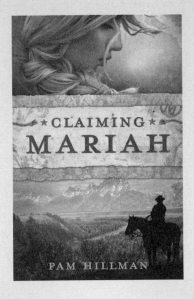

"(Hillman is) gifted with a true talent for vivid imagery, heart-tugging romance, and a feel for the Old West that will jingle your spurs."

Julie Lessman,
author of the Daughters of Boston series

★ AVAILABLE IN STORES AND ONLINE ★

www.tyndalefiction.com

CP0921

Wisdom, Wyoming Territory
Late spring, 1882

DUST SWIRLED as the two riders approached the house.

They stopped a few feet shy of the steps, and Mariah Malone eyed the men from the shadowy recesses of the porch. Both were sun-bronzed and looked weary but tough, as if they made their living punching cows and riding fences.

One man hung back; the other rode closer and touched his thumb and forefinger to the brim of his hat. "Afternoon, ma'am."

"Afternoon." Wavy brown hair brushed the frayed collar of his work shirt. A film of dust covered his faded jeans, and the stubble on his jaw hinted at a long, hard trip. "May I help you?"

"I'm here to see Seth Malone." His voice sounded husky, as if he needed a drink of water to clear the trail dust from his throat.

At the mention of her father, a pang of sorrow mixed with longing swept over her. "I'm sorry; he passed away in January. I'm his daughter. Mariah Malone."

The cowboy swung down from his horse and sauntered toward the porch. He rested one worn boot on the bottom step before tilting his hat back, revealing fathomless dark-blue eyes.

"I'm Slade Donovan. And that's my brother, Buck." He jerked his head in the direction of the other man. His intense gaze bored into hers. "Jack Donovan was our father."

Oh no, Jack Donovan's sons.

A shaft of apprehension shot through her, and Mariah grasped the railing for support. Unable to look Mr. Donovan in the eye, she focused on his shadowed jaw. A muscle jumped in his cheek, keeping time with her thudding heart.

When her father died, she hadn't given another thought to the letter she'd sent Jack Donovan. She'd been too worried about her grandmother, her sister, and the ranch to think about the consequences of the past.

"Where is . . . your father?" Mariah asked.

"He died from broken dreams and whiskey."

"I'm sorry for your loss," she murmured, knowing her own father's sins had contributed to Jack Donovan's troubles, maybe even to his death. How much sorrow had her father's greed caused? How much heartache? And how much did his son know of their fathers' shared past?

The accusation on Slade Donovan's face told her, and the heat of fresh shame flooded her cheeks.

"My pa wanted what was rightfully his," he ground out. "I promised him I would find the man who took that gold and make him pay."

Tension filled the air, and she found it difficult to breathe.

"Take it easy, Slade." His brother's soft voice wafted between them.

Mariah caught a glimpse of Cookie hovering at the edge of the bunkhouse. "Miss Mariah, you need any help?"

Her attention swung between Cookie and the Donovan brothers, the taste of fear mounting in the back of her throat. An old man past his prime, Cookie would be no match for them. "No," she said, swallowing her apprehension. "No thank you, Cookie. Mr. Donovan is here to talk business."

She turned back to the man before her. Hard eyes searched her face, and she looked away, praying for guidance. "Mr. Donovan, I think we need to continue this discussion in my father's office."

She moistened her lips, her gaze drawn to the clenched tightness of his jaw. After a tense moment, he nodded.

Malone was dead?

Leaving Buck to care for the horses, Slade followed the daughter into the house. She'd swept her golden-brown hair to the top of her head and twisted it into a serene coil. A few curls escaped the loose bun and flirted with the stand-up lace of her white shirtwaist. She sure looked dressed up out here in the middle of nowhere.

Then he remembered the empty streets and the handful of wagons still gathered around the church when they'd passed through Wisdom at noon. He snorted under his breath. Under other circumstances, a woman like Mariah Malone wouldn't even deem him worthy to wipe her dainty boots on, let alone agree to talk to him in private. He couldn't count the times the girls from the "right" side of town had snubbed their noses at him, their starched pinafores in sharp contrast to his torn, patched clothes. At least his younger brother and sisters hadn't been treated like outcasts. He'd made sure of that.

He trailed the Malone woman down the hall, catching a glimpse of a sitting room with worn but polished furniture on his right, a tidy kitchen on his left. A water stain from a leaky roof marred the faded wallpaper at the end of the wide hallway. While neat and clean, the house and outbuildings looked run-down. He scowled. Surely Seth Malone could have kept the place in better repair with his ill-gotten gain.

Miss Malone led the way into a small office that smelled of leather, ink, and turpentine. She turned, and he caught a glimpse of eyes the color of deep-brown leather polished to a shine. The state of affairs around the house slid into the dark recesses of his mind as he regarded the slender young woman before him.

"Mr. Donovan," she began, "I take it you received my letter."

He nodded but kept silent. Uneasiness wormed its way into his gut. Did Miss Malone have brothers or other family to turn to? Who was in charge of the ranch?

"I'm sorry for what my father did. I wish it had never happened." She toyed with a granite paperweight, the distress on her face tugging at his conscience.

He wished it had never happened too. Would his father have given up if Seth Malone hadn't taken off with all the gold? Would they have had a better life—a ranch of their own maybe, instead of a dilapidated shack on the edge of Galveston—if his father hadn't needed to fight the demons from the bullet lodged in his head?

He wanted to ask all the questions that had plagued him over the years, questions his father had shouted during his drunken rages. Instead, he asked another question, one he'd asked himself many times over the last several months. "Why did you send that letter?"

Pain turned her eyes to ebony. "My father wanted to ask forgiveness for what he had done, but by that time he was unable to write the letter himself. I didn't know Mr. Donovan had a family or that he'd died." She shrugged, the pity on her face unmistakable.

Slade clenched his jaw. He didn't want her pity. He'd had enough of that to last a lifetime.

She strolled to the window, arms hugging her waist. She looked too slight to have ever done a day's work. She'd probably been pampered all her life, while his own mother and sisters struggled for survival.

"I hoped Mr. Donovan might write while my father was still alive, and they could resolve their differences." Her soft voice wafted on the still air. "I prayed he might forgive Papa. And that Papa could forgive himself."

"Forgiveness is too little, too late," Slade gritted out, satisfaction welling within him when her back stiffened and her shoulders squared.

She turned, regarding him with caution. "I'm willing to make restitution for what my father did."

"Restitution?"

"A few hundred head of cattle should be sufficient."

"A few hundred?" Surely she didn't think a handful of cattle would make up for what her father had done.

"What more do you want? I've already apologized. What good will it do to keep the bitterness alive?"

"It's not bitterness I want, Miss Malone. It's the land."

"The land?" Her eyes widened.

He nodded, a stiff, curt jerk of his head. "All of it."

"Only a portion of the land should go to your family, if any. Half of that gold belonged to my father." Two spots of angry color bloomed in her cheeks, and her eyes sparked like sun off brown bottle glass. "And besides, he worked the land all these years and made this ranch into something."

Slade frowned. What did she mean, half of the gold belonged to her father? Disgust filled him. Either the woman was a good actress, or Malone had lied to his family even on his deathbed.

"All of it."

She blinked, and for a moment, he thought she might give in. Then she lifted her chin. "And if I refuse?"

"One trip to the sheriff with your letter and the wanted poster from twenty-five years ago would convince any law-abiding judge that this ranch belongs to me and my family." He paused. "As well as the deed to the gold mine in California that has my father's name on it—not your father's."

"What deed?" She glared at him, suspicion glinting in her eyes. "And what wanted poster?"

Did she really not know the truth? Slade pulled out the papers and handed them to her, watching as she read the proof that gave him the right to the land they stood on.

All color left her face as she read, and Slade braced himself in case she fainted clean away. If he'd had any doubt that she didn't know the full story, her reaction to the wanted poster proved otherwise.

"It says . . ." Her voice wavered. "It says Papa shot your father. Left him for dead. I don't believe it. It . . . it's a mistake." She sank into the nearest chair, the starch wilted out of her. The condemning poster fluttered to the floor.

A sudden desire to give in swept over him. He could accept her offer of a few hundred head, walk out the door, and ride away, leaving her on the land that legally, morally, belonged to him. To his mother.

No! He wanted Seth Malone to pay for turning his father into a drunk and making his mother old before her time. But

Seth Malone was dead, and this woman wouldn't cheat him of his revenge.

No matter how innocent she looked, no matter how her eyes filled with tears as she begged for forgiveness, he wouldn't give it to her. Forgiveness wouldn't put food on the table or clothes on his mother's and sisters' backs.

"No mistake." He hunkered down so he could see her face. "You have a right to defend your father's memory, I reckon. But I'll stick by what I said. The deed is legal. And that letter will stand up in court as well. You've got a decision to make, ma'am. Either you sign this ranch over to me, or I'll go to the sheriff."

Silence hung heavy between them until a faint noise drew Slade's attention to the doorway.

An old woman stood there, a walking stick clasped in her right hand. Her piercing dark gaze swung from Mariah to him. He stood to his full height.

"Grandma." Mariah launched herself from the chair and hurried to the woman's side.

The frail-looking woman's penetrating stare never left Slade's face.

He held out his hand for the deed. Silence reigned as Mariah handed it over.

"I'll give you an hour to decide." He gave them a curt nod and strode from the room.

DISCUSSION QUESTIONS

1. Louisa is unhappy with how her life has turned out: children always making a mess and a husband who is too busy with work to notice her. Have you ever felt stuck in your own life? How did you overcome this?

2. With the appearance of Jazz Sweet, Collin realizes the sacrifices his wife makes each day to keep their family running smoothly. Have you ever taken someone you love for granted? Why do you think this so easily happens?

3. Louisa and her daughter do not see eye to eye, but Jazz and Madison have an instant rapport. Do you struggle to communicate with your children or parents? What's the best way to work toward understanding and reconciliation?

4. When Tim falls asleep in her arms, Jazz hesitates to move him. Why do you think this scene triggers memories of her sons?

5. Jazz embodies all the fun and excitement Louisa wanted to experience in her own life, but Jazz soon wishes she could remember what it was like to be Louisa. Have you ever wished for another's life? What would you miss most if you weren't yourself?

6. Jazz tells Collin it is imperative they and the children go to church as a family. Do you agree? What do spiritual disciplines and church attendance look like in your own family?

7. Upon finding out about his wife's memory loss, Collin wonders if this is "a second chance, a gift from God to make his marriage work." What would you change in your life if you had a do-over?

8. When Tim is lost, Collin has a revelation: "He began promising God he would be a better father if only Tim could be found unharmed. Then he switched to asking for God's guidance, realizing his promises to God meant nothing." Why does he think it's a better idea to ask for God's guidance than to promise God he'll do better in the future? Do you agree that these kinds of promises can sometimes be difficult to keep? How can we avoid making empty promises to God?

9. Louisa loses her memory in part because of the trauma she's fighting to block out. What is the source of that trauma? How did it impact her adult life and her relationships with her family members? What

happens when the truth of this childhood experience surfaces at the end of the book?

10. In the same way that Louisa conceals her affinity for writing romance stories, have you ever hesitated to share a passion or dream for fear of others' opinions? If you did end up telling someone else about it, what happened?

11. When Collin envisions his family's camping trip, he is hoping to create lasting, fun memories. But the trip doesn't turn out the way he planned. Can you think of a time when you tried to build happy memories with your family, only to have everything go awry? How did you respond to these unexpected events?

ABOUT THE AUTHOR

Christian author DIANA LESIRE BRANDMEYER writes historical and contemporary romances, including *Mind of Her Own* and *A Bride's Dilemma in Friendship, Tennessee*. She's also written a work of nonfiction, *We're Not Blended—We're Pureed: A Survivor's Guide to Blended Families*. Once widowed and now remarried, she writes with humor and experience on the difficulty of joining two families, be they fictional or real-life. Visit her online at www.dianabrandmeyer.com.

Bigger. Better. Together.
Stories of love, blending, and bonding.

GREAT INSPIRATIONAL FICTION

TYNDALE
FICTION

www.tyndalefiction.com

CP0638